Too Hot

"The passion…is hot enough to singe the fingers…a pleasing tale."

—*Romance Reviews Today*

"Captures the readers from the first scene…Holt weaves this erotic romance like a master…an enjoyable afternoon read."

—*Romance Divas*

"A delightful historical with a slight twist."

—*Midwest Book Review*

Further Than Passion

"Fantastic…a keeper…Holt has finely tuned the art of delving into secret fantasies and drawing out what women want. In this deliciously sensual story, she keeps readers glued to the pages by infusing every one with plenty of sizzle. Very sensual."

—*Romantic Times* (starred review)

"Holt pens a compelling, erotic tale…a sensual feast of love, betrayal, and sensual pleasure, *Further Than Passion* takes the reader beyond the typical consequences of desire for happily-ever-after…[a] powerful story that readers will find impossible to put down…each character springs vibrantly alive, living in the reader's imagination long after the last page is turned."

—*Midwest Book Review*

"A deeply passionate book…very seldom does a historical novel find its way to my shelf, but this is one author for whom I will always make an exception. Fans won't be surprised to find this book on their keeper shelf."

—*A Romance Review*

"Holt's most exciting story of all. *Further Than Passion* is an intriguing and spellbinding love story."

—*Fallen Angel Reviews*

"Highly erotic…a poignant and emotional love story…only Cheryl Holt can write such sweet, erotic romances that touch the heart, body, and soul."

—*Historical Romance Club*

"Holt is an extremely talented author. Every book she writes is so sexy, the characters so real, that I'm sorry when the story comes to an end."

—FreshFiction.com

More Than Seduction

"Fantastic...a keeper...Holt demonstrates why she's a grand mistress at keeping sensuality at a high boil in her latest and most tempting romance. She adds depth to this sensual tale with her mature characters, a touch of poignancy and a strong plot. Holt truly understands what readers crave."

—*Romantic Times*

"Hang onto your hats! Cheryl Holt gives you hot romance with characters you love and admire in all her books, but I think she outdid herself with her latest book. To me it's her best work yet. It's a winning story you can't read fast enough. Excellent, stirring, steamy, and so darn good you just about melt in a puddle of desire if you aren't careful. Cheryl Holt is magnificent once again. I wonder what she will do next? I can hardly wait!"

—*Reader to Reader Reviews*

"*More Than Seduction* is another winner for Cheryl Holt. This book pulls you in and you won't be able to put it down. The sexual tension is extreme and the love scenes are blazing hot. This is definitely a keeper."

—*The Romance Studio*

"An enticing story, rich with sensuality...a tantalizing read."

—*Romance Reviews Today*

"A tempting treat."

—*Romance Junkies*

Deeper Than Desire

"Just about the best writer of erotic romance that we've got."

—*Statesman Journal* (Salem, Oregon)

"Sexy, titillating love story…add some suspense, abductions, a mad villain, and an exciting climax and you have all you need in an erotic romance."

—*Romantic Times*

"A jewel…intriguing, compelling, and passionate."

—*Old Book Barn Gazette*

"The thing that I like best about Cheryl Holt's writing is that she makes her characters come alive as their stories unfold. You get mad, glad, sad, and sexy as the devil while reading her glorious books that not only are well-written erotic stories but have substance and a good storyline concerning the characters' lives that make them human and realistic. Now this is a writer to watch because she is going places. Ms. Holt delivers stories that you love reading. They are hot and spicy…filled with compelling characters that set your heart to racing with her imaginative and titillating storytelling."

—ReaderToReader.com

"An intricate tapestry of intriguing characters."

—RomanceReaderAtHeart.com

"Romance fans will enjoy this erotic tale of forbidden love that feels and is right. Holt turns up the heat with this superior historical."

—TheBestReviews.com

"Cheryl Holt will ravish her reading audience with this well-written tale. Her clever plot will lure the reader on as she seduces one to continue reading page after page. Filled with sexual tension and loaded with secondary story lines, one comes away satisfied. If a delightful taste of erotica is what you are looking for, you will find your senses replete in *Deeper Than Desire*."

—Simegen.com

Total Surrender

BEST SENSUAL NOVEL OF THE YEAR   —*Romantic Times* Magazine

"Cheryl Holt is something else again. I was totally blown away by *Total Surrender*, a tale both erotic and poignant. Sensational characters, and a very compelling read that readers couldn't put down unless you're dead! It's also the dynamite sequel to last year's *Love Lessons*...don't miss this author. She's a sparkling diamond."

—ReaderToReader.com

"A lush tale of romance, sexuality, and the fragility of the human spirit. Carefully crafted characters, engaging dialogue, and sinfully erotic narrative create a story that is at once compelling and disturbing...For a story that is sizzling hot and a hero any woman would want to save."

—*Romance Reviews Today*

"A deliciously erotic romance...the story line grips the audience from the start until the final nude setting, as the lead characters are a dynamic couple battling for *Total Surrender*. The suspense element adds tension, but the tale belongs to Sarah and Michael. Cheryl Holt turns up the heat with this enticing historical romance."

—*Writerspace*

"A very good erotic novel...if you like a racy read, you'll enjoy this one!"

—*Old Book Barn Gazette*

"Cheryl Holt is very good at what she does."

—*Statesman Journal* (Salem, OR)

Love Lessons

"With her well-defined characters, even pacing, and heated love scenes, Holt makes an easy entry into the world of erotic romance...readers will enjoy *Love Lessons*."

—*Romantic Times*

"Hot, hot, hot! The love scenes sizzle in this very sensual romance between two people from different worlds...readers enjoying an erotic romance will not be disappointed."

—Writers Club Romance on AOL

ST. MARTIN'S PAPERBACKS TITLES BY CHERYL HOLT

Too Wicked To Wed

Cheryl Holt

ST. MARTIN'S PAPERBACKS

This is a work of fiction. All of the characters, organizations and events portrayed in this novel are either products of the author's imagination or are used fictitiously.

TOO WICKED TO WED

Copyright © 2006 by Cheryl Holt.

ISBN: 0-312-93799-7
EAN: 9780312-93799-7

Printed in the United States of America

St. Martin's Paperbacks edition / September 2006

St. Martin's Paperbacks are published by St. Martin's Press, 175 Fifth Avenue, New York, NY 10010.

10 9 8 7 6 5 4 3 2 1

Too Wicked To Wed

1

LONDON, ENGLAND, 1814 . . .

The front door to the house was wide open.

Helen Mansfield looked up and down the busy street. No one was paying any attention to her, and without pausing to reconsider her plan, she slipped inside.

Due to the delicacy of her mission, she'd come alone, without benefit of maid or footman, and her heart pounded with dread. The clandestine visit was the first really bold, exotic thing she'd ever done, and she yearned to conclude her business quickly and quietly, and without making a fool of herself.

After she had been out in the bright July sunshine, the vestibule seemed very dark. She tarried, her eyes adjusting to the shadows, while hoping that the butler would step forward to welcome and announce her, but it was eerily silent.

She studied her surroundings, finding the lodging to be

well built and appropriately fashionable, but it had an air of abandonment. The entryway was empty, with a lone table positioned down the hall, and it was covered with a sheet as though the current occupant hadn't yet had occasion to tug it off so the space would be more habitable.

Of course, that occupant being a notorious, barbaric pirate, perhaps he didn't realize that civilized people lived any differently.

She tamped down the uncharitable thought, refusing to proceed on a sour note. Her feelings were sufficiently conflicted, her temper adequately ignited, and she was determined to remain calm and courteous, regardless of how humiliating her appointment proved to be.

Noise erupted on the stairs, and she leapt away as a barefoot, scantily clad woman came racing down. Her clothes—if one could call the garment an *outfit*—consisted of only a summery shift, the hem of which fell to mid-thigh. It was constructed from a slinky red material that hugged her torso like a glove, revealing each of her curves and hiding nothing that ought to be concealed.

Her breasts were enormous, and they bounced gleefully as she passed, the mounds swaying in tandem, her nipples jutting against the bodice.

The woman was obviously a strumpet, and Helen couldn't stop gawking.

What sort of bawdy abode had she entered? What mischief was occurring that a gentlewoman—such as herself—could stumble into it? Who was in charge?

As the woman reached the foyer, she gazed up the stairs and shouted, "Catch me if you can, you surly lout." Laughing, she vanished down the corridor.

A man scurried after her, his arms stretched out to grab her, but she was too fast and easily evaded him. He was a grubby fellow, with a scraggly beard, a gold earring, a knife in his belt, and numerous teeth missing, and he embodied every low trait Helen had expected to observe among the residents.

With how her luck was running, he would likely turn out to be Mr. William Lucas Westmoreland, the man she was seeking. What if he was? How would they have a rational conversation?

He had hesitated, struggling to detect how his prey had escaped, when he espied Helen cowering in the corner. With unrepressed lechery, he scrutinized her, and the odor of alcohol around him was so strong that she was amazed he could walk. She gagged and lurched away.

"You'll be next, my pretty little thing," he promised. "Don't go anywhere."

"Your *next* what?" she mumbled as he tottered off.

She checked to be certain she'd brought the kitchen knife she'd sewn into the seam of her skirt. After all, she wasn't stupid. She was in the lair of treacherous, violent bandits for whom no deed was purported to be too evil. If she was threatened, she hadn't the temerity to use the weapon, but still, she felt better knowing she could yank it out and wield it with great relish.

Her fury with her younger brother, Archibald, surged anew. How typical that he would immerse her in such a wretched jam! His dominant attribute was his total ability to wreak havoc. He was immoderate in his appetites, passionate about his pleasures, and never fretted over anyone but himself. As a twenty-five-year-old spinster, she'd eschewed marriage to stay at her beloved home of Mansfield Abbey, where she diligently worked to curb his worst excesses.

He was her sole kin, so she'd always been too protective of him, had rescued him from too many scrapes, and he was positive that she would rescue him from this latest one, too. The notion had her so angry that if he'd been standing there with her, she'd have clasped him by the throat and strangled the life out of him.

From down the hall, commotion drifted toward her. People were talking, and there seemed to be a party in progress—in the middle of the day!—but the social event sounded different from any to which she'd ever been invited.

Their voices were odd and furtive, as if the participants had been naughty—or were about to be. Women were cooing and sighing, oozing with a bliss Helen didn't comprehend.

She yearned to investigate, but she was staunchly convinced that, whatever was transpiring, she couldn't bear to learn the details. Without a doubt, she should simply stomp out and let Archie handle the mess for once—it would serve him right—but she wouldn't.

He was incredibly spoiled, so she shouldn't have been surprised when he'd informed her that he'd lost Mansfield Abbey in a card game. But even for him, the behavior was extreme. He'd frittered away every last chattel, every candle and fork, every horse and hoe.

There was nothing left.

The villain Mr. Westmoreland had won it all, and if she couldn't persuade him to give it back, she couldn't predict her and Archie's fate. She had to reason with Westmoreland. She had to! The estate was a small place, a pittance, a veritable hovel compared to the other grand properties in their neighborhood. Why couldn't he have coveted somebody else's home?

Despite his savage reputation, he was alleged to possess a shred of integrity. During a terrible sea storm, he'd risked life and limb on a ship of drowning British sailors.

Using daring sailing skills, he'd maneuvered through the gale, plucking those he could from the turbulent waters. Then he'd personally pursued the floundering stragglers, braving thirty-foot waves in a dinghy and finally even diving into the raging tempest to prevent what would have been instant death for some of the Navy's finest.

Every man had been saved.

As a result, Westmoreland was the darling of the kingdom, his courage bandied over in every tavern in the land, and as a reward, he'd been pardoned for his previous crimes by the Prince Regent.

Surely, such a dashing hero could find it in his heart to heed an anxious woman's plea for mercy.

Ready for anything, she squared her shoulders and marched down the corridor to the closed door at the end. It was ajar, and she peeked through the crack into a cavernous room that had probably been the prior owner's library. The walls were lined with bookcases, but they were empty of books, and there were dilapidated pieces of furniture that didn't match. It appeared as if the individual who'd purchased the items had no clue as to what was needed to fill a fancy house. Boxes were stacked, waiting to be unpacked, but there were no servants who might be set to the task.

A dozen gorgeous women were present, and they sprawled like lazy mermaids on pillows and daybeds, sipping wine and purring to one another. They were scandalously garbed in only their undergarments, fancy corsets and colored pantaloons that were festooned with ribbons. Their slender calves were concealed by lacy stockings, their tiny feet balanced on spiky heels.

They were attractive and alluring, and in contrast, she felt dowdy and provincial. With her brunette hair tucked into a tidy chignon, her hazel eyes that were too wide and saw too much, her drab brown traveling dress and shabby cloak, she was a boring, unsophisticated country girl. She was too skinny, too old, too plain, and so far out of her element that she might have laughed had she not been so desperate.

In their midst, a man lounged on a lavish sofa. While he was strikingly handsome, with golden-blond hair and piercing blue eyes, he exuded a tough and dangerous air that made her pause. He reminded her of a wolf on the prowl, alert and prepared to attack with the slightest provocation. He was muscular and fit, tall and robust, and his features were arresting, but in a rough fashion that added to his aura of menace and peril.

She imagined he'd had a hard life. Years of toil were etched in his face, yet he was so imposing and unusual that she was fascinated.

He was naked to the waist, attired in a peculiar pair of trousers stitched from a light, flowing fabric that was likely intended for hot weather. The material hinted at burly thighs and long legs, and was the style a sultan in Arabia might wear while entertaining his harem.

His shoulders were brawny, his stomach flat as a board. To her astonishment, he had a matting of hair across his chest. She'd never seen a man's chest before, so she hadn't known hair would grow there, and she suffered from an outlandish urge to tromp over and riffle her fingers through it.

A covey of the blond sirens hovered around him, with one snuggled on his lap. They were caressing him all over, and they took turns leaning down and . . . and . . . kissing him on the lips!

She tried to remember if she'd ever viewed two people

kissing, but she couldn't recollect a single occasion where it might have happened. Her world was so staid, couples so restrained, that a display of affection was beyond anyone of her acquaintance.

She was spellbound.

The man would dally with one woman, then another, and while Helen wasn't positive, it seemed as if they were putting their tongues in each other's mouths. The discovery did something to her insides. Butterflies swarmed through her tummy; her womb shifted and stirred; the mysterious feminine spot between her legs was relaxed and moist.

The female on his lap moaned and arched up and, mesmerizing Helen even further, the man nibbled down her neck, where he proceeded to bare her breast and suck on her nipple.

"Oh, my Lord!" Helen murmured, as a man spoke from directly behind her.

"May I help you?"

Cheeks burning, she jumped and whipped around to confront a fellow who was a clerk or secretary. He was younger than herself—probably twenty or so. Dressed impeccably in a conservative suit, a portfolio tucked under his arm, he was the only normal person she'd encountered since entering.

His dark hair was neatly clipped, his demeanor proper and polite, his speech educated and refined, but his disdainful blue eyes made it clear that he knew how avidly she'd been spying. There was no way to pretend she'd been doing anything else. She was mortified, but determined to forge on with some amount of aplomb.

"Yes, you may help me. I'm looking for Mr. Westmoreland."

"You found him." He pointed to the man in the library with the bevy of admirers fawning over him. "Shall we go in?"

She gulped with dismay. She'd been anticipating a grimy, disgusting criminal. Not some Greek god.

"*He* is Mr. Westmoreland?"

"Yes, but it's *Captain* Westmoreland. And you are . . . ?"

Obviously, she had to reassess her plan. Westmoreland was unlike any other man she'd ever met, and in dealing with him she would be completely out of her league. How could they casually chat when she'd seen his lips wrapped around that . . . that . . .

She blushed bright red.

"I'm no one of any importance, and he's rather busy. I'll stop by tomorrow when he's not so . . ." She hadn't the vocabulary to describe Westmoreland's conduct, so she vaguely waved toward him, then spun to depart.

"I can guarantee that he won't be behaving any better later on." The man gripped her elbow and halted any retreat. "He has a definite *way* with the ladies, if you catch my drift. Whatever your purpose, you might as well get it over with. Then, you won't have to come back."

"No. I believe I'll be off."

He clutched her arm even tighter. "Stay. I insist."

A guard stepped in and expertly blocked any exit. The clerk pushed at the door, and to her horror, everyone in the room froze and gaped at her.

Westmoreland ceased his love play and glared—but not at her. In her dreary costume, and with his being surrounded by dazzling beauties, she was invisible. He focused on the clerk, a scowl marring his flawless brow.

"What is it this time, Mr. Smith?" Westmoreland demanded. "Can't you see I'm involved? I asked you not to interrupt again."

"You have a visitor, Captain."

"Who is it?"

"She hasn't said."

Westmoreland still hadn't noticed her, and out of the corner of her mouth she whispered, "Mr. Smith, if you have any sense of decency, you'll let me slip away."

"Sorry, but I have no *decency* remaining. I lost every ounce of it when the Captain purchased me in a slave market."

"He . . . he . . . what?" she stammered.

"Go on," Smith coaxed. "Go on. He looks as if he bites, but he doesn't really."

Smith urged her in, the guard hurrying her along by giving her a firm shove. She stumbled, furious when several of the hussies snickered. She pulled herself up to her full height of five feet five, and she stared them down, quickly cowing them to silence.

Westmoreland's attention locked on her, and he rose. He'd forgotten the trollop on his lap, and she plummeted down, but he failed to note that he'd practically tossed her on the floor. He was imperious and rude as a king, and Helen was surprised. She wasn't certain what she'd expected from the infamous brigand, but it wasn't such an ample quantity of arrogance and conceit.

Like a large, predatory cat, he approached, his gaze not wavering, and her pulse thudded like a small bird's. While she'd figured he'd be tall, he was much bigger than she'd calculated. He loomed over her, and though she'd never pictured herself as petite, in his towering company she felt absolutely tiny.

She stood her ground, deciding that she couldn't have him detect how terrified she was. In the tales being spread around the country, he'd been credited with every foul felony from kidnapping to cannibalism. He was reputed to have killed thousands of men, to have eaten babies for his supper.

While she discounted the more incredible yarns, all stories originated with a sprig of truth, and until she knew him better, she couldn't predict of what he might be capable.

"Well, well, Mr. Smith," he mused to the clerk. "Guess who we have here."

"I haven't a clue, Captain."

"Can't you tell? It's Miss Mansfield."

Her name rippled through the crowd like a wildfire, the coven of slatterns abuzz with speculation. From how they were evaluating her, it was clear that they were all aware of Archie's folly. Was the entire city cognizant of his gambling debacle? Was the general populace tittering over his stupidity?

How humiliating! How galling! When she got home— *if* she got home—she'd murder him. She'd have no despicable sibling; she'd be an only child.

"How do you know who I am?" she snapped.

"You and your brother could be twins," he explained. "I must admit that I'd about given up on you. Does your appearance mean you're finally ready to begin? Shall we do it right here and let everyone watch? That way, there'll be a ton of witnesses, and we won't have any question as to the terms of the wager being appropriately commenced."

He stepped in, and she stepped back. She had no idea to what he referred, and she frowned as Mr. Smith scolded, "Captain, if I may say—"

"No, you may not, Mr. Smith. Butt out. It's none of your affair."

"But she's a respected gentlewoman, and you can't—"

"Mr. Smith!" he hissed, his temper barely controlled. "Have you gone deaf?"

"No, sir."

"Then, I suggest you be quiet."

Smith's cheeks reddened, but he braved a retort. "But you can't debauch her. It's simply not done."

"It's *done* all the time," Westmoreland asserted, his concentration not leaving Helen. "If you don't believe me, ask her brother. Ask her dear, departed father."

She ignored their barbs and honed in on the mention of *debauchery*. Though she had no inkling what it might entail, it boded ill for an acceptable outcome.

"What's this nonsense about debauching me? I wish to confer with you about my brother's debt, about having it forgiven—as is the fair and honorable conclusion. You can't walk away with our estate after a measly turn of the cards. You know it's wrong."

"I know nothing of the sort."

"You can't do it!"

"I can, and I will. It was your brother's idiocy that led you here. Not mine. Besides, it's totally within your power to have the property restored to him, which I presume is why you've come." He grinned like the Devil himself. "I'm eager to start whenever you are. In fact, I can hardly wait. Just say the word, although I'm not much for *talking*."

"Well, that's my plan, so resign yourself to a boring parlay of the details."

"I'm afraid a meager discussion won't get you anywhere. I'm resolved to your fate."

"My . . . my fate? You make it sound as if I'm about to be hanged."

"Oh, it won't be that bad. Any lady present will verify that I'll make it quite good for you."

"Make *what* good for me?"

Her rejoinder elicited out-and-out guffaws from the

throng, and she flashed a menacing scowl to quell the merriment. He was unaffected, though, and he reached out and toyed with a lock of hair that had fallen loose from her chignon. For some absurd reason, her heart fluttered when he touched her, and she didn't care for the experience, at all. She batted him away.

"Stop babbling in riddles," she commanded.

"In riddles? What is it you don't understand?"

"What power have I regarding the return of the estate? I haven't the vaguest notion to what you allude."

He chuckled, his voice a rich, deep baritone that tickled her innards and rattled her bones. "I take it your brother wasn't completely frank with you as to the conditions of our wager."

"I know my home is in your hands, which is sufficient information."

"No, your home is in *your* hands."

It seemed as if he were speaking in a foreign language she didn't comprehend. "My hands?"

"Yes. After your brother squandered Mansfield Abbey, he tried to win it back by betting *you*."

She had so few possessions, no cash or other valuables. What could Archie possibly have staked? "By betting my . . . what?"

"You're a female." His potent gaze wandered down her torso. "You have only one thing that would interest a man like me."

As his implication dawned, she huffed with outrage. "You contemptible cad!"

"Aah, I see you grasp my intent."

"You and my brother actually gambled over my . . . my . . ."

"Yes. And *you* lost."

"I'm to surrender my . . ."

She couldn't utter the word *virtue* in front of him, and she'd always been so sheltered that she didn't know what such a submission would require. It involved a husband and wife and their actions in the marital bed, but other than that indistinct point, she hadn't the slightest hint of what had been promised.

"It's a tad more than a mere *surrender*," he advised.

"What is?"

"For thirty days, you're to please me in any fashion I desire. If you do, and I'm *satisfied* with your performance, he can have his paltry farm. I'll have no need of it."

"Thirty days?"

"Yes. I'm to enjoy a month of dissipation, although now that I've met you, I have to confess that you're too skinny for my tastes. And I'd prefer a blonde. But I suppose once we're snuggled under the covers, I can shut my eyes and pretend you're someone else."

He'd hurled so many insults that she couldn't tabulate them all, and she was too stunned to respond. His claim was too awful to be genuine, too horrid to be implemented.

"I don't believe you," she finally said. "Archie would never . . ."

"Wouldn't he?" He nodded at Mr. Smith. "Show her the contract her brother signed."

She was aghast. "You wrote it down?"

"Of course. Do you take me for a fool?"

She studied him more carefully, weighing character, assessing temperament, and she was sickened to realize how thoroughly she'd misjudged him as an opponent. He was more intelligent, more shrewd and driven, than she ever could have fathomed.

"No," she murmured, "you're definitely not a fool."

"Your brother swore I'd be getting a virgin, and you should both hope he's telling me the truth. I hate to be lied to, and I'll kill him if you're not." He gestured round the room. "I'll let it be your choice. Shall we amuse ourselves here in the library? Or would you like to go upstairs to my bedchamber?"

2

Mr. Smith?"

"Yes?"

Helen flashed her sweetest smile. "Would you usher the guests out of here? Mr.—that is, Captain—Westmoreland seems to be laboring under the oddest impression. We must talk privately."

"I'm not mistaken," Westmoreland interjected.

"He's not," Mr. Smith added, looking terribly sorry. "I have their agreement . . . if you'd like to read the terms?"

"No, I don't need to see it."

She was amazed at her composure. A thousand thoughts were careening through her head, most including maiming and murder, although under the circumstances, she'd be hard-pressed to decide with which man to begin.

"If you'd ask everyone to go?"

"Certainly," he offered, though he didn't move, and she realized that he was waiting for Westmoreland's permission.

With Smith being very young, and Westmoreland purportedly his *owner,* she could imagine how tricky it would be for him to assert himself. Helen, however, was a free person and not afraid of Westmoreland in the least.

"Ladies . . . ladies . . ." Helen clapped her hands, rousing them as she would a group of schoolgirls. "The party's concluded."

No one stirred, so she grew more aggressive. As if *she* were the hostess, she started snatching up wineglasses and blowing out candles. "Thank you for coming," she said over and over. "Please stop by again. The Captain will be delighted to entertain you later."

She grabbed the drapes and yanked them open, causing shrieks of dismay as sunshine flooded the room.

"Honestly, Westmoreland," a harlot complained, "aren't you going to do something?"

Westmoreland gave a subtle signal to Mr. Smith and the guard. Within seconds, the library was emptied, and Helen was intrigued by how swiftly Westmoreland's minions hurried to obey.

How did he instill such loyalty and devotion? Through kindness? Through brute force? What type of man was he deep down? If she hoped to reason with him, she had to find out.

He stood silently, observing events as if they had no connection to him, as if he didn't care what any of the people present elected to do. As the last curvaceous bottom slithered out, the guard and Smith following, the door was closed, and Westmoreland spun toward her. An irresistible smile dimpled his cheeks.

"What a tigress you can be," he said.

"I've flayed men with my claws."

"I'll bet you have."

"You'd best be cautious around me," she warned.

"I will."

"I always get what I want."

"I can see that, and you've spoiled my fun in the process."

"You're like a sheik with his concubines."

"Yes, I am. Aren't I lucky?" He was completely unrepentant.

"I'm sure your harem will return shortly."

"I'm sure they will," he cockily concurred. "How could they bear to stay away?"

He sauntered over to a mahogany desk that had been shoved into the corner, and he perched on the edge. Arms folded over his massive chest, his strong muscles rippling, he scrutinized her, his blue, blue eyes probing for signs of weakness or apprehension.

She kept her expression blank, recognizing that if he glimpsed any vulnerability, he'd pounce like a hawk on a rabbit, but it was difficult to pretend nonchalance. Other than her brother and his friend Adrian, she was rarely in the solitary company of men, especially one who acted like a rapacious Romeo. She wasn't positive how to behave.

Considering the assemblage of trollops that had just fled, Westmoreland had definite opinions about how women should comport themselves and, wager or no, he would be vastly disappointed by her sober demeanor. She had no raucous tendencies, was never driven to caprice or whimsy, and for the briefest moment, she regretted that she wasn't more madcap and uninhibited.

What would it be like to toss off convention and do something totally outrageous? She had no idea.

She couldn't envision what it would be like to cavort with him. Merely from pondering such iniquity she tingled with an excitement and zeal that she'd never noted before, which had her confused.

Was she secretly pining for male attention? Had she a covert wish to lead a different sort of life? Perhaps with her being surrounded by the familiar at Mansfield Abbey, she was unhappy with her lot but hadn't realized it.

It was so dreary, having to watch over Archie all the time, to be constantly hovering on the brink of ruin because of his selfish habits, so it was only natural that she'd crave some variety in her situation. But still, she was frightened by the ferocity with which she suddenly yearned for an adventure. The strange perceptions unnerved her, and she shook them away.

"Now that we're alone," she said, "let's begin again."

"By all means," he mocked, "let's do."

"Shall we sit?"

"I'm comfortable right where I am."

At his response, she couldn't sit, either. He was so tall, and if she seated herself, it would exacerbate their disparities. He was already too conceited by half, and she couldn't have him feeling even more superior.

She walked over but kept several feet of space between them. "I'm begging you to restore my brother's property to him."

"No."

"Captain Westmoreland—"

"Since we're about to be lovers, you might as well call me Lucas. Or Luke. Whichever you prefer is fine by me."

"I'll do no such thing, and we're *not* about to be lovers."

"How badly are you wanting to save your home?"

"Very badly."

"Then call me Luke."

She sighed with frustration. "You're the most exasperating individual I've ever met."

"So I've been told—on many occasions."

He studied her, his torrid gaze leisurely journeying from the top of her head to the tips of her toes. As if he'd prodded her with a hot poker, she sizzled and burned in every spot where he lingered. Her lips were tingly and moist, her breasts heavy and full, the nipples alert and rubbing her corset.

"You're prettier than I thought you'd be. Too skinny, but pretty."

"Really, Captain, you mustn't—"

"Come here." He extended his hand, expecting her to blithely take it.

"No."

"Are you scared of me?"

"Of you?" She laughed, but it sounded feeble. "Why would I be?"

"Maybe because I eat small children for my supper? Or because I ravage women wherever I go?"

As he mentioned some of the shocking tales that were circulating, she detected that he was amused by the gossip. On discovering that he could joke about himself, she calmed, and as she did, she experienced the most bizarre awareness. Of him as a man. Of him as a friend. She seemed to know everything about him, and she had no clue as to why she would, but it was an interesting and welcome insight, and she hoped she could use it to further her cause.

He wasn't the ogre others painted him to be. While indisputably a criminal, with a penchant for mischief and trouble, he was very smart, and he could be fair and compassionate. She could feel it to the marrow of her bones.

"I don't believe any of that folderol."

"You don't?"

"No, though I think you enjoy having the stories spread."

"Why would I?"

"It keeps everyone terrified of you."

He chuckled. "Touché, Miss Mansfield."

A relaxed silence ensued, where they evaluated each other; then he repeated, "Come here."

"No."

"Why?"

"Because you're up to no good."

"I am?"

"Yes, and whatever you're planning, I'll have no part of it."

"You're positive?"

"Yes."

He moved from his perch on the desk and narrowed the distance between them. He was so near that his boots dipped under the hem of her skirt. She could feel his heat; she could smell the soap with which he'd bathed, could see a nick under his chin where he'd cut himself shaving. She was so overwhelmed—by his size, by his charisma and allure—that she was dizzy, and it was all she could do to keep from reaching out to him in order to steady herself.

"You shouldn't have bet with my brother," she scolded.

"*He* bet with me. I didn't start it."

"Then at the end, when all was lost, you shouldn't have wagered over me."

"He offered you; it was none of my doing. I didn't even know he had a sister."

"He might have proposed the deed, but you were wicked to agree. Have you no honor remaining inside you?"

"Not a shred," he confessed, and he shrugged. "The little braggart dug his own hole. He didn't even need a shovel. I was simply an innocent bystander, but after the rants and insults I had to endure, if you suppose I'll ignore his debt, you're mad."

"You males and your blasted pride."

"My pride is enormous. I don't deny it. So I won't back down, and I demand payment. It matters not to me what compensation you choose to render. You can have your property, or you can have your chastity, but you can't have both."

"Aren't you the least bit embarrassed at what you've done?"

"I'm a man," he stated, as if that explained the mysteries of the universe. "I was presented with the opportunity to have a beautiful, eager woman warm my bed for a month. Why would I refuse?"

"Because it's wrong! Because—despite what my idiotic brother might have claimed—I'm not willing!"

"You're more *willing* than you care to admit."

"How can you say that? I'm a spinster, so I have no notion of what it is you wish from me. How could I *want* it to happen?"

"You're desperate to keep your home, so ultimately, you'll be amenable. It has naught to do with what might pass between us, though I'm certain you'll like it much more than you suspect."

"Why is that?"

"I'm a skilled lover. I can make it wonderful for you."

"You're correct: Your pride is enormous. Your head is so swelled with vanity that I'm surprised you can fit it through the door."

"I've never been humble."

"I can tell."

He leaned in, his torso connecting with hers, and she could feel him all the way down. Chest, tummy, thighs, they were forged fast, and his proximity rattled her. Her skin prickled; her heart pounded. Every sense came alive with a renewed energy, and she was confounded by her reaction. She didn't want to like him, but her anatomy had other ideas.

She could scarcely resist wrapping her arms around him and pulling him even nearer. Was she insane? Even in her sheltered condition, she recognized that she desired him. How could that be? He was her enemy, her nemesis. She shouldn't be intrigued, yet there was a powerful voice in her mind, inciting her to try all sorts of conduct that she oughtn't. The urgings were so diabolical that she could barely keep from clasping her hands over her ears to drown out the racket.

What if . . . what if . . .

The question goaded her. What if she submitted? She could let him attempt whatever he wanted. They were alone, and no one would ever know. She'd heard women whispering about the endeavor and some of them enjoyed it, so it couldn't be that awful. She could yield, then return to Mansfield, safe in the knowledge that she'd done a noble thing, that she'd sacrificed herself for the greater good.

He broke into her tormented reverie. "What's it to be, Miss Mansfield?"

She stared into his weathered, attractive face, debating, considering, ruing, and finally, she murmured, "I can't. I'm sorry."

"Why would you be sorry?"

"I want to help my brother, but it would go against everything I believe and everything I've been taught."

"Are you sure this should be your decision?"

"Very sure."

"All right, then. I'll be by next week to take possession."

"Next week!"

"Yes. Inform your brother that I'll expect him to vacate the premises before I arrive."

"But next week!"

"You were supposed to have come to me two months ago, so you're already very late. Your brother kept begging for more time so you could prepare yourself. I've been gracious enough to grant him every extension, but my patience is exhausted. I'm weary of both of you. Please go."

"It's my home," she pathetically mentioned.

"I understand."

"Do you?" she bitterly inquired. "Do you really?"

"I've learned—more than anyone—what it means to lose all."

There wasn't a hint of sympathy in his gaze, and to her horror, tears welled into her eyes. She'd been so confident that she could reason with him, and earlier, she'd sensed a kindred spirit. How could she have been so wrong?

"Why are you doing this to us?"

"Your brother did it, Miss Mansfield. Not me."

"But you don't have to follow through."

"I want to, I guess."

"But why?"

When no answer was forthcoming, a few tears overflowed and splashed down her cheeks. She swiped them away.

"Crying never affects me," he callously advised, "so it's a waste of energy. It won't fix anything."

"Maybe not, but it will definitely make me feel better."

He laughed, and she wanted to hit him, so she spun away. Struggling for calm, she gulped huge breaths, while trying to figure out how to exit with some amount of aplomb, yet she couldn't force her feet toward the door. Once she walked out, any chance she had to sway him would be over. She'd have to proceed to Mansfield and pack her bags, and the prospect was so grim that she couldn't hurry the moment along.

"Did you ever hear talk," he startled her by querying, "about a Miss Mary Lucas, who was a ward of your father's?"

"Over the years, my father had many wards. I couldn't begin to list them all." She peered over her shoulder, hating him for how handsome he was, for how unflappable and in control. "Why would you ask about him anyway? He's been dead for over a decade. What link has he with any of this?"

"How old are you?"

"Twenty-five."

"You're too young, then," he mused. "You wouldn't have known her."

Her father had had many despicable traits, including vice and thievery. He'd been a spendthrift, who'd constantly scrambled for funds, and he'd often fostered orphans so he could pilfer their inheritances. It was a contemptible legacy—not that she'd confess as much to Captain Westmoreland, but it sounded as if he had a grievance against her father on behalf of this Mary Lucas, who, from the name, might be one of his relatives. She sighed. How could she rectify a transgression that had happened before she was born?

"Is there anything I could say that would change your mind?"

"Yes."

Hope sparked eternal. "What?"

"Tell me that you're ready to go upstairs." He arched a brow. "Tell me and mean it."

"You're obsessed with my ruination."

"Not obsessed. Just determined to collect what's due me."

"No, you're obsessed, when I have no notion why." It was pointless to continue imploring, and she trudged out. "I pray your ownership of Mansfield brings you the happiness you so obviously crave, but were I you, I wouldn't count on it."

"Oh, I'm plenty happy, Miss Mansfield. I don't need Mansfield Abbey to make me more so. Farewell. Thank you for stopping by. It's been extremely amusing."

She'd been dismissed, and he immediately forgot about her. He went to a table that was covered with bottles of liquor, and he picked up one and commenced imbibing without benefit of a glass. She watched him, the amber liquid swilling down his throat, his rumination miles away from her petty troubles.

At being snubbed she was furious, and she dawdled, studying him. She was much more curious than she should have been as to what was milling about in his autocratic, devious, twisted head. Coming up for air, he paused, and glanced in her direction.

"Are you still here?" He seemed genuinely surprised. "I thought you'd gone."

"To where?"

"To wherever rich, frilly females like you go in the day."

The remark rankled, pricking at her temper and civility. Frantic for leniency, for mercy, she'd debased herself before him, had let him embarrass her in front of his paramours, and she was seething.

"Oh yes," she retorted, "since I'm so wealthy and indolent, I'm off to Mansfield Abbey. No, wait! I can't go there. It doesn't belong to me anymore."

"It never did. It was your brother's."

"It was mine—in my heart and my soul."

"And now it's mine. Isn't it interesting how a few minutes can alter everything?"

She stewed, wondering how to get through to him, how to make him listen. Could any plea influence him? He stared, cold as a fish, clearly wishing she'd depart and quit pestering him.

She pictured him with her brother, the two of them chuckling merrily as they gambled and drank. Why should they be allowed to inflict so much misery on so many? Why should they have the prerogative to decide what would occur?

Suddenly the pressures of her life were crushing her. She was tired of being clever and pragmatic, the one who fixed every mess, who cleaned up after every catastrophe.

Age thirty was approaching fast, and what had she to show for her time on earth? No husband, no children, no home of her own, and no possibility of any of those things ever becoming reality. She was alone and always would be. She had no possessions other than a few shabby, unflattering dresses, no cash to spend on herself. Why . . . if she'd wanted to run away and start over, she hadn't the wherewithal to go!

All she had was Mansfield Abbey. It was *her* world that was being destroyed. Not theirs. The two wastrels weren't concerned about Mansfield. She was their pawn in a fight she didn't understand, but with the security of Mansfield her paramount objective, what else mattered?

Archie had demolished whatever good name they'd

had, so her reputation was in shreds. Her chastity—
protected for twenty-five years for some obscure future
spouse—would never be needed. She could never wed,
for she could never be shed of Archie. She didn't dare
leave him to his own devices, didn't dare walk away from
Mansfield and give him free rein. Without her mitigat-
ing presence, there was no predicting what disasters he'd
instigate.

If Westmoreland took Mansfield Abbey, where would
she go? What would she do? Her existence was so tied to
the place that should she be obliged to abandon it, she
might simply cease to be.

A flicker of resolve ignited, then blazed into a burning
inferno. She wouldn't lose Mansfield. She couldn't. Not
when it was within her power to save it.

"I'll do it," she muttered, almost before she realized
she'd spoken aloud.

"You'll do what?"

"I'll grace your bed for a month. I don't think any
woman has ever died from performing the marital act, so
it can't be too repulsive."

"Repulsive?"

"Yes. I'm sure I have the stomach to force myself
through it."

"Well, that stellar attitude certainly makes me want to
lie down with you." As if her declaration were the funni-
est ever, he laughed and laughed, and when he'd re-
gained control, he said, "Sorry, but I've had a change of
heart. After meeting you, I'd rather eat hot coals than
sleep with you. You can slink back to the country. In fact,
if it will hurry you along, I'll have Mr. Smith escort you."

"Oh no, you don't, Captain Westmoreland." She
stomped over, her determination hardening with each

stride, and she poked a finger in his chest. "A deal is a deal. You demanded this result; you pushed for it. I'm here, and you'll have me—and you'll be glad about it!"

He assessed her as if she'd gone mad. "*Glad* is it?"

"Stark-raving, gleefully, unbearably delighted. I guarantee it."

"Do you now?"

She *was* feeling a tad insane. "Yes, so direct me to your bedchamber. You have a bedchamber in this monstrosity of a house, don't you?"

"Oh aye, I have a very grand one."

"Then take me to it. The sooner we commence this charade, the quicker I can be rid of you."

She strutted into the hall, not tarrying to learn if he'd follow, but he did.

3

In here."

Luke shoved open the door to his suite, and he studied Miss Mansfield's delectable bottom as she sauntered in ahead of him.

She really was pretty, though she'd tried her darnedest to hide her best attributes. Her body was slender but shapely, so she was tempting and lush in all the ways a man enjoyed. She had the biggest, most expressive hazel eyes, and the most fabulous brunette hair, but with it pulled into a neat bun, and a dress that covered her from chin to toe, she could have been a stern schoolteacher or grumpy governess.

He pitied her for her lack of feminine wiles. She'd come to him hoping to entice, hoping to persuade, and she'd worn *brown*! How could she think to titillate when she looked so drab?

He liked his women buxom and blond, flashy and sophisticated. His debauched tastes were a sad indicator of
how long and how frequently he'd fraternized with
whores. He couldn't recall having ever fornicated with a
virgin, especially one of Miss Mansfield's lofty social
status. The notion of having intimate relations with her,
of instructing her as to what she should do with her
hands and her mouth, was extremely disconcerting.

With his recent acclaim, every hussy in London was
flocking to his stoop. They were eager to consort with
him, and he'd been seriously entertained, so he was busy.
The last thing he needed was to fuss with a silly, frightened shrew who had a sharp tongue and domineering
manner.

He loathed the Mansfield family. Three decades earlier, his mother, Mary Lucas, had been a ward of the late,
despicable Mr. Mansfield. He'd done such a poor job of
seeing to her welfare that she'd often been without ade-
quate supervision. While scant more than a girl, she'd
been seduced by the infamous Duke of Roswell, Harold
Westmoreland.

When she wound up pregnant, Mansfield had tossed
her out without a penny. She'd managed to survive until
Luke was five, but she'd never been a strong person, and
their dire circumstances had quickly exhausted her.

She'd gone to her grave pining away for the Duke,
Luke's disgraceful father, even though the Duke had never
given her a single farthing or acknowledged his baby son.
Her imprudent affection had taught Luke a hard lesson:
Love was foolish. It only brought grief and devastation.

Over the years, he'd made his own way in the world.
He'd grown up on the streets of London as a successful
and notorious criminal, and he'd served an eternity in the
penal colonies in Australia—from which he'd escaped

after many desperate attempts. Through gambling and vice, he now owned a fast sailing ship, and he was rapidly becoming a wealthy man with no recognition or assistance from his aristocratic sire.

He'd never met the Duke and didn't want to meet him. Luke's Christian name—William—was a Westmoreland family name, one conferred on sons throughout the centuries. Luke rarely used it, preferring his mother's surname of Lucas, instead. He considered the choice to be a snub of his father and all that the affluent, pretentious man represented.

With the Navy rescue Luke had effected, with his being feted at every turn and even publicly praised by the Prince Regent, there were rumors that the Duke was finally interested in an introduction, but Luke detested the vile libertine and planned to reject any overture.

Luke's dislike of the Mansfields was no less potent. He had a score to settle with them, a desire to seek justice on his mother's behalf. The objective had driven him forever, had provided resolve and solace during tortures and incarcerations.

When he'd won Mansfield Abbey from Archie Mansfield, he'd been delighted. When the brother had offered up the sister, Luke had been even more thrilled. What could be more appropriate than to have a precious Mansfield daughter ruined by a Westmoreland as Luke's own mother had been?

He'd thought he could force the issue, but he couldn't. He'd expected Helen Mansfield to be an exact copy of the father, of the brother, but she wasn't, and Luke felt sorry for her. She seemed to be a very sincere individual—a tad bossy, to be sure—but with a sibling like Archie Mansfield who wouldn't be difficult? She'd been ensnared in her brother's folly, and Luke wouldn't ravage her because of it.

He had a few scruples—not many, but a few—and she had weighty problems winging in her direction. She didn't need the added complication of a sexual frolic with a disreputable pirate.

Nor did *the pirate* relish the trouble and bother that would ensue should he keep her for the next thirty days. She assumed that she was resigned to forfeiting her chastity, but she never would. Not for him, anyway. He wanted her gone, but she was a proud woman, and pride was something about which he knew quite a bit. He would send her home, feeling redeemed in her quest to save her estate.

She frowned at the empty space. "Why don't you have any furniture?"

The comment irked him. His mother had been the daughter of a baronet, his father a duke. Luke secretly yearned to behave as if he were at ease in their realm so that he could more swiftly advance into their society, and his lack of refinement was so annoying. He had money to obtain the necessary items, but he had no idea what those items should be.

"I'm renting the place temporarily," he lied, "and I haven't had the opportunity to shop."

"If I'm to spend a month here, you must make arrangements for my comfort."

"Such as?"

"For starters, you must hire a lady's maid for me. And I'll have to have cupboards and dressers in which to keep my things. Clothing has to be delivered."

"By all means, Your Majesty, I'll see to it right away. But I intend for you to be completely occupied." His appreciative male gaze roamed down her torso. "You won't need anything to wear."

"Of course I'll need clothes, you oaf! As opposed to

the slatterns with whom you typically fraternize, I am a gentlewoman."

"But *I* am not a gentleman. I like my feminine companions to be naked."

She whipped away. "Have you a bed upon which to sleep?"

"In the adjoining chamber, but we won't be *sleeping*."

He nodded toward it, and she stomped over. She was putting on a very bold front, and he was humored by her displays of bravado. He was curious as to how far she'd wander down the carnal road before she panicked and called a halt.

She stopped in the threshold, her eyes wide. His bed was massive and ornate, with a carved headboard, thick quilts, and a plush mattress. It was the sole thing in the entire room and covered most of the floor.

"For pity's sake," she groused, "it's fit for a king."

"It certainly is."

"I'll need a ladder to climb onto it." She glared over at him. "You've taken time to purchase one piece of furniture, and *that* is what you buy?"

"None of my paramours has complained."

He wasn't about to explain his past, the hovels and icy stairwells as a child or the dank, slimy cells as an adult. Sweet dreams, when he could find them, were a must. He had the resources to slumber in luxury, and he indulged to the limit.

He pushed her inside, and he followed, tugging at the curtains and lighting the lamp. She watched, the silence growing awkward, the tension so extreme that he could nearly taste it.

"What . . . what now?" she inquired as he crossed to her.

"*Now,* we begin."

"With what?"

"With you keeping your part of the bargain."

"I don't know what to do."

He was charmed by her confession. "I'll show you."

He untied her cloak, and as he drew it away, he noticed that his hands were shaking. He was a bundle of nerves! How extraordinary! How hilarious!

"Turn around," he commanded.

"Why?"

"I want your hair down."

"My hair?"

"Yes. I like it flowing down your back."

"Must you?"

"I'm afraid I insist."

She pondered refusal; then she spun and held herself very still as he yanked at the pins and combs. The tresses swished down in a brunette wave that hung to her waist. It was a rich mahogany, shot through with strands of auburn and gold, and she stiffened as he riffled his fingers through it.

He was excited to be touching her so intimately, and his level of enjoyment disturbed him. The wrongness of his conduct, the excess, was exhilarating, and he pulled away, not liking the sensations she engendered.

He fluffed the lengthy mass over her shoulders, as he grumbled, "Much better."

"Are we going to lie down?"

"Eventually." He rotated her so that she was facing him.

"Will it hurt?"

"Will what *hurt*?"

"What you're about to do to me."

"No." He smiled. "Why would you think it would?"

"I heard some women talking once. They said . . . well . . ."

"They were mistaken," he fibbed, not seeing any reason to confirm her fears. He wasn't about to breach any maidenheads, so she didn't need to know the true details. "It will be very pleasant."

She licked her bottom lip, the guileless move making his cock shift and stir. Without warning, and to his utter shock, a fine erection was forming. Apparently, he desired her more than he'd realized, and considering how avidly he'd been romping in recent days, how could he have any unsated lust remaining?

He was no better than a rutting dog!

Just like your father! a voice scolded, but he ignored it.

"May I ask you a question?" she queried.

"I'm not sure I'll answer, but try me."

"If we're not married, how can we . . . we . . ."

She blushed. Naughty discussion was beyond her, and her hesitancy emphasized how contemptibly he was acting. He'd lost his virginity at age thirteen, as a boy running errands for whores in a brothel. For most of his life, his lovers had been the crude, coarse women of port towns and taverns. Lately, with his spreading celebrity, the caliber of his partners had risen, but they'd always been mature, experienced females who knew what they wanted and how to go about getting it.

Miss Mansfield was like a fresh breeze on a hot summer afternoon. Who was he to shatter her innocence?

"How can we what?"

"Well, men and women do things that are . . ." She groaned with frustration. "Oh, I can't describe what they *do,* but I thought you had to be husband and wife to do it!"

Had he ever been that young? That naïve? His upbringing had been so different from hers. He couldn't remember a time when he hadn't understood the facts of adult behavior, and though he was only thirty, compared to her he felt a hundred and thirty.

"Haven't you ever seen two lovers kissing after a dance or at a fair?"

"I don't believe so."

"Have you ever been kissed?"

"No."

"Really?"

She glanced away, embarrassed at having to admit her spinsterish status. In her world, maidens didn't cavort with gentlemen unless marriage was the goal. They didn't sneak around in parlors, seeking passion. Still, she was very pretty. She should have had a dozen swains.

Why hadn't any man dared? How marvelous that he would be the first!

"Shut your eyes."

"Why?"

"I'm going to surprise you."

"How?"

"Just do it, Miss Mansfield."

"I don't trust you."

"Which is very wise, but do it anyway."

She stared at him, then complied, her lashes fluttering down. He stepped in, his trousers brushing her skirt. Sparks ignited, their surroundings crackling with an energy that greatly disconcerted him.

He was so jaded and cynical, while she was so pure and unsullied, and he wanted to grab her and hold her until some of her decency and wholesomeness rubbed off.

Shaking off the odd impressions, he rested his hands on her shoulders; then he leaned down and kissed her. In the history of kisses, it wasn't much about which to brag. He didn't clasp her body to his own, didn't maul or grope her, but the interlude was stunning and fulfilling in a fashion he hadn't encountered prior. Her lips were soft and moist, her breath sweet and warm, and he tarried, relishing the dear moment.

He enjoyed kissing and did quite a lot of it, but it was always a swift and brief prologue to the main event. Why dawdle when the ultimate bliss was so near? Yet, with Miss Mansfield, he had no intention of pursuing a squalid ending, so he could revel in the embrace without racing to the conclusion.

He lingered much too long, and he had to force himself to break it off. Scowling, flustered, he scrutinized her, wondering what he'd set in motion. He'd never be satisfied with a single kiss, not when he craved so much more.

"Can I open my eyes now?" she asked.

"Yes."

She peered up at him with a new and keen interest. "That was very nice."

"Yes, it was." Numerous comments were possible, but what emerged was, "I want to do it again."

Without waiting to hear if she did, too, he wrapped his arms around her, and there was nothing chaste or restrained about his advance. He was overcome by a wild, reckless urge to have her. Luckily, she was as swept up, as frantic, as he, and she participated with an equal fervor.

He teased and taunted, moaning with pleasure as he dipped his tongue inside. A strange fever was driving him, a need he'd never felt before, and he couldn't seem to get close enough to her. He lifted her, carrying her backward until she was trapped against a bedpost. He moved between her legs, her thighs balanced on his own, her skirt rucked up.

At the salacious positioning his phallus was ecstatic. He flexed, his hips matching the rhythm of his tongue.

He kissed her forever; he couldn't stop. His fingers found her breast, kneading and fondling the plump mound, the action increasing his ardor.

He kept on until he was so aroused that he worried he'd spill himself in his pants like a callow boy. He was so titillated that he couldn't predict what he might do. A loud voice inside his head was spurring him to finish— despite her wishes—to take her and be done with it, and he was startled by its ferocity.

He never lost control with a woman, was never overwhelmed by lust, so he couldn't figure out what was occurring. He viewed sex solely as a corporeal alleviation, usually as a business deal, too—with money paid for services rendered—yet she'd incited him to madness.

She had the good sense to pull away, and her hesitation yanked him to sanity. He nibbled across her cheek, her nape. He should have released her and slid away, but she fit perfectly in his arms, and he couldn't bring himself to let her go.

"Please, Captain," she begged.

"It's all right," he soothed.

"This is all happening too fast," she said. "I need to catch my breath."

"Of course." He was kicking himself for acting like such a beast. She had to be reeling, as confused by their amazing bond as he was himself. He'd had almost two decades to adapt to the spiral of desire, while she'd had no opportunity, at all.

He shouldn't have rushed her. If he'd been more patient, they could have continued until . . .

He didn't complete the reflection, for he refused to ponder where his enthusiasm might have led them. She provoked him in ways he'd never imagined, had unlocked an old reservoir of yearning that he'd assumed he'd buried ages ago.

She was dangerous to his equilibrium, and he had to get rid of her before he did something stupid, something irrevocable. He straightened and slackened his grip, gliding her down his body till her feet touched the floor.

"There's a connection between us, isn't there?" she ventured. "That's . . . unique?"

"Yes."

"Why are we feeling it?"

"It's a mystery. Some people are just suited, as others aren't and never will be. There's no explanation."

"But I don't even like you, so how could that be?"

He chuckled. "Perhaps you like me a bit more than you realize."

"No, I don't. I'm positive I loathe you."

He bent down and kissed her again, a simple brush of his lips to hers. Briefly she allowed the contact; then she turned away.

"I can't do this," she whispered. "I thought I could, but it would be so wrong."

"It's not wrong, Helen." A deranged, insatiable part of him wanted her to stay, wanted her to give him all the things she'd promised.

"It is," she insisted. "It's so much more physical than I envisioned."

"We have a special attachment. We shouldn't walk away from it."

What was he saying? Was he crazy? He had to shut his idiotic mouth! At once! His goal was for her to huff out in a snit, and he couldn't have his unruly cock guiding his words.

"I can't."

She was embarrassed and staring down at the rug. The sight of her—so rumpled and adorable, disheveled from his attentions—tugged at deep, unfamiliar emotions that had him desperate to keep and protect her.

He was eager to coax her out of her decision and her drawers, to cajole and beguile until she relented. He could, too. He was a master at seduction, and she was a lonely, isolated female. With hardly any effort, he could woo her into doing what she oughtn't, but it would be detestable to coerce her into a relationship that would leave her devastated in the end.

She had no business being swept into his sordid life.

"This doesn't change anything," he felt duty bound to mention.

"I know."

"I'll seize the estate."

"I understand."

"Are you certain?"

"Yes."

She started to cry in earnest, pretty tears dripping down her cheeks, but she did nothing to hide them. It seemed as if her heart was breaking, and his dormant conscience shifted uneasily. He reached out and swiped them away, and the feel of those salty drops on his fingertips was nearly his undoing. He almost yielded, almost told her he wouldn't go through with it, and he managed to bite down the offer before he uttered it.

How had she captivated him? Why had he let her?

"Don't be sad," he entreated.

"But I've failed everyone."

"No, you haven't. It wasn't your job to rescue them."

"It's always been my job," she bleakly replied. "That's all I do is take care of everybody else. I'm so tired of it."

"Then maybe it's time they took responsibility for

themselves," he gently advised. "You needn't shoulder it all."

"So many will be lost without me." She slumped with resignation. "I recognize that I have no right, but might I ask you a favor?"

"I can't guarantee I'll grant it."

"Will you permit my servants to stay on? Some of their families have been at Mansfield for generations. I hate to have them suffer because of my brother."

It was a fair request, and he'd need help with the property. "I'll have Mr. Smith interview them."

"Thank you."

"Their remaining will depend on if they can work for me, if they can be loyal. I'm renowned as a brutal taskmaster."

"You're not as vicious as you pretend to be."

"I'm not?"

"No."

He smiled, thrilled that she had such a heightened opinion of his character. What would it be like to live up to her expectations? For a flickering instant, he was disappointed that he'd never have the chance to find out.

"Good-bye, Helen."

"Good-bye, Captain Westmoreland."

Neither of them could bear to separate. The encounter had been too enchanted, and though the coming weeks would bring fighting and enmity, for the moment they dawdled like a pair of half-wits, assessing, remembering, cataloguing features. He linked their fingers, squeezing tight to reassure and console; then he dipped down for one last kiss. She joined in, groaning with pleasure and despair, and she pressed her face against his chest.

As if he was precious to her, as if she was afraid to let him go, she cradled him to her as he stroked his hands up and down her back. Then, without another word, she stepped away and ran, not stopping to so much as grab her cloak.

He stood in the quiet house, listening as her fleet strides carried her down the stairs and out the front door. For the longest while, he tarried, wondering . . . if she'd had a parting comment . . . what it might have been.

4

I couldn't go through with it," Helen explained for the hundredth time. She was weary of the entire argument. "I'm sorry."

"You're *sorry*?" her brother grouched. "What have you to be sorry about? I'm the one who's lost everything."

She watched as he paced the floor. He was a pretty man, with shiny brown hair and big hazel eyes. He had such appealing features that he was often mistaken for a girl. At age twenty-three, he was the consummate London gentleman who thrived on his life in the city, and he viewed the estate as a necessary evil that funded his lavish routine. He'd never felt the bond to the land or the people that weighed so heavily on Helen.

He was polished and suave, his clothes perfectly tailored, his hair neatly trimmed, his nails delicately manicured, and at that moment Helen would have loved nothing more than to walk across the room and slap him silly.

Since she'd arrived home from the debacle with Captain Westmoreland, she'd been listening to a relentless diatribe of all the ways she'd failed. During the awful encounter, Westmoreland had delivered sufficient humiliation, and she didn't need Archie piling on more.

"You shouldn't have made such a terrible bet," Helen said. "You know I'd never agree to consort with him."

"If you had any feminine instincts, you could have pulled this off. How could you be related to me and be so lacking in style? Look at you!" He gestured at her modest green dress. "You're a veritable drab. Of course he didn't want you! You were supposed to be charming! You had to give him something to . . . to . . . desire! Have you no concept of the type of woman that a knave like Westmoreland enjoys?"

Her cheeks burned with embarrassment. She knew precisely the kind who tickled his fancy. She'd seen them lounging in his library like a gaggle of gorgeous mermaids, and though she'd never admit it, Archie was correct: If she'd been more glamorous or attractive—if she'd been more *loose* with her favors—she could have persuaded Captain Westmoreland. He'd seemed to like her, had definitely lusted after her, and if she'd enticed him, she could have saved them all.

"Perhaps if you'd hinted at what was expected of me," she snapped, "I might have been a tad more prepared."

"And how would prior knowledge of my wager have made any difference?" he retorted. "Would it have gotten you into his bed? I think not!"

"Now, now, Archie," his friend Adrian Bennett cut in, "you're in a dither, and it's not helping. You must calm yourself." As he deflected Archie's rancor, he flashed a conspiratorial wink at Helen. "You're being too hard on Helen. She tried her best; you know she did."

"I know nothing of the sort," Archie replied. "She's ruined me!"

"There's no reasoning with Westmoreland," Adrian continued. "You remember what he was like. He's completely perverse. Helen hadn't a better chance than either of us."

"Oh, what time is it?" Archie wailed as he glanced at the clock. "One-thirty! Gad, he'll be here any minute. He and his crew of dirty pirates will swarm over all my property. I'm sick, I tell you, just sick!"

He stomped out, his irrational complaining drifting off as he went. As usual, he couldn't fathom how any of the catastrophe was his fault, and Helen could only shake her head in disgust at how self-centered he was. He'd always acted like a little prince, and he'd grown from being a cute, wicked boy to a cute, nasty man, and she'd long ago abandoned hope of improved conduct.

As his footsteps faded, Adrian smiled and shrugged. "What shall we do with him, hmm?"

"He's out of control."

"Don't worry, Helen. I'll take him to London with me. We'll have him squared away in a thrice."

Helen was vastly comforted by Adrian's pledge of assistance. He was Archie's constant companion, and they'd been confidants for over a year, so close that Archie had invited Adrian to move into his town house, where he and Adrian had adjoining bedchambers. In many ways, Adrian was Archie's double, beautiful and slender, though with blond hair and blue eyes. He relished fashionable clothes, fine wine, and Archie's world of parties and balls.

With Adrian being thirty-five and so much older than

Archie, she'd initially deemed it a strange relationship, but anymore, she didn't question their association. Adrian was good for Archie. He was a positive influence and curbed many of Archie's worst impulses, so Helen welcomed his presence and was happy to see him when the two men visited Mansfield. He was a gracious, educated, and interesting guest.

"Will you leave this afternoon?" she asked.

"As soon as the Captain's entourage is spotted out on the road."

Helen breathed a sigh of relief. She didn't have to place Archie and Captain Westmoreland in the same room to predict that it would be a disaster.

Noise erupted out in the drive, and Adrian walked to the window to discover the cause.

"Is it Westmoreland?" she inquired.

"Yes. He's brought only one carriage, though. He's on horseback, with another rider accompanying him."

"No horde of pirates?"

"No. I guess he's not afraid of us."

"Why would he be? We're a bunch of housemaids and farmers. What could we do? Beat him to death with mops and hoes?"

"It's a thought," Adrian said, chuckling; then he quivered with an uncharacteristic annoyance. "He sits on that horse like a king! He's smug and proud as a peacock."

"Why shouldn't he be? He's got everything, and we have nothing."

"He's a handsome devil, isn't he?"

"He is at that." She flushed with memories of how dashing he was, how tall and broad. In the week since she'd trifled with him, she'd relived their encounter over and over. Each detail was as vivid and arousing as when it had actually transpired.

Suddenly she felt overheated, her pulse beating too fast, as she rose to greet him. She was much more excited than she should have been. After all, the blackguard was coming to evict her. Her bags were packed and in the foyer, her and Archie's gig ready to carry her to the vicar's residence in the village, where she would spend a few days while she decided what to do next.

"Would you like me to go down with you?" Adrian queried.

"There's no need. One of his minions swore to me that he doesn't bite."

"With all those weapons hanging off his belt, he certainly looks vicious. Are you sure?"

"Quite sure. He talks tough, but he's harmless."

"Harmless! He's rumored to have murdered a thousand men."

"All poppycock." She started into the hall. "Why don't you find Archie and keep him occupied? It's probably best that they don't bump into each other."

"A prudent suggestion." He nodded and followed her. "I'll distract him and spirit him away before he realizes that Westmoreland is here."

"Thank you."

She descended the stairs alone, savoring a final solitary stroll through her home. The staff was awaiting the Captain on the lawn. They were dreading his appearance but curious, too, about the infamous swashbuckler and hero. Everyone wanted to take his measure, and they were eager to curry his favor so they wouldn't lose their jobs.

She didn't blame them. It wasn't their fault that Archie was a fool. They had bills to pay and families to support. She simply wished she'd had the gumption to offer Westmoreland something he valued so that she could have stayed, too.

As she stepped outside, she wondered why she wasn't more distraught. She should have been crumpled in the grass and weeping like a babe, but the occasion was so unbelievable that her mind couldn't process it. Events were happening slowly, as if she were trudging through water or having a peculiar dream.

The gardener grumbled, "Will he eat the children? Shall we hide them?"

The entire assemblage bristled at the prospect, and Helen scolded, "For heaven's sake! He won't eat anyone's children!"

"Will he ravish the women?" The maid Peg shivered as if she was hoping he'd commence with her.

"No," Helen insisted. "The stories you've heard are nonsense. He's a perfect gentleman." Which was a lie but would calm nerves.

Westmoreland reined in and dismounted, and in the brilliant sunshine he was even more dynamic than he'd been in London. With his golden hair and bronzed skin, he shimmered like an apparition. He was attired as the bandit he was, in a rough-hewn tan shirt, brown trousers, and high black boots, and he had a gold earring in his ear that she hadn't previously noted. As if anticipating resistance, he was armed to the teeth, with a large pistol strapped to each hip and ferocious daggers dangling from several locations.

The slim, alert guard she'd seen in the city lagged behind him, watching his back. The guard was as heavily armed as Westmoreland and scanned the landscape, searching for trouble and risk. The only normal one of the bunch was the young, efficient Mr. Smith, who climbed out of the carriage to join them.

Westmoreland stood, feet braced, studying his new domain with a keen interest. As he finished his survey, a barking hound rushed from the stables, and it was stupid enough to lunge at the imposing stranger.

As if wild dogs were a common occurrence, Westmoreland hardly reacted. He casually turned and ordered, "Sit!"

The command was so forceful and authoritative that the whole line of servants shifted as if the direction were for them as well as the animal, and Helen was surprised that none of them plopped down on the ground. As for the dog, it was completely cowed. It whimpered and fell to its haunches.

Westmoreland leaned down and extended his fingers, letting the creature learn his scent; then he straightened and—as if they weren't aware of his identity—proclaimed, "I am Captain William Lucas Westmoreland. If any of you has a problem with my arrival, you're to leave immediately. Those who would like to remain are welcome, but you'll have to swear an oath of fidelity to me. I demand absolute loyalty, and I'll brook no disobedience. Talk it over among yourselves, then apprise Mr. Smith of your decisions."

He started toward the house, but she was positioned in front of the door, and he couldn't enter unless she moved.

"Good day, Miss Mansfield," he hailed. "We meet again."

Ridiculously, she was hurt that he'd referred to her as *Miss Mansfield*. In London, when they'd been intimately thrown together, he'd called her Helen.

"Captain Westmoreland," she said, nodding.

"You're looking particularly fetching this afternoon." His avid gaze raked over her, his lusty nature apparent for all to witness. The men were green with envy, the women fanning themselves, and Helen blushed a bright pink as she was assailed by recollections of her and Westmoreland's magnificent kisses.

Before she could regroup, he gripped her by the waist, picked her up, and set her to the side, strutting past as if she were invisible.

She couldn't say what behavior she'd wanted from him, but she'd never have guessed that he'd act as if they were scarcely acquainted. Their brief, wicked tryst had rattled her so that she could reflect on naught but him.

Absurdly, she'd assumed that the rendezvous would have had a similar effect on him, that he'd have been missing her and glad to see her again. The fact that he'd barely glanced at her was a painful and humiliating reminder of how insignificant the assignation had been on his end.

He was the consummate cad, who regularly engaged in seduction, and she'd been so inept at amour that he probably didn't even remember what they'd done.

Ablaze with mortification, she kicked herself for mooning over him. What had she been thinking?

Determined to depart with aplomb and courtesy, she followed him inside. Though it galled her, she'd give him a polite tour, would chat and describe the rooms and furnishings, then she'd go without a nostalgic tear or moment of begging.

She'd just firmed her resolve when her brother waltzed into the foyer. There was an instant of astonished recognition; then Archie sneered, "So, Westmoreland, you've finally slinked in. You filthy thief, I could smell you at twenty paces."

.At the slur, the spectators gasped. Compared to Westmoreland with his superior size, Archie was a tiny man. He'd always had an elevated opinion of his place in the world, and he felt that others should defer to him because of it. He didn't grasp that social standing meant nothing to the Captain.

Westmoreland towered over Archie, but Archie didn't notice or comprehend that he was in danger.

"You're supposed to be gone, Mansfield," the Captain remarked. "Why are you still here?"

"I live here, you despicable swine."

"Not anymore. This is my property, and I don't have to suffer your annoying presence."

"I'll go when I'm good and ready, you foul bastard."

A deadly menace swept over the Captain, and he grabbed Archie by his shirt, lifted him with one hand, and tossed him against the wall. Archie flew through the air like a rag doll, his arms flailing, his head hitting the plaster with a loud thump; then he slid to the floor and huddled in a ball.

Westmoreland bent over him and muttered, "If you ever insult my mother again, I'll kill you."

As if Archie were dung in a pasture, Westmoreland stepped over him and proceeded on. Adrian was lurking in the shadows, observing the altercation with alarm.

"Aren't you Mr. Bennett?" Westmoreland questioned.

"Yes," Adrian admitted.

"Drag your queer friend out of here, and if you value your meal ticket as much as you seem to, you won't let him return."

"I won't," Adrian vowed. "We'll leave for London right away."

"You do that." Westmoreland stormed by him, bellowing over his shoulder to his guard, "Sergeant Reilly, I want them off the premises in fifteen minutes. Have my driver take them in the carriage, so that I can be certain of it. I won't have them riding off on my new horses. Keep them out of the stables."

Reilly acknowledged the order with a smart salute, then went over to prod Archie to his feet.

Helen watched the mêlée, stifling her glee at Archie's receiving the thrashing he'd so richly deserved. Still, she was terrified over the fate of her tenants and servants. Westmoreland obviously had a temper that could quickly have him rampaging, so what would become of them?

When she and Westmoreland had been sequestered in his bedchamber, she'd had such a different view of his character. She'd pegged him as a tough, uncultured individual, but one who was reasonable and wise enough to manage the estate in her stead.

She hadn't foreseen drama and intimidation and . . . and . . . violence. How could she have been so mistaken?

She couldn't allow the fiasco to continue. Not when she had the power to prevent it. She sidled around her brother, where Adrian was hunkered down and assisting him, and she hastened to Westmoreland's side.

"What?" he growled, his eyes shooting fire.

"I've changed my mind," she whispered, not anxious to be overheard.

"About what?"

"About you. I'll . . . I'll have you."

Realization dawned as to her intent, and he scoffed. "Well, *I* won't have you. Go away. I'm busy."

He espied Mr. Smith, who was tiptoeing by the brouhaha in the threshold. Smith was clutching papers, his astute gaze assessing the surroundings, his pen poised to jot an inventory of her belongings.

"Mr. Smith, come here," Westmoreland commanded.

Smith hurried over. "Yes, Captain?"

"Miss Mansfield is pestering me. Find out where it is she's planned to settle, and see to it that she gets there without delay."

"But what about my cataloguing the chattels?"

"It can wait."

Mr. Smith moved to usher her out, and she leapt out of reach, hiding behind Westmoreland's broad frame. She snuggled herself to him, boldly wrapping her arms around his waist so that Smith would have to physically yank her away to comply.

Westmoreland snarled with frustration and pried at her fingers, but every time he pulled them apart, she laced them together again.

He peered around and groused, "Miss Mansfield, stop it."

"No."

"What is it you want from me?"

"Give me another chance. Please?"

He pondered and wavered, his male attention drifting down her body. Ultimately, he warned, "I don't have the patience for your games. You better mean it."

"I do."

"Then haul your ass upstairs. Now!" She released him and raced away, scrambling as fast as her legs would carry her. Down below, he was talking to Smith.

"Guard these stairs," he said, "and don't let anyone up them till I come back down."

"But . . . but . . ."

"Just do it, Mr. Smith."

Then he was tromping after her, his strides heavy and purposeful. She was quaking with trepidation, shocked by what she'd instigated. Their prior foray had provided her with some idea of what was about to happen. He would touch and kiss her, would fondle and pet, would do more and try more than she could begin to imagine. And she was ready to permit him any liberty!

She wanted him so desperately, and she couldn't figure

out why. Her amorous hunger was wrong and sinful, and she had to fight it with every fiber of her being. She couldn't participate with the enthusiasm she'd shown previously, wouldn't embarrass herself with the same sighs and moans of ecstasy.

She had to control herself, as any properly bred Englishwoman ought!

She dashed into her room, entering before she had the opportunity to reflect on why she'd brought him to *her* chamber instead of another. There were a dozen bedrooms. She could have chosen any one of them, but she hadn't, and it was too late to select another location.

If he came in—for even a second—the rumors would be excruciating. She'd never live them down.

Did it matter? With the security of Mansfield at stake, was there any other option? Considering the good she'd render by proceeding, how could her reputation signify?

She stared at her bed, seeing it in a whole new light. It was so small and cozy, so different from his king's bed, and her stomach tickled. As she perused it—her thoughts in disarray, her resolve weakening—he stomped in behind her.

She whipped around as he sealed her fate by slamming the door and turning the key in the lock.

"Lie down," he ordered, "and be quick about it. I'm positive this will be very unpleasant, and I want to get it over with as rapidly as possible."

5

Luke watched as Miss Mansfield climbed onto the mattress and stretched out. Her eyes were tightly closed, and she was stiff as a board, her ugly dress covering every inch of intriguing skin, and she was so miserable that he wanted to laugh.

It was painfully obvious that she'd rather be tortured on the rack than fornicate with him, and he wasn't about to waste his time bedding a cold, hostile woman. He had to gain control of the estate so that no one questioned his ownership, but her insistence on a reprieve had rankled at his better sense, had sent him skipping off to her bedchamber like a lunatic.

That damned kiss was the reason, he admitted. That accursed, irritating, aggravating kiss! He couldn't get it out of his head. It had felt so right to hold her, and since she'd fled London he hadn't been able to stop thinking about her.

He had to kiss her again so that he could figure out how he'd been bewitched. If he had to kiss her for the next hour—for the next day!—that's what he'd do. He planned to keep on till he'd purged himself of his irksome, over-whelming desire to be with her.

He clumped about, jerking at his belt, tossing his knives and pistols on the table. Each noise had her flinch-ing, and he enjoyed tormenting her. Let her suffer as he'd been suffering!

"What are you doing?" she inquired.

"I'm removing my clothes."

"You're what?" She scrunched her eyes even more firmly shut.

"When a man makes love to a woman, he likes to do it naked."

"Naked! I'm not about to—"

"Helen?"

"What?"

"Be silent."

"You can't expect me to simply lie quietly while you . . . you . . . ." Her pretty cheeks burned with embar-rassment.

"The terms of the bet are that you're to do whatever I ask, and if I *ask* you to be naked, then naked is what you shall be." He paused. "Unless you'd like to go back down-stairs . . . ?"

She gnawed on her bottom lip. "No. You may carry on."

He yanked off his shirt and pitched it on the floor. He wasn't sure why he was disrobing. Perhaps he wanted to infuriate her, or rattle her, or maybe—just maybe—he wanted to feel her soft hands on his bare skin.

He walked over and gazed down at her. She'd heard him approach, and her panic rose even higher. Her body was rigid with fear, as her virginal mind conjured ruthless scenarios.

What kind of beast does she suppose I am?

As the surly rumination swirled by, he realized exactly what she assumed. He worked hard to cultivate a contemptible image. In his chosen profession, he had to appear vicious and unbending, and when the circumstances called for brutality, he could definitely be cruel.

She'd listened to the stories, so she had to be terrified, and his temper faded like leaves on the wind. She wasn't like any woman he'd ever met before, so, where she was concerned, he had no frame of reference, but his attraction was eating away at him. He was eager to tarry with her, to bask in her glow, to rescue her from the lonely, awful life she seemed to be leading.

The sudden burst of emotion was exasperating, but he let it wash over him as he sat on the edge of the mattress and leaned forward, his palms balanced on either side of her.

"Helen?"

"What?"

"Open your eyes."

"No. Just do what you have to do, and get it over with."

He chuckled. "Look at me."

"No," she repeated.

He kissed her, using the slightest pressure, but doing nothing to enhance the passion. Restraint was torture, but he held himself in check. She was impatient, prepared for him to behave outrageously, and when she finally grasped that he wasn't about to proceed, she pulled away and scowled.

"You're toying with me," she charged, correctly deducing that he wouldn't ravish her. "You have no intention of giving the estate back to my brother."

"No, I don't."

"Then why come upstairs with me?"

"Because you begged, and I couldn't resist."

The curt comment hurt her, but she should have no elevated opinion of his character. If she ever discovered that he'd raced to her room because of how thoroughly he'd been captivated, she'd have too much power over him. It was better that she deem him a blackguard with ulterior motives, which was his condition most of the time.

Despicable as it sounded, the servants would know he'd been with her. They would speculate about what he'd done, and if they believed he had the temerity to rape such a fine woman, it would augment his status as a callous criminal.

"You are a lout!" she accused.

"Yes, I am."

"A devious, conniving villain!"

"I don't deny it."

"I'm alone with you—my reputation shot to Hades—for no good reason, at all."

"And I'm not even sorry."

"Ooh . . . you are a lying, deceitful pig!"

"I wouldn't go that far."

"But you've taken off your shirt!"

"Yes, I have."

"Why?"

"So you can touch me. From how I've had to put up with you I'm entitled to a little pleasure before we're through."

"I'd rather have my hand chopped off."

She squirmed away to storm out, but he wasn't ready to oblige her. He hadn't had his fill of her fascinating company. Plus, he wanted more rumors to spread, wanted more people conjecturing over his amorous, malicious tendencies.

He rolled on top of her and pinned her down. Her breasts were pressed to his chest, the delectable nipples poking into him like shards of glass. Her tummy was flattened to his own, her mons a cushy cradle for his rock-hard phallus. He wedged his torso between her lush thighs, their feet and legs tangled.

She tried to push him off, but it was like shoving a boulder, so she batted at him with her clenched fists. He gripped her wrists and trapped them over her head.

"Let me go!" she demanded.

"Not just yet." He grinned like the cat that was about to eat the canary.

"I refuse to stay up here."

"It's not up to you. It will *never* be up to you."

He was petting her nape, her shoulder, his naughty fingers dropping in slow circles, each swipe bringing him nearer to her perfect bosom.

"Stop it!" she entreated.

"No."

"It's so obvious you don't desire me. Why continue this torment?"

He frowned. "Me? Not desire you? Why would you say a silly thing like that?"

"I keep throwing myself at you, and you're humored by my inept advances, but it's clear you're more interested in a plot of land and some buildings than me."

"It's a very *nice* plot of land, though."

"Shut up."

He laughed and fitted himself more snugly between her legs. His cock was perched right where it liked to be, and though she was a sheltered virgin, her anatomy recognized that it needed the decadent placement very much. She shivered with the initial stirrings of ardor.

"I think it would be very grand if we were lovers," he told her.

"You do?"

"Oh yes. I can't imagine anything I'd like more."

"But we aren't going to be, are we?"

"You don't really wish to proceed, Helen."

"I do! I'm desperate to save the estate."

"I understand that you are, but you're not capable of accomplishing it in the fashion your brother envisioned, and despite what you've heard about me, I won't force an unwilling woman."

"I'm willing! I am!"

He couldn't bear to argue with her, so he kissed her instead. She groaned—whether with despair or ecstasy he couldn't decide—and joined in. The embrace was hotter and more frantic than what had transpired between them in London.

As he ripped the combs from her hair and stroked her all over, she followed his lead, her slender, crafty fingers working across his back and arms. At first, she was tentative, but she quickly grew more bold, participating with a confidence and enthusiasm that thrilled him.

He put her hand on his chest, her palm directly over his heart, the matting of hair tickling her skin. She sifted through the thick pile, her fingernails innocently brushing his aroused nipples, making him ache, making his cock throb with agony.

He was so provoked, so ready to lift her skirt and take her, and the strength of his craving frightened him. He didn't comprehend why he was being so reckless, but he couldn't desist. He could only hold on and enjoy the wild ride.

He caressed her breast, massaging the soft mound, dipping into the bodice of her dress to pinch her nipple. She arched up, gasping and writhing; then he eased away.

Without a word, he sat up, letting his lust recede, his equilibrium settle; then he stood and went to the window to gaze outside. With a distracted but grim satisfaction, he noted that her brother was climbing into the carriage that would whisk him away.

Luke should have been more elated, but his phallus was about to burst out of his trousers, and he prodded at it, trying to relieve the pain, to cram it into a manageable spot. The need to return to her, to spill himself, was bone deep, a fierce, merciless urge that hammered at his resolve.

"Are we . . . are we . . . finished?" she asked from behind him. He listened as she sat up, the mattress creaking with her shifting weight.

"Yes."

"I feel all . . . all . . . quivery inside. Am I still a virgin?"

He smiled and peered over at her. "Most definitely."

"So you didn't . . . ?"

"No. There's quite a bit more to it."

"What else happens?"

For once, he was at a loss. He couldn't explain what behavior was required. He fornicated with women who *knew,* and he had no idea how to describe the event. She likely wouldn't believe him anyway. To her chaste ears, it would sound too bizarre.

"I'm hardly the man to advise you. It's your husband's job."

"Hah! As if anyone would have me after this story swirls around the neighborhood!"

He ought to apologize, but he couldn't generate any remorse. He'd have moved heaven and earth to kiss her one more time, and he was depressed to realize that his obsession hadn't diminished in the least. He wanted her more than ever, and given the slightest encouragement, he'd march over and start in again.

"You're blushing," she claimed. "Has my question embarrassed you?"

"I guess it has."

"Are you telling me that big, bad Captain William Lucas Westmoreland can be naughty—often and with great relish—but he can't talk about it?"

"Some deeds are better in the demonstrating."

"Meaning your amatory skills?"

"I didn't hear you complaining."

She shook her head and chuckled. "You are so vain."

"When you're as marvelous as I am, it's difficult to be humble."

She grabbed a pillow and threw it at him, and it tumbled to the floor and bounced away. They stared and stared, a thousand comments floating through the air, but neither could speak any of them aloud.

He had to stop dawdling. He was needed downstairs to take charge of the chaos his arrival had caused, but he couldn't depart. At the sight of her, with the afternoon sun shining in, the blankets mussed, the atmosphere heavy with their incomplete passion, his heart did a little flip-flop.

Wondering if he wasn't mad, he rubbed a weary hand over his eyes. He couldn't send her away as he had her brother. Not yet, anyway. Not until he had a few more chances to purge his system of her strange influence.

"I have a proposition for you," he murmured.

She gave a mock shudder. "Having previously been the recipient of another of your *proposals,* I'm quaking with terror over what it might be."

"Very funny."

"I'm a veritable bundle of stimulating remarks."

"Such a tiny woman. Such a sarcastic mouth."

"Would you rather I was meek and fawning?"

"Yes, as a matter of fact. I like females who are timid and biddable."

"Then you're going to hate me."

He never could. "A woman should know her place."

"And that is?"

"Beneath me. In my bed."

"You are incorrigible."

She was vastly amused, trembling with mirth, her voice husky and mellow, and it trickled over him like a soothing waterfall. He liked how merriment dimpled her cheeks, was intrigued by how fetching and wholesome she was, and his level of infatuation had him disconcerted anew.

He retrieved a chair and brought it over, but once he'd seated himself, he couldn't begin. He'd figured out the perfect scheme by which to keep her, at least for a while, but if she scoffed at his request, he'd be mortified, which—for a man of his vanity and conceit—was saying a lot.

"So what is it, Captain?" she prompted. "What is this grand offer? I'm on pins and needles."

"I need your help."

"With what?"

"First, you have to promise not to laugh."

"Laugh? At you? Never. Unless, of course, you do something totally idiotic, and now that I've learned how deranged you are, I have to admit that it will always be a possibility."

"Would you quit joking? I'm serious."

She assessed him, then sobered. "Yes, I see that you are."

"If you choose not to assist me, you have to promise that you'll never tell anyone I asked."

"My goodness. What is it?"

"Swear to me!"

"Yes, I swear. I won't ever tell a soul."

He scrutinized her, his astute perception sinking in, and he sensed that he could trust her.

"Have you heard any of the stories about my past?"

"Some. You're an escaped felon—"

"A *pardoned* escaped felon." The distinction seemed significant to make.

She nodded. "You fled the penal colonies when you shouldn't have, and you're a pirate who robs and pillages and steals."

"Yes, yes." He waved away the truth. "But have you heard anything important?"

"Such as?"

"I rescued those sailors."

"You were very brave."

"*They* were very stupid, but because of it, my father wants to be introduced to me."

"Your father."

"Yes."

"You've never met him?"

"No."

"Who is he?"

"I thought everybody knew."

"I don't."

"I'm the natural son of the Duke of Roswell."

"Your father is Harold Westmoreland?"

"Yes, that's him. Honestly, Helen, the entire country is agog over the tidings. Have you been living in a cave?"

"Your father is Harold Westmoreland, the Duke of Roswell."

She was stunned, and she kept repeating herself, so he interrupted: "Have you ever met him?"

"Twice."

"What's he like?"

"Let's just say that I now comprehend why you're so unbearably arrogant. It must be something in your blood."

"I'm *nothing* like him."

"Your wishing won't make it so."

"I'm not!" he insisted.

"All right, you're not." She bit down a grin.

"I might be presented to the Prince Regent, too."

"The Prince! Well, you're certainly wallowing in lofty company."

"Supposedly, the Prince is impressed with my valor, and he's grateful for my service to the Crown. He's considering some blasted ceremony where I'd become a knight."

"A knight!" She started to giggle; then, remembering her vow not to, she swallowed it down.

"See? You're laughing."

He rose and went to the window again. It had been a silly notion, hoping she might help. He never sought assistance. When others aided him, it was because he ordered them to and they were bound to obey by oaths of loyalty. He'd always been on his own, had carved his own destiny. He didn't need anybody else. He didn't *want* anybody else.

Suddenly she was beside him, and she laid her hand on

his arm. "I'm sorry, Luke. You surprised me. I shouldn't have teased you."

"Don't worry about it. It doesn't matter."

"Yes, it does. This is important to you. Tell me what you need from me. I'm happy to give it."

Peering outside, he took in the fertile fields, the sturdy buildings, the horses grazing in the paddock. It was all his. He'd come so far and would go so much farther. He'd fought and scrapped and won, had murdered and maimed, and had lived to brag about it. He'd sailed the Seven Seas, had survived doldrums and hurricanes, but he trembled at the prospect of speaking with a paltry duke.

He was determined to make a place for himself in the Duke's world, to seize a seat at the exalted man's table. The Duke and his kind had killed Luke's mother with their apathy and condescension, and Luke would have his revenge. He would become one of them, would fraternize and mingle and cajole, while he fleeced them blind.

Money was what they understood, and he intended for them to lose a lot of it. They owed him, and he would make them all pay, but he'd never have the chance if he couldn't pass himself off in their snooty society.

"I'm a proud man, Helen."

"Yes, you are."

"If I agree to an appointment—I'm not positive I will, mind you, but *if* I do—I have to learn how to act. I have to know how to dress and what to say, and I'm not sure how to figure it out on my own."

"What is it you would like from me?"

"Show me what to do. If I decide to go through with it, I don't have long for you to teach me."

"I could help you," she said, without pausing to mull

the request. "In fact, I'd like to try. You're turning into a rich, renowned gentleman, and you could definitely use some smoothing around the edges."

He snorted. "Do you think so?"

"Absolutely."

"I'll compensate you."

"I'll do it for free. As a friend."

"No, you should have some cash to settle yourself after you leave."

"Thank you."

"And I'll let you stay at Mansfield Abbey. For another year. You can advise me about the tenants and the farm."

"For a year?"

Her relief was palpable. If he'd tossed her out as he'd despicably planned, had she had anywhere to go?

"Swear it!" she demanded, throwing his taunt back at him. "Swear to me that you mean it."

"You'll have to take the word of a pirate, but I swear."

She studied him, then said, "I trust you. You wouldn't lie to me."

"Well, not about this."

She elbowed him in the ribs. "Here's your first lesson: Don't be obnoxious."

He smiled. "Have we a deal, Miss Mansfield?"

"Yes, I believe we do."

6

I wonder if we could have him killed."

"Killed? You can't be serious."

Adrian Bennett nearly choked on his brandy. Archie was at the front end of a major tantrum. He'd hopped out of bed and was pacing the floor, so Adrian relaxed against the pillows, ready to ride out the storm with a placating, sympathetic smile on his face.

"Oh, but I am," Archie griped. "The filthy swine! Swaggering in and assaulting me as my servants watched! He ought to be cut down like the cur he is!" Archie halted and whipped around, his silk robe flapping open, his small, sated phallus limp on his leg. "Is there anyone we could hire?"

"To murder Captain Westmoreland?"

"Yes! Yes! Focus, would you, darling? I can't abide

that he's ensconced at Mansfield Abbey. It's not right, I tell you. It's just not right! Something must be done."

Adrian stifled a grin. The notion of Archie doing injury to Westmoreland was very funny. And ridiculous. The daring Captain was larger than life, so vital and robust that it was impossible to envision him being brought low. Any harm would simply bounce off.

"Murder isn't the answer," Adrian responded, struggling to keep the discussion on a rational plane. "Even if he died, the property wouldn't revert to you. It would go to his heirs. You know what the lawyers said. The transfer was completely legal. A dozen people were witnesses as you signed the agreement that gave it to him."

"He forced me!" Archie shrieked. "You were there. You saw him."

"He can be daunting," Adrian concurred, hoping to mollify.

"I don't care what my solicitors say. I'll fight it in the courts. My peers won't permit such an injustice to stand. If I have to, I'll bribe them. They'll screw the dirty bastard for me."

He resumed his pacing, ranting about the unfairness of his lot, and Adrian tuned him out.

Would a bribe work in the courts? Adrian had no idea, but he was extremely curious as to where Archie would get the money to accomplish such a maneuver.

Archie hadn't yet realized the extent of his fiscal disaster. The farms at Mansfield had financed his lavish habits. For a few months, maybe as long as a year, he'd survive on credit, but soon bill collectors would come knocking. He wasn't a nobleman; he couldn't refuse to pay. What then?

Before calamity struck, Adrian would have to arrange a new situation for himself. He'd been so certain of his place with Archie, but who could have guessed that the spoiled little despot would prove to be such a disappointment?

"Do you suppose he's partial to buggery?" Archie asked, breaking into Adrian's reverie.

"Westmoreland?"

"He's a bloody pirate. Aren't they all sodomites?"

"I believe many are, but definitely not Captain Westmoreland."

"Are you sure?"

"I'm positive."

Westmoreland was many things—shrewd, valiant, arrogant, imperious—and he oozed sexual magnetism, but he had no abnormal tendencies. Adrian would stake his life on it.

"More's the pity," Archie grouched. "If he had an ounce of deviancy, we could blackmail him."

"He doesn't seem the type who'd yield to extortion."

"Well, perhaps *you* could seduce him, then persuade him to do what we want. Heaven knows you're pretty enough. A fellow would try absolutely anything to keep you in love with him. Look at me and how thoroughly I've debased myself!"

Prior to their meeting, Archie had never had a relationship with a man, and Adrian had smoothly groomed him into their decadent affair. Archie had been lured further and further down the road to perdition, until now the foolish child had no clue how to find his way back to the straight and narrow.

Adrian sighed, his patience for Archie's diatribe wearing thin. Archie had been given more boons than any single individual ought to have, and he didn't appreciate any of them. With his squandering of Mansfield, Adrian had to consider other avenues of enrichment. There were so many lonely, gullible people, and when Archie crashed in economic ruin Adrian wouldn't stay around to pick up the pieces. He'd be happily established elsewhere.

"Westmoreland is very handsome," Adrian goaded, relishing the opportunity to prick at Archie's temper.

"I saw you drooling over him."

"With a body such as his, I can't help but fantasize."

"You're such a whore."

"I bet his cock is massive, which would be a nice change from yours. At least I'd be able to feel it."

"You dog! You wound me with your insults! Why do I put up with you? Why? Why?"

Mildly aroused by Archie's tirade, Adrian observed impassively. If Archie didn't calm himself, Adrian would have to intervene, which was always amusing. Archie could be easily pressed into performing deeds he detested.

Adrian wasn't averse to engaging in any carnal exploit, no matter how disgusting or depraved, and he didn't care if his partner was a man or a woman. He regarded sex as an act of power, and he had few scruples, especially over an endeavor as silly as physical ardor. He reveled in the thrill that came with coercion, the titillation that followed violence, the pleasure that accompanied supremacy.

"Archie, be silent. I'm weary of your harangue."

"Then stop tormenting me. My world is collapsing, and all you can do is nag over the prospect of having Westmoreland in your bed instead of me!"

"Who wouldn't want him?" As if pondering an assignation, Adrian gave a mock shudder.

"Oh, you beast. You are too cruel!"

Archie grabbed a vase and smashed it on the floor, but Adrian ignored him and sipped on a brandy. He yawned and stretched. "You're being entirely too petulant. Desist at once, or I won't tell you what I've decided."

"About what?"

"I've figured out how we'll defeat Captain Westmoreland."

"How?"

"We'll use your sister."

"My sister! Don't mention her to me. This is all her fault. If she'd succumbed, as I commanded, none of this would have happened."

"I don't know about that. Westmoreland seems determined to harass you."

"And he is! He is!" Archie complained. "Why couldn't she spread her legs as any other female has to twice a day? With how she's guarded her precious chastity all these years, you'd think she was a nun."

"She's not very passionate."

"No, she isn't. I should have taught her a lesson or two about desire when I had the chance."

"Maybe you should have," Adrian said. "I've heard that incest can be incredibly entertaining."

"She has such a smart mouth. I'd like to show her what to do with it besides sass me."

Adrian chuckled. "I'd like to watch."

"You are such a pervert."

"I don't deny it."

At the thought of Helen and Archie fornicating, at how he, Adrian, might lead and dominate the encounter, his phallus stirred. Helen would be tied to the bedposts and begging for mercy as Archie forced himself upon her. The event would be wicked and totally evil, and thus precisely the sort upon which Adrian thrived.

"Listen to me," Adrian ordered. "If we handle her correctly, we can control Westmoreland."

"There's no *controlling* him. He's a lunatic."

"That's as may be, but he's utterly besotted with her."

"With Helen? You're mad."

"Didn't you notice?"

"I didn't exactly have the time," Archie sneered.

"No, I guess you wouldn't have."

"I've seen the kind of flashy women he enjoys. Helen is a drab; he wouldn't have glanced in her direction. She tried to seduce him, remember? He wasn't interested."

"He's a *man,* you idiot," Adrian retorted. "He's ruled by his cock—just like the rest of us. Of course he was *interested.* And that wasn't what Helen said. She said *she* couldn't go through with it. That's a huge difference."

"Still, how could we use her? What could she do?"

Helen was gullible and trusting, even more malleable than her brother. She assumed that he and Archie were merely friends, that Adrian was concerned about Archie's welfare. She was too naïve to suspect their complex relationship and too innocent to peer to the heart of Adrian's motives, which would be her undoing.

"I'm not certain yet," Adrian mused, "but I'll reflect on it. Now then, all this talk of Helen's ravagement has left me hard as stone, and I'm ready for you to attend me."

Archie looked as if he'd refuse, as if he'd make Adrian climb out of bed and fetch him, but Archie knew how irritated Adrian would be, how much defiance would hurt. He didn't dare disobey.

Like a lamb to the slaughter, he walked over and slid under the covers.

❧

"The Captain says you're to put down your pen and come to supper."

At the comment being spoken from so close by, Robert Smith jumped. He'd been engrossed in his inventory and unaware that footsteps were approaching. He glared at the Captain's first mate and bodyguard, Pat Reilly.

Robert couldn't explain why, but Reilly rattled him. Whenever they were thrust together, Reilly was constantly spying on him. Robert always felt as if Reilly was about to ask him a question or share a vital secret, and Robert was continually on the verge of shouting, *What? What is it?* But he never did, for he wouldn't give Reilly the satisfaction of knowing he'd caught on to the other man's petty game.

Reilly appeared to be a few years older than Robert's age of twenty, though in light of a sailor's brutal existence, it was difficult to conjecture with any accuracy. He and Robert were the same short height of five feet eight, and with their black hair and blue eyes, thin faces and high cheekbones, they had comparable features, but the similarities ended there.

While Robert was slender and bookish, pale and soft from hours spent at a desk, Reilly was rugged and tough, slim, too, but a whipcord lean that was acquired from rough living, from brawling and scrapping. His skin was bronzed from the sun, his hands calloused from hard work.

Whenever Robert was in Reilly's presence, he was reminded of all the things he was *not*: He wasn't flamboyant, he wasn't dangerous, and he definitely wasn't brave. He'd never studied fencing or pugilism, had never loaded or fired a pistol, was too embarrassed to curse or spit, and had never raised his voice in anger.

He regularly fretted over his failings and couldn't stop wishing he'd been born with some skill besides an ability to add and subtract. Still, he was lucky enough to be traveling with Westmoreland's band of notorious pirates, and

the Captain often bragged that Robert was the most dis-
gustingly honest person he'd ever known.

Westmoreland was frighteningly clever and shrewd
like a fox, but he'd had no formal education and could
barely read or write, so Robert's talents were necessary,
and he tried to be consoled by that fact, meager though it
was.

"Must you sneak up on me, Sergeant?"

"I wasn't *sneaking*. I can't help it if you have your
nose poked in one of your stuffy books."

"It's not a book," he grumbled. "It's an accounting
ledger."

"Same difference."

"Only to someone who's illiterate—such as yourself."

At having uttered the rude remark Robert was appalled, but Reilly shrugged off the insult and hurled his
own.

"When I was growing up, I had more important things
to do than chew the fat in some stupid schoolroom."

"I'm sure you did, Sergeant."

"The Captain's waiting on you, so let's go." Reilly
nodded toward the door. "He says you're to eat with him
and Miss Mansfield. He says she'll like your fussy manners."

Robert blanched. "I'm to dine with the Captain and
Miss Mansfield?"

"Every night."

"That's what he intends?"

"Yes, sir."

Which meant that there'd be no arguing with the invitation. If there was one detail he'd learned about Captain
Westmoreland early on, it was that he never changed his
mind after he settled on an idea. He was stubborn and

unbending, but annoyingly, he always turned out to be correct, so there was no convincing him to heed the opinions of others.

"I don't care to go," Robert protested.

"Don't tell me; tell the Captain. I'm certain he'll be more than happy to have you refuse."

Reilly chuckled maliciously, as if he hoped he'd get to watch such a confrontation, the likes of which Robert would never dream of instigating.

"I suppose I could join them—just this once," Robert muttered. "It won't kill me."

"Eating never does."

"But the *talking* is another story entirely."

"You're quiet as a mouse," Reilly said, "so I doubt there's any chance you'll perish during supper."

"I might surprise you. I might chatter like a magpie. I might talk myself to death."

"Well then, the Captain will tire of it real quick and put you out of your misery, so you needn't worry."

Robert gathered up his pens and papers, as Reilly bristled with impatience.

"Hurry up. While you dawdle, the Captain's food is getting cold."

Robert stacked his documents and clutched them to his chest. "Reilly, considering that we've come to seize Mansfield Abbey, don't you find it disconcerting to be in Miss Mansfield's company?"

"No. She's a fine lady."

"I agree, but doesn't it make you uncomfortable, knowing that we're here to . . . to . . . toss her out?"

"The Captain wouldn't do anything underhanded"—a debatable point!—"and he won the property fair and square."

Ah . . . the world was so simple for an individual of

Reilly's limited capacities. Robert grasped the full dynamic of the situation—as Reilly never could. It wasn't Miss Mansfield's fault that she'd lost her home, and Robert wanted no part in wresting it from her.

He added his jars of pens and ink to the load of papers, and as he turned, the pile shifted and nearly fell. Reilly jumped forward to assist, and their jostling landed them in an awkward position, with Reilly's thigh wedged between his own, Reilly's fingers on Robert's hip.

The predicament was sordid and wicked, and Robert leapt away as Reilly grinned. His curious gaze raked Robert's torso, and at the attention Robert flushed, his pulse sped, and the queerest sensation sizzled through him. It was centered in his middle regions—particularly his groin—and he was struggling to discern what it was when the cause raced through him like a wildfire.

Desire! Though he was a virgin, he wasn't a monk, and he knew what he was feeling: hot, potent lust.

At the discovery he was aghast with dismay.

Reilly was blushing, too, his cheeks a fetching shade of pink. Nervous and shy, as he'd never seemed before, he shuffled his feet and glanced away. Robert was horrified to note that, at that moment, the other man looked terribly young and downright pretty.

"I won't say I'm—" Reilly began, but Robert cut him off.

"Dear Lord, don't even think about finishing your sentence."

Reilly hemmed and hawed, then murmured, "I'll tell the Captain you're on your way."

"You do that," Robert said.

Reilly rushed out, and as his strides retreated down the hall, Robert dropped his supplies onto the desk and sank into the chair.

He was a sodomite! He had to be! There was no other explanation.

He buried his head in his hands, recalling the taunts he'd suffered as a boy from his two older, meaner brothers. He'd been small and quiet, a scholar and intellectual, while they'd been big, stupid louts. They'd tormented him over the differences, but gad, had they been correct? Had they seen some effeminate aspect to his character that he'd never noticed himself?

Their teasing, and his need to prove himself more masculine, had pushed him into joining them for his disastrous grand adventure to Italy that had been abruptly terminated in the Mediterranean. After a grueling bout of drunken bullying, his brothers had thrown him overboard, then they'd sailed off and left him adrift, which was how he'd come to be picked up by Mussulman traders.

They'd taken him to Africa, where Captain Westmoreland had stumbled upon him, starved and beaten, in a slave market. The Captain had taken pity on a fellow Englishman and bought him, then given him refuge and employment. For the unwarranted displays of kindness Robert would follow Westmoreland to hell and back, but how could he continue working on the ship when it was filled with so many virile, swaggering males?

Obviously, his close proximity to all that manly vigor had rattled loose a deviant nature. Was the appeal like a drug? Once released, would it become more and more unmanageable until he was a raving reprobate, chasing young boys into secluded alcoves?

Buggery was a capital offense! What was he to do?

He'd have to remain on the property till Westmoreland let him leave, but how was he to show his face around the house? If he ran into Reilly again, he'd die of mortification. With every fiber of his being he had to fight his infatuation.

"A sodomite!" he wailed. "What next?"

He grabbed his things and darted out.

7

If you poke me again," Helen heard Captain Westmoreland bark as she walked down the hall, "I'll cut off your hand!"

The threat had her hurrying into the front salon, where the local tailor, Mr. Haversham, jerked away as if he might lose the appendage at any moment.

"He'll do nothing of the sort, Mr. Haversham," she insisted as she stormed in. "Don't fret."

"I apologize, Miss Mansfield," the beleaguered tailor said. "I'm trying my best."

"I know you are."

"He's squirming so much that it's like working on a pile of ants. He won't stand still."

Westmoreland growled, "The oaf acts as if I'm a bloody pincushion."

She scowled at the Captain. "You! Be silent."

"Perhaps I should come back and finish tomorrow?" Haversham suggested, clearly wanting to leave as rapidly as possible. The initial proposition of crafting a fashionable wardrobe for the notorious Captain had sounded intriguing, but obviously the gild had rubbed off the golden notion.

"That's a wonderful idea," Helen agreed. "Have you all the measurements you require?"

"Yes."

"So you needn't return. You could sew a few things and have them sent over."

"But what if they don't fit exactly right?" He huffed with indignation. "I have my reputation to consider."

"You're a genius with needle and thread. Whatever you produce will be perfect." She glared at Westmoreland. "And if there's any question, I'll make sure it's understood in the village to be the fault of the wearer. Not the creator."

Haversham scooped up his tools and raced out, but he was so inconsequential to Westmoreland that the Captain didn't spare him a glance. Westmoreland went to the window and stared across the fields to where horses ran in the pasture.

Though it was a disloyal thought, it was so pleasant to have him in the house instead of her brother. Archie and Westmoreland both fostered drama and upheaval, but Westmoreland's was a different type of chaos. He was brash, loud, and demanding, but though he behaved outrageously, the conduct was driven by his desire to have tasks accomplished to his specifications.

He scarcely noticed that she'd tarried in the room with him, and his disregard was really beginning to grate. Since they'd arrived at their strange bargain, he'd been very busy with the property, so she rarely saw him. On two separate occasions, he'd kissed her senseless, and the abbreviated seductions had left her in a fine fettle.

Her body was aching, her mind restless, and she couldn't stop obsessing over him, which was so aggravating. She despised the hours wasted in rumination as she pondered how he could have frolicked with such abandon but remained unaffected. She was dying to inquire, but she was too timid to engage in such a frank discussion.

How can you ignore me? she yearned to shout. *How can you pretend we've never kissed?*

She crossed to him and scolded, "Must you intimidate everyone with whom you come in contact?"

"Yes."

"With such constant bullying, how can you expect to convince others to do what you want?"

"People always obey. They wouldn't dare defy me."

"They *obey,* but wouldn't it be better to have them participate simply because they were eager to be helpful?"

"If we did things that way, how would anyone know who's in charge?"

"Trust me, Captain, there could never be any doubt as to who is the boss."

"Damn straight."

He smiled at her, his striking blue eyes glimmering with a heightened interest. He had the most incredible knack for focusing in, for absorbing every detail, and she couldn't tamp down a shiver of excitement. Though it was a sorry statement on her pitiful life, there was no more splendid feeling in the world than to have his undivided attention.

"You're looking very fetching today," he said.

"Why . . . why, thank you." She fought the urge to pat her hair or tug on her sleeve.

"But I loathe that dress."

"My dress?"

"It's deplorable. In fact, I detest all your clothes."

"Captain, you can't—"

"Lucas," he interrupted. "When we're alone, you must call me Lucas. Or Luke. I've told you before, but you never do it, and your reluctance is starting to annoy me."

"We wouldn't want you *annoyed*, would we?"

She was being sarcastic, but he responded in all seriousness. "No, we wouldn't. Now, you were saying?"

"In polite society, you can't comment on a woman's apparel or make disparaging remarks about how she's attired."

"Why?"

"It's just not done."

"Maybe some females need a little guidance."

"Not from you."

"What if I don't like what she's wearing?"

"You should keep it to yourself," she snapped.

He laughed and gestured to her torso. "You should show more skin."

"I'm displaying plenty."

"You could be a prissy governess."

"I'm a country hostess, who's entertaining company, not some London doxy."

"You're much too pretty to hide your best attributes."

She was about to chastise him again, but she couldn't move beyond the discovery that he found her attractive. The flattery did something funny to her insides, had her wanting to shed her conservative gown, to take down her hair, to do whatever would induce him to repeat the accolade.

Her need for praise was pathetic! She hadn't realized she was so starved for masculine esteem, and she abhorred her weakness. She was irked that she liked him so much, that she was mooning after him and hanging on his every word.

Luckily, a maid was coming with the tea cart, so Helen had an excuse to step away, to reassert her aplomb and regain control of her careening emotions. When she was with him, she stuttered and fumbled like a ninny, so in awe of his magnificence that she could barely function.

She had to buck up! Had to quit wallowing in his glory. He was just a man—a very dynamic, handsome, intriguing one, to be sure, but a man none the less. There was no reason to be quite so agog.

"I've planned a treat, Captain," she announced as the maid entered. "Won't you join me on the sofa?"

He peered at the sofa, then at her, then at the sofa again, giving her such a salacious, naughty grin that it twisted her stomach and curled her toes.

"I'd be delighted, Miss Mansfield."

"For tea, Captain Westmoreland. For tea."

"I hate tea."

"You'll learn to like it."

"It hasn't happened yet, and I'm thirty years old."

"I recognize that it goes completely against your nature, but could you humor me and at least try to be accommodating?"

"I can *try*," he offered, "but I'm not positive I'll succeed. You're awfully hard to please. What do you think?" he suddenly inquired of the maid. "Does she seem kind of fussy to you?"

"Captain!" Helen hissed. "Shut up! You're embarrassing me."

"Why?"

She walked over so the maid wouldn't eavesdrop, and she spoke very softly. "It's not appropriate to be so familiar with the servants."

"What did you say? You're talking so quietly I can't hear you."

He bent down, as she rose on tiptoe and glanced up. He was gazing at her so wickedly that it was clear he'd been intentionally luring her closer.

"You bounder." She leapt away and grumbled, "You can hear me just fine."

"Yes, but it's amusing to have you so flustered. I love it when your cheeks are all red with temper."

The observation rattled her further so that she was a mumbling, bumbling bundle of nerves. Praying for patience, she took a deep breath. "Could we get down to business?"

"I'm ready whenever you are."

"You can't fraternize with the servants."

"I wasn't *fraternizing*. I was merely asking her opinion."

"Well, don't."

"Why?"

"It's not fitting."

"According to whom?"

"Captain, do you want my assistance or not?"

"Yes."

"Then be silent, and do as I tell you."

She pointed to where he should sit—far on the opposite end of the couch from herself—and once he was comfortable, she could see that ease wouldn't be possible. He was too large, too grand, too . . . too . . . everything, and the piece of furniture was absolutely tiny with him on it. He extended his legs, his strong thighs so evident, and it was disconcerting to have all that solid male flesh rippling next to her. She could scarcely recollect her purpose.

She'd meant to explain the ritual of tea, the pouring,

the passing around, the calming effect, but before she could utter a sound, he grabbed a teacup and held it out to the maid.

"What's your name, lass?" he queried.

"Peg."

"Fill this with brandy, would you, Peg? All the way to the brim."

"Yes, Captain." She hurried to the sideboard, as Helen gnashed her teeth.

"We're not here to drink brandy," Helen chided. "It's the middle of the afternoon."

"So? I'm dying of thirst. I could use a good, stout nip."

"I'm trying to educate you about tea!"

"I know you are, Helen"—he gave her wrist a placating pat as Peg delivered his liquor—"but when I meet my dear old da I doubt we'll carry on like a pair of persnickety society matrons. I'm fairly certain we'll tip a few pints." He chuckled. "Probably more than a few."

Her exasperation bubbled over. "Talking to you is like talking to the wall."

"You're not the first person who's said that to me." He gaped at the plates, arranged with dainty pastries and petite biscuits. "That's not enough food to keep a bird alive. Peg, I'm starving. Would you go to the kitchen and have Cook slice me up some beef and bread? Big, thick slices, if she has them. A hunk of cheese would hit the spot, too."

"Oh yes, Captain! Right away, Captain." Peg assessed him with a look that bordered on hero worship; then she rushed out, thrilled at having the chance to attend him and scurrying faster than she ever had at Helen's behest.

"We're having tea!" Helen seethed as Peg disappeared. "With biscuits! We'll have a full meal later this evening."

"What time will that be?"

"Nine or so."

"But I've been working since dawn. I'm famished now."

Helen threw up her hands. "I give up. You're a heathen, a savage, a . . . a . . . brute."

"Which of those is the insult?"

"There's no teaching you anything. You already know it all."

"You're correct about that."

"I can't imagine why you sought my help. You don't really want it."

"No, I don't," he admitted, and he reached for a pastry and wolfed it down.

"Then why am I here?"

"You're entertaining me. You're doing an excellent job of it, too. I haven't had this much fun in ages."

With no thought at all, he gobbled all of the food she'd debated over at length and with such relish. Then he went to the sideboard and refilled his brandy. When he returned, he poured a dash of tea on top of it, and she couldn't decide if he was trying to pacify or further aggravate her. As he was too arrogant to attempt civility, it had to have been done to irritate, and the realization made her unbearably sad.

Though she couldn't deduce why, she yearned to matter to him. She wanted him to be glad he'd let her stay on at Mansfield, glad that she was his friend and guide in his quest to better himself. It wounded her to ascertain that he couldn't care less, that she could be present or not. She felt like a pet lapdog that he could absently stroke when he was in the mood, and that he could disregard when he wasn't.

Disheartened and humiliated, she murmured, "I'll just be going."

"Going? Where?" He scrutinized her, his curious gaze digging deep, and he frowned. "I've hurt you."

"No, you haven't." She forced a laugh and waved away his comment. "Don't be ridiculous. I merely have plenty of chores, and as I'm obviously not needed here, I should get after them."

"I don't excuse you."

"I wasn't aware that I had to have your permission."

"Oh, you do," he said. "You definitely do."

He amazed her by picking up a napkin and wiping his fingers with it. After his continuously claiming not to have learned such conduct, she was confused by the polite gesture. She was watching him intently, so she was caught off guard as he leaned in and trapped her against the arm of the sofa.

"Do you recall the day I arrived at Mansfield?" he inquired.

How could she forget? He'd stormed in like a hurricane battering the coast, like a rebel army breaching the fortress. "Of course."

"We were up in your room."

"Yes."

"I have to tell you a secret."

He scooted nearer, nearer. She scooted back, back, but there was nowhere to go.

"What is it?"

"I adore kissing you."

"You do not." She scoffed, scared to believe him.

"I do, too. And how about you? Do you like kissing me?"

"No, not a bit." She wasn't sure why she'd told the whopping fib, but it didn't seem proper to have enjoyed it so much.

"Helen, you shouldn't ever lie to me. It's so apparent when you are. If we were on my ship, I'd have you whipped for playing me so false."

"Maybe I liked it a little," she allowed.

"Only a little?"

"Well, perhaps quite a lot."

"Would you like to try it again?" he probed.

"I think about it occasionally."

"I'm so glad."

"You are?"

"Yes, because I think about it constantly."

"That can't be true."

"It is, my darling Helen."

He closed the distance between them, his lips falling lightly on hers, and she sagged with relief. She felt as if years had passed since they'd been together. She'd missed him so much! How had she survived without him?

She clutched at his shirt, demanding that he enhance the embrace. At her blatant invitation he chuckled smugly, having been confident that she couldn't resist. His tongue glided into her mouth to tangle with her own, and his fingers were in her hair and deftly removing the combs so that it slid down to hang over the edge of the sofa.

She wasn't certain what might have happened, but Peg's footsteps sounded in the hall as she brought his requested meal. Helen gave a squeal of alarm and Westmoreland ended the kiss, but he didn't shift away or release her.

As Peg waltzed in, he hovered over Helen, their torsos intertwined, his hand on her hip. Their positioning was appalling and decadent, and Peg gasped.

Westmoreland didn't glance up. "Leave the food on the table, Peg," he quietly ordered. "Then shut the door on your way out."

Peg did as she was bid, though she slammed the tray harder than necessary, and she marched out with a disapproving stomp in her stride.

"That was a disaster," Helen wailed, huddling into the cushion.

"What was?"

"Her seeing us like this."

"So?"

"She'll notify the staff. They'll assume we're . . . we're involved."

"We are involved," he reminded her. "Besides, that's what they already suppose. It won't come as a surprise to anyone."

"What do you mean?"

"Haven't you heard the gossip about us?"

"No. What are they saying?"

"They claim I've had my wicked way with you—and more than once, too."

"But we haven't done anything," she protested, "except kiss, and that doesn't count."

"The details don't matter to a servant. As far as they're concerned, you've been ruined. And"—he wiggled his brows—"you liked it! But I was your partner, so what's not to like?"

"I have to get out of here."

"No."

She pushed at his shoulders, but he wouldn't budge. "Captain!"

"Be still."

"This is bad enough. I have to go before it grows any worse."

He studied her, then shook his head. "I've been entirely too patient with you. I should have made you mine long ago."

"I have no notion of what that entails, but I'm not having any part of it. Now let me up."

"No."

"What is your plan? To ravish me?"

"Yes, but I guarantee that you'll enjoy it."

She was prepared to argue, but he halted any tirade by pulling her beneath him. In a thrice, she was flat on her back, with him on top, as she'd been that day in her bedroom, but this time, the situation was much more intimate and exciting. The door wasn't locked; anyone could walk in and catch them misbehaving. The prospect of discovery was thrilling and added a degree of naughtiness that baffled her. When had she become so wanton?

The couch was so small that there was no space to maneuver or escape. He settled himself between her legs so that his privates were pressed to her center. The touch was electrifying, and at the contact her body celebrated.

"We can't do this," she contended.

"We have to."

"No, we don't."

"Hush."

She didn't actually want him to cease, but she was terrified of progressing. There was a raging beast inside her that was urging her to commit any depraved deed he suggested. Nothing could dissuade her, not worries about her reputation, or about the stories that might spread, or about the consequences later on. She had to revel in the moment, and the future be damned.

The spiral of pleasure had commenced, and it was heaven to dally with him, to have lust roaring in her ears and pounding through her veins. He was whispering endearments in an exotic language she didn't understand, and she held him tighter, needing him nearer, and she wished she could draw him into herself and keep him there forever.

His crafty fingers stroked her breasts, kneading the pliant mounds through the bodice of her dress. Each caress was like a bolt of lightning, and she hissed in agony as he slipped under corset and chemise to fondle her nipple. When he finally clasped one, when he pinched and squeezed, she moaned with relief.

"Stop, stop," she pleaded. "I can't bear it."

"You have to let me."

"It's too much."

"No, it's not. With you, it's never enough."

He tugged at fabric, exposing her bosom, her nipples pouting in the cool afternoon air. He gazed at them and preened with his possession.

"So very pretty," he murmured, "and all mine."

He bent down to nip and lick, to nudge and play; then he sucked the taut nub into his mouth. His dastardly seduction was driving her insane with need. He was flexing his hips in a fascinating way that had her trembling with a craving she couldn't describe. Her anatomy recognized the movement and exulted in it, her own hips meeting his thrust for thrust.

He was easing up her skirt, massaging her thigh. With each swipe, she shivered in anticipation of an exquisite apex that would either bring her reprieve from misery or kill her with its power.

"Have you any idea," he asked, "how a man and woman join together?"

"I don't know what you mean."

His fingers glided into her drawers, traveling down to tangle through her womanly hair; then he slid them into her. He was probing, searching, and she definitely hoped he found whatever he was seeking.

She arched up. "Captain! Please!"

"This is how I want you, Helen: wet and eager and begging me."

The sensation was riveting, her heart hammering so

violently that she was afraid it might simply quit beating. She needed him to halt, but at the same juncture, she was desperate for him to keep on until . . . until . . .

Oh . . . she didn't know till when! There had to be an end point. A person couldn't continue through such tumult without conclusion.

"Captain! Lucas! Luke!"

"Yes?" He grinned. "Call me Luke, and I am putty in your hands."

"I can't go on. It's too . . . too . . ."

"Wonderful?"

"Yes."

He paused, reining in his baser inclinations. She felt as if she were balanced on a cliff, as if she were about to leap over, but it was obvious he was finished. Was he mad? He couldn't leave her in such a disordered state!

He released her and sat up, and he pulled her up, too. Without comment, he arranged her clothes as he silently evaluated her. His desire was blatant and discernible, but there was something else in his look—an almost tender affection—that had her pulse fluttering.

"Are we done?"

"Yes."

"But I feel all ragged inside."

"I expect you do."

"You can't stop!" she complained.

"I have to."

"Why?"

"Because you always push me farther than I intend to go," he confessed.

"I do?" A vain, feminine part of her was tickled.

"And, while I admit to being a terrible cad, I'm not about to deflower you on the sofa in the front salon."

"What does deflowering require?"

He snuggled himself to her and whispered, "I'll show you later."

"Why wait? Show me now."

"No. I'll come to your bedchamber after dark."

"You'll do no such a thing," she protested. "We've aroused too much speculation as it is. I'm not about to fuel more gossip."

As if she hadn't spoken, he advised, "About eleven o'clock. Don't lock your door."

"Captain—"

"Luke," he insisted.

"Luke, you can't."

"I can. I won't let you tell me no."

"I don't want you there. It's wrong."

"Yes, it is, but we're going to do it anyway."

"You are so stubborn! Will you listen to me?"

"The house will be quiet," he claimed. "No one will know."

"Lucas Westmoreland, you—"

"Wear something sexy. Better yet, don't wear anything, at all."

He stood and strolled out, leaving her to brood and stew.

8

Pat Reilly dawdled, quietly and unobtrusively, in the corner of the frilly salon, observing Miss Mansfield as she stitched on a sampler. With her stylish hair and pretty dress she was an elegant woman, worth watching, worth emulating.

She was distraught, though, brooding and so agitated that she hadn't noticed Pat, so Pat continued to spy. It was soothing, being in the fancy house, studying how Miss Mansfield lived, and Pat couldn't help but ponder what it must have been like to grow up in the beautiful, serene spot.

Did Miss Mansfield realize how lucky she was?

Captain Westmoreland was an admirable skipper, but life with him was grueling, and wearisome circumstances the norm. Pat had never known a different existence. From the earliest memories of childhood, it had been struggle and privation, work and more work. This period at Mansfield Abbey was a marvelous respite, a boon beyond any imaginable.

What would it be like to stay on? To stay forever? To never return to the ship and the rough, brutal sea?

Pat tried to envision asking Miss Mansfield's permission to remain, but it was unlikely she'd heed the plea of a common sailor. The Captain would have to concur, too, but even if he agreed, it would be impossible for Pat to leave him. Captain Westmoreland had sworn that he'd always protect Pat, and after all his kindnesses over the years, loyalty was the least of the gifts Pat owed.

Miss Mansfield jumped and muttered, "Drat it."

"Are you all right, miss?" Pat inquired.

At the sound of Pat's voice, Miss Mansfield whipped around. "I didn't know you were there, Sergeant. It's nothing. I'm a tad distracted, so I'm having trouble concentrating. I poked myself with the needle."

There was blood oozing from her fingertip, and as she dabbed at it with a kerchief, Pat dared to sidle closer. "Would you like me to fetch somebody? I could bring the Captain. He's a genius with—"

"No, I don't need any assistance," she quickly interrupted. "Especially not from Captain Westmoreland."

She smiled, but it was a trifle strained, and Pat yearned to lean over and give her a consoling squeeze on the shoulder. It was hell, falling for the Captain. No female was immune, and if Miss Mansfield hadn't already landed in his bed, she'd find herself there soon enough.

For a woman with her lofty morals the plunge had to be dreadful, and the ending would be even worse. They all loved him, but the sentiment was never reciprocated. The longest Pat had seen the Captain revel with the same partner was three weeks, and that was because they'd been stranded by storms in an isolated harbor and he'd had no choice.

Poor Miss Mansfield. Pat wouldn't change places with her for all the gold in the King's palace.

"Would you like me to finish the stitching for you?" Pat uttered the suggestion without considering.

"You?" Miss Mansfield replied, but she hastily covered her rude implication. "I . . . I . . . that is . . . do you sew?"

"Of course. I'm a sailor. I sew all the time."

Miss Mansfield's disbelief was obvious, an indication that she wasn't aware of how much effort it took to make a sail flutter in the wind. Pat was the most skilled of the crew at the tiny repairs the other men hated. Miss Mansfield's sampler was a delicate embroidery of some bluebirds, and Pat would give anything to labor over so fine a piece.

"It's very sweet of you to offer," Miss Mansfield said, "but I'll fuss with it later. I can't settle down. I guess I'll walk in the garden."

Pat nodded. "That's a good idea."

Miss Mansfield headed for the French windows that led onto the verandah, and as she passed, Pat was fascinated by how petite she was, by how clean and flowery she smelled. More words popped out where they oughtn't.

"Don't do it."

"Don't do what?" Miss Mansfield queried.

"If you don't want him in your bed, tell him *no* and mean it. Deep down, he's a gentleman. He'll quit pestering you."

Miss Mansfield blushed a bright scarlet. "Sergeant Reilly, as we're scarcely acquainted, I can't fathom why you'd make such an indiscreet comment to me."

"I can see how distressed you are. Don't fret over him. He's not worth it."

"I have no notion of whom you're speaking," she fibbed.

She stomped out, and for a few minutes Pat tarried to be sure she'd truly gone. The embroidery on the sofa invited idle hands to pick it up and indulge, but the moment was lost as noises down the hall revealed that the Captain had arrived. Pat met him at the door to the salon.

"Afternoon, Captain."

"Pat, where have you been? I've been looking everywhere."

"I was chatting with Miss Mansfield."

"Were you now? Did Her Majesty deign to be civil to your lowly self?"

The Captain teased about Miss Mansfield, but it was plain that he'd taken a shine to her. Pat had witnessed enough of his romantic escapades to recognize the signs. "She was very pleasant."

"Really?"

"Really."

"I must be rubbing off on her."

"You must be."

Pat grinned. The Captain was irresistible, so Miss Mansfield didn't stand a chance. Oh well, the excitement might be beneficial, might loosen her up a bit.

Pat had stepped aside to allow the Captain to enter when Robert Smith rushed to catch up with him, and at the abrupt and unanticipated reunion Pat couldn't stifle a gasp of surprise. Since their peculiar encounter in the library Pat hadn't seen him. They were both hiding. Not that Pat had necessarily wanted to evade him, but Smith rattled free too many emotions and memories that were best left undisturbed. He tapped a fount of longing and discontentment that Pat was desperate to ignore.

As unprepared as Pat for them to be thrust together,

Smith flushed with mortification, the color heightening the blue of his eyes, the black of his hair. With the same perfect manners and snooty schooling as Miss Mansfield, he was such an attractive man. He knew how to dress, how to talk, how to carry himself, and Pat was fixated on him in a fashion that was dangerous and crazed.

He hemmed and hawed, then cleared his throat. "Ah . . . Captain . . . ?"

The Captain whirled around and studied him carefully. "What is it, Mr. Smith?"

"I forgot my ledger. It's out in the stable."

"Why can't you use the one you're holding in your hand?"

"I need the other one. I'll go get it, and I'll be right back."

"Don't disappear on me as you did yesterday."

The previous morning, the three of them were to have had breakfast, but Smith had failed to show, and though the Captain had searched and searched, he couldn't locate Smith anywhere. Pat was impressed that Smith had dared to disobey a direct order.

"I'll just be a minute," Smith vowed, and he scurried away.

With blatant interest, Pat evaluated Smith's retreating bottom, and the Captain couldn't help but notice.

"What are you doing?" he asked.

"Nothing."

Determined not to gape, Pat jerked away, but the Captain was too astute to be fooled.

"You're completely infatuated," he correctly charged.

"With Mr. Smith? Are you mad?"

"Don't lie to me."

Pat shifted with discomfort, then admitted, "It's a passing fancy. It doesn't mean anything."

"Does he know?"

"No, and I don't need you telling him, either."

"But he's smitten by you."

The prospect was absurdly thrilling. It had been an eternity since anyone had been. "You think he likes me?"

"It's so bloody obvious. He's miserable, which must be why he's vanishing every other second. You're being cruel to keep it a secret."

"I am not."

"Maybe I'll have a chat with him," the Captain threatened. "Man-to-man. I'll explain the facts of life."

Pat's heart pounded. "What good would it do?"

"Well, that would be up to you, wouldn't it?"

"I suppose."

"Why don't you reflect on it?"

His words were perplexing. What was he saying? Was he claiming that he wouldn't mind if Pat sought a path that didn't include him? Suddenly it seemed as if the Earth had tipped off its axis, as if the stars had altered their positions and it had become impossible to chart a course.

"But I have to stay with you," Pat said. "It's my destiny. And what about you? What would you do without me? We swore an oath."

"Sure we did, and I'll always need you. But having Mr. Smith and serving me don't have to be mutually exclusive."

"They don't?"

"Mr. Smith is a fine man," the Captain pronounced. "He's a tad fussy, at times, but he's honest and decent. You could do a whole lot worse."

He strolled out and, more confused than ever, Pat traipsed after him.

❧

"Miss Mansfield was kissing him? You're positive?"

"I saw it with my own two eyes. I couldn't believe it."

Adrian scrutinized the maid Peg, and he forced a smile that she would assume was sincere. She was a moonfaced, chubby girl whom he detested, but from his first meeting her, he'd identified her as an easy mark. Nearly everyone had a price by which they could be bought or blackmailed, and she was such a modest creature, with such minor expectations, that hers had been much lower than most.

Her dominant trait was her laziness, but she was brilliant at pretending to be busy. As a consequence, she was forever flitting about but doing nothing, so she was often at the center of the action and thus an excellent spy.

"You've done well."

At the praise, she preened. "Thank you, Mr. Bennett."

He and Archie had been fretting in London, dying to learn what was occurring at Mansfield, so Adrian had visited the estate. He'd spent the afternoon with Helen, while taking great pains not to cross paths with Captain Westmoreland. The shrewd pirate had guessed at Adrian's perverted relationship with Archie, and Adrian had no desire to fuel Westmoreland's temper or give him further reason to question Adrian's conduct.

Adrian wasn't finished with the Mansfield siblings—there was still a gold mine to be culled—and he couldn't have Westmoreland whispering suspicions to Helen. Helen thought Adrian was wonderful, and Adrian intended to keep it that way.

He turned to go and had reached the carriage when a nervous Peg called, "Mr. Bennett!"

"What is it, Peg?"

"What about . . . the . . . the . . ."

He leveled a glare that was so malevolent, she shrank back. They were out in the woods, far from the house, the sun setting, and she was scared of the dark. It was a weakness she never should have mentioned.

"I'm off to London, Peg, and I can't dawdle. Spit it out."

"What about my money?"

He usually paid her a few coins, but never enough for her to be satisfied. "You know that you have to earn it with special favors."

"But . . . but . . . in the beginning you said I only had to notify you of what I saw."

"Yes, but you provide such paltry information that it's not worth the effort of speaking with you." The comment was a lie. She had a genuine knack for eavesdropping. Such a sneaky individual, working for the wrong person, could be dangerous.

"I told you everything."

"And it was so insignificant that I'm not certain why you bothered." He jangled his purse, the coins clinking together. "Do you want your reward or not?"

She gazed hungrily. "Yes, I want it."

"Then climb in the carriage."

He spun away and clambered in himself, not pausing to worry if she'd follow, for he knew she would. She was imprudent and greedy, which was a bad combination, and she'd been courted with such expertise that she didn't realize she was being manipulated. As the sole gentleman who'd ever glanced in her direction, he brought excitement and intrigue to her dreary world, and she actually presumed he'd been captivated by her homely, dull self.

She was such an idiot.

Momentarily, she lumbered in, and she perched on the opposite seat, fiddling with her skirt and staring at her feet. The silence grew oppressive, his anticipation spiraling. He relished the power he had over her, how he could control and frighten, could coax and coerce.

"Well," he started, "for what are you waiting?"

"It's . . . it's difficult for me."

"I don't care." He gestured to her bosom. "Bare yourself."

She dithered, but couldn't commence, so he yanked at her bodice, exposing her huge, saggy breasts.

Another man, a different man, might have found them appealing, but *he* wasn't one of them. He was sickened by the sight and unaccountably furious, which increased his loathing for her.

"Stroke them," he commanded.

Tentatively, she caressed the foul mounds. "Like this?"

"Yes. Now pinch the tips." Timidly, she took hold, scarcely applying any pressure, so he snapped, "Harder."

"I'm embarrassed," she whined.

"Before we're through, you'll be more than *embarrassed*." He grabbed her arm and dragged her onto his lap. "You're such a stupid, stupid child. You can't do anything right."

He considered sucking at her nipple, while he bit her, while he marred her, but he couldn't abide the notion of having the rubbery piece of flesh in his mouth.

"Get down on your knees," he ordered instead, and he tried pushing her to the floor, but she resisted, fighting him to the bitter end. "Get down," he repeated, "or I will beat you first, and then you'll have to do it anyway."

She whimpered, but complied. With shaking fingers, she unbuttoned his trousers, and she leaned over his erect and ready phallus, but she couldn't proceed.

"Please . . . I can't . . ."

"Do it!"

"I . . . I . . ."

He clutched her by the throat, making her look up at him. His feigned regard swept over her, and she soaked in his appreciation like a sponge.

"Promise you won't hurt me afterward," she begged.

"My dear, Peg," he crooned, "how could I think of it?"

"Last time you were so angry."

"You disobeyed me, Peg. Can you recall how you disobeyed me?"

"Yes." Her lashes fluttered down, her cheeks reddening with humiliation.

"It won't happen again, will it?"

"No."

"Then there's nothing to fear, is there?"

"I guess not," she said more softly.

"Focus on the cash you'll have when you've finished. Imagine all the pretty baubles you'll purchase with it."

His stirring her avarice did the trick. She bent down and sucked at him, swallowing deep as he'd taught her. She was clumsy and inept, but he reveled in his dominion over her, in his having her prostrate and vulnerable. He could strangle her, or kill her with a few vicious blows to the head, then bury her in the forest, and no one would ever know.

He closed his eyes and began to thrust.

❧

"What have you learned?"

"So much that I can't decide where to start."

Archie paced his library, a drink in hand, his temper on a short leash. He had numerous bank accounts, but no means of replenishing them. Creditors were circling, so something had to be done.

He'd sent Adrian to Mansfield to parlay with Helen, but the bastard had been gone a week, and Archie was livid. He didn't like Adrian being off on his own. With Adrian's carnal proclivities, there was no telling what mischief he might have stumbled upon while he was away.

"What was Helen's explanation for why she's still on the property?"

Adrian shrugged. "Westmoreland permitted her to stay."

"For how long?"

"Another year."

"A year!" Archie was aghast. "Why would he let her?"

"Helen claims he wants her advice about the farm, but I don't buy it."

"Why not?"

"I heard from another source that they're involved."

"Sexually?" Archie was stunned.

"The servants are abuzz. Apparently, he deflowered her the day he came to take possession."

"Helen is such a prude. Can you truly believe she'd spread her legs for anyone?"

"I'm not certain," Adrian said. "She seemed the same as ever, but then, they've been seen kissing, too."

"Right out in the open?"

"Yes."

Trying to make sense of the news, Archie resumed his pacing. If Westmoreland was copulating with Helen, then the bet was in force, the chance of regaining the estate a viable option. Yet Archie hadn't been apprised of the situation. Allegedly, Westmoreland was a reputable criminal—honor among thieves and all that—who'd abide by the terms of the wager.

If Helen had succumbed, then Archie deserved to know. How could the two of them presume to keep their liaison a secret?

"It galls me that Westmoreland might have taken her virginity," Archie complained.

"Why? Every sister loses it sooner or later."

"But Westmoreland!" Archie shuddered with revulsion. "I wish I'd ravaged her before she wasted it on that petty villain."

"You haven't the nerve for such a despicable deed."

"I have, too."

"Quite the boast, darling. I'd love to have you prove it. If I thought you were man enough, I'd hold Helen down, myself, while you raped her."

A horrid notion occurred to Archie. "You don't suppose they're in league together, do you?"

"To what end?" Adrian inquired.

"To cheat me out of my heritage!"

"How could they defraud you? You can't be swindled out of what you don't own."

"Well, if they're fucking, then after a month, the estate should be mine. What if they've agreed to be quiet about their affair? If he's genuinely fond of her, he might give her Mansfield as a lover's parting gift. Or what if she's seduced him with marriage in mind? She'd have my legacy, and I'd be cut off at the knees!"

"Anything's possible, Archie." Adrian's voice was laced with derision.

"The conniving bitch!" Archie seethed. "What if she's betrayed me?"

"Shut up." Adrian went to the sideboard and poured himself a brandy. "You talk and talk, but you never *act*. I'm weary of listening to you rant."

"But what can I do?"

"You see?" Adrian chided. "That's your main problem. You have no imagination." He turned to leave.

"Where are you going?"

"I'm exhausted from my travels"—Adrian smiled snidely at what his words implied—"so I'm off to take a nap."

"You can't be serious. I've been waiting for you for days."

"Well, I'm tired, so you'll have to keep on waiting."

He walked by, and as he passed, he patted the front of Archie's trousers, the slight touch making Archie's cock sit up and beg. Archie was disgusted with himself. Why was he so eager for Adrian's approval? He was so willing to debase himself in the pathetic hope that Adrian would want him with an equal fervor.

"How many lovers had you whilst you were away?"

"Too many to count," Adrian taunted. "The variety was so refreshing. My rod is completely worn-out."

"Bastard!" Archie hurled.

He threw his drink, but Adrian was gone. The glass thumped against the wall and fell to the rug, so that he didn't even get the satisfaction of a loud shatter.

Adrian poked his face through the door. "Must you always behave like a child?"

"You're a whore, Adrian. An absolute whore, and I hate you."

"Perhaps if you were more of a *man,* I wouldn't grow bored and require other company so often."

He strutted out, as Archie raged all alone.

❧

Robert tiptoed through the dark kitchen, clutching a robe, towel, and change of clothes, as he proceeded to the small bathing room beyond. The staff was wonderful about preparing hot water after supper so that he could have a bath. It was an effortless business, a bucket dipped into the reservoir behind the stove, then the contents dumped into a real tub, where he could actually recline and soak.

As he'd learned during his failed trip to Arabia and his subsequent year at sea with the Captain, he couldn't tolerate being filthy. He'd been raised in a tidy house, where clean laundry and nightly washing were routine, so it had been difficult to endure lengthy stretches without the simple luxury that he'd once taken for granted. He indulged whenever he could.

He was so distracted, having been busy hiding from Pat Reilly and avoiding the Captain, that he'd entered the room before he realized someone was already inside and enjoying the amenity, and he cursed his luck. In all the evenings he'd crept down, he'd had the spot to himself, and he had begun to assume that he was the only one who used it.

He could see the occupant's back, and as he focused in, trying to identify the interloper, he recoiled in horror.

It was Reilly! He'd recognize those shoulders anywhere! Reilly's ponytail was unbraided, the strands curly and shimmering in the dim candlelight. He was relaxed, his bare arms resting on the edge of the tub, his slender fingers gripping the rim.

In an instant, Robert was hard as a rock. He had to flee or he'd be humiliated beyond redemption, but his trousers were so tight with his erection that he didn't know how he'd exit without assistance.

Oh, why couldn't he have been born a normal man? What purpose was served by making such a vile discovery at age twenty? He was still a virgin! How could Fate be so cruel?

He had stepped away, intending to sneak out undetected, when suddenly Reilly glanced around.

"Hello, Robert."

Robert gulped with dismay. In his fevered state, Reilly seemed very pretty. "Hello, Sergeant."

"I heard someone coming. I was hoping it was you."

"You were?"

Reilly's lips were full and ripe in a manner Robert hadn't noted prior. His skin was silky, his cheeks aglow, and at the transformation Robert was so mesmerized that he couldn't storm out as he ought.

"Would you wash my back?" Reilly asked.

"Your . . . your . . . back? I don't think so."

Robert gazed at the door and ordered his feet to march toward it, but they wouldn't obey. He was frozen in place.

"Then why don't you climb in with me?" Reilly needled. "If you won't wash my back, I'd be more than happy to wash yours."

Robert started to shake, trembling with a violent need to do precisely as Reilly had suggested, and he fought the urge with every ounce of his being. Despite how vigorously he desired Reilly, he'd had a sound Christian upbringing, he knew right from wrong, knew piety from buggery, and he wouldn't yield to temptation.

"Come, Robert," Reilly entreated. He was up on his knees and shifting around. "Come to me."

"No. No, I can't."

"You can, Robert. I know you want to."

"No . . . please . . ."

Reilly had spun all the way, and he halted, his chest squared, his hair tossed over his shoulders, and Robert saw . . . a pair of female breasts, a slim waist, a rounded hip, and a dusting of crotch hair with no phallus in the middle of it.

He gawked, his confused mind racing. Ultimately, he accused, "You're a woman."

"Yes."

"You've always been a woman."

"Since the day I was born."

"I'm not a sodomite. . . . I'm not a sodomite. . . . I'm not a sodomite. . . ." Though he wasn't a Catholic, he made the sign of the cross several times; his relief was so great that he collapsed against the wall.

"Are you all right?"

"No, I'm not. I'll never be all right again. My heart is about to quit beating."

Reilly laughed and rose, facing him without a hint of modesty. He—*she*—left the tub and sauntered over, water dripping off her and sluicing down her thighs. She was wet, slippery, and moist, and the most exotic, fantastic vision he'd ever witnessed.

"My name isn't Pat. It's Patricia."

She was tall, as tall as himself, and she looked him straight in the eye as she pressed her drenched body to his and kissed him directly on the mouth.

He'd been kissed before, by tavern wenches who frequented a sailor's world, so he understood how it was accomplished, but nothing in his previous experience had prepared him for Patricia Reilly. He was quite sure he'd died and gone to heaven. She was so willowy, all long arms and legs, all smooth curves and lines, and she threw herself into the embrace as if she wanted to keep on for the rest of eternity.

"Why aren't you a woman?" he demanded as he yanked away. The question was absurd and made no sense, but she answered it anyway.

"Because it's safer being a man."

"Does the Captain know?"

"Of course. It was his idea."

"Why?"

"Because I was owned by a rich and powerful sultan in Egypt." She'd been enslaved! How awful! "When the Captain rescued me, it was an affront that had to be avenged. The man will never stop searching."

"So you've been hiding in plain sight."

"With the Captain constantly watching over me."

"I thought you were his bodyguard."

"No. He's mine."

"Have the two of you ever . . . ?"

"God, no. He ruts like a dog. I have *some* standards." She clasped his hand. "Come with me."

"Where?"

"I'll show you."

She led him into the adjoining room, a scullery maid's alcove with a narrow cot and a dresser. Her shirt was draped across a chair, her boots tucked under it.

"You sleep in here?"

"Yes."

"You've been spying on me as I bathe!"

"Every night, through the crack in the door."

He flushed with chagrin. "For shame, Miss Reilly! For shame!"

"Why? I liked what I saw." She lay down and stretched out. "And since we're about to be lovers, you should probably call me Patricia."

She was a naked, enticing siren, her pert breasts teasing him, her nipples erect and luring him to misbehave. Down below, her womanly hair was . . . was . . .

Gad! He couldn't even look! He was too much of a coward!

He wasn't positive what to do next. He'd heard bawdy rumors about how sexual mating was conducted, and he'd occasionally glimpsed the Captain with his partners, so he had some concept of what transpired, but not much. His monumental failings swept over him, once more. How could he have lived to be twenty, have sailed the oceans and traversed Arabia, but not have learned how to make love to a woman?

"The crew jokes about you," she said. "They claim you're a virgin. Is it true?"

He peered up at the ceiling. "Dear Lord, let the floor open and swallow me whole."

"Do you know what I think?"

"No, what?"

"I think there's a tiger lurking inside, one that's waiting to be set free."

"A tiger!" he scoffed.

"Lie down, Robert."

She patted the mattress, and he disgraced himself further by confessing, "I don't know what to do."

"Well, I do. Don't be afraid."

He hated that she could perceive his fear, and he yearned to prove that he wasn't scared, but still, he couldn't move. He was torn between a hunger to proceed and the desperate need not to humiliate himself, and she saved him by rising and taking charge.

She guided him to the bed and eased him down. He felt paralyzed, unable to speak or react, as she arranged his torso just how she wanted it.

Then she climbed on top of him and balanced on her haunches. She unbuttoned his trousers, and he realized that he should dissuade her or participate, but he couldn't do either one. The entire episode was like a dream, and he wondered if he wasn't walking in his sleep.

"You're not dreaming," she whispered, as if she could read his mind.

She reached under the placard, and as a female palm encircled his phallus for the first time, he knew she was correct: He was definitely awake.

"Oh, sweet Jesu," he groaned, and he arched up.

The stimulation was so intense that he prayed he wouldn't spurt all over the sheets, but embarrassment seemed likely. Struggling for calm, he steadied his breathing, he recited mathematical tables, he named the capitals of Europe—in alphabetical order.

She tugged his pants down around his flanks, his privates bared for her inspection. "You're very fine, Robert. Very fine."

Her voice was little more than a purr, the word *very* sounding like *verra,* and hinting at a Scottish heritage that hadn't been disclosed. She grabbed hold and centered him; then she lowered herself, her sheath gliding down to encompass him. In a thrice, he was impaled inside her, and before he could thrust or enjoy, a wave of uncontrollable pleasure inundated him, and with great relish, he emptied himself. A boisterous, mortifying cry bellowed from his lips as he bucked and writhed.

He was no stranger to the naughty gratification of orgasm and had stooped to appeasing himself when his swelled loins became too much to bear, but none of those furtive incidents could begin to compare with the bliss she'd bestowed. He was so titillated, his cock immediately ready for another go, and he would do anything, would give anything, would tell her anything, so long as she agreed to a repetition.

With a bit of practice, he could be better at it. He just knew he could!

"I'm sorry," he mumbled.

"For what?"

"For . . . for . . ." He couldn't say *for being such a virginal idiot.*

She chuckled, but in a kind way, and she leaned down and kissed him. "The initial one is simply to take the edge off. We'll do it again—and again—till you start to get the hang of it."

"Do you mean it?"

"Oh yes, I absolutely do."

She dug her knees into the mattress so that she could rock back and forth across him. With immense gusto, he clutched her hips and joined in.

9

Open it—this very second—or I'll break it down."

Luke frowned at the locked door, his hopes for a pleasant, wild romp rapidly fading. He'd assumed that he and Helen were in complete accord, that she realized they shared an attraction that had to be acted upon.

He knocked more loudly. "Open up, Helen. Now."

He pressed his ear to the wood, but silence greeted him, and his temper spiked. He thought he'd been clear, and she'd agreed, that a hot, spicy amour was precisely the cure for what ailed her.

"I know you're in there. Say something."

No response.

He sighed, wishing—just once!—he could take the easy road with her. "Fine. Have it your way."

He raised his foot and delivered a jarring blow, which brought a frantic rustling on the other side.

"Go away," she hissed.

"No."

"Don't you dare bash in my door!"

"Then haul your pretty arse over here and unlock it."

He kicked again, and she raced over, fumbled with the key, then yanked it wide. She loomed in the threshold, and he laughed at how conservatively she'd covered herself. Obviously, she presumed the clothes—a flannel nightgown, unflattering robe, mobcap, and woolen stockings— would thwart his masculine drives. It was pathetic, how little she knew about male inclinations. If she'd attired herself in a suit of armor, he'd still desire her.

"Be quiet!" she scolded. "You're causing a big ruckus."

"Which is all your fault."

"My fault?"

"Yes."

"It's the middle of the night. I'm in my own room, minding my own business, whilst you are storming around in the hall and raving like a lunatic. And it's *my* fault?"

"If you'd do as I say, we'd get on so much better."

"You are mad."

"Mad about you."

"Get out of here."

"No."

She was in a snit and prepared to deny him entry, so he simply picked her up, set her to the side, and walked in.

"You can't just . . . just . . ."

"I already have."

He turned the key, sealing them in, and he slipped it into his jacket, wanting her to comprehend that she couldn't leave until he decided to let her.

"Give me the key!"

"No."

"I'm beginning to believe that *no* is the only word in your vocabulary."

"If you'd be a tad more cooperative, I wouldn't have to use it all the time."

"You are the most obstinate person I've ever met."

"I'm sure that's true."

He hadn't been inside her bedchamber since the day he'd arrived, and on that occasion, he'd been too busy to notice any details. He wasn't certain why he'd delayed in coming again. Every item in the house belonged to him, so he could have ordered an inventory, but for some reason, he'd permitted her a private sanctuary.

Still, he was dying of curiosity, desperate to learn more about her, and he roamed about, handling her possessions, peeking in her dresser drawers, rummaging through her wardrobe.

"What are you doing?" she asked.

"I'm snooping. What does it look like?"

"Well, stop it. I won't have you pawing through my things."

"Too late." He reached over and pulled off her cap, and her braid swished down. "There. That's better."

"Don't even think about removing anything else."

"I'm not about to go to all the trouble of being secluded with you, then have you moping around like a grouchy, old widow."

"I'm not out to impress you," she griped.

"Trust me, Helen. I know women. I'm a veritable connoisseur. You try to be invisible, and it just won't do. I don't like it."

"We wouldn't want you to be unhappy, would we?"

"No, *we* wouldn't. Now loosen up. Untie your hair. You're aware of how I like it."

He tugged at the ribbon that secured her braid, and it came undone. He riffled through the silky mass, intrigued by how it fanned across her back.

She'd been reduced to speechlessness—praise be!—and she watched him as one would a dangerous beast. She was positive he had an evil intent, which irked him to no end. Why couldn't she understand that he wouldn't harm her?

He never had to convince a female to have sex with him—they required no encouragement—so he hadn't any idea of where to start with such a persuasion. He kept nosing around, studying her meager collection of gowns. She either had the worst taste of any woman alive or didn't care about her appearance, which couldn't be right.

He evaluated a pair of stockings that had been mended too often to count, and he was about to comment when she snatched them away. She stuffed them in a drawer and slammed it shut.

"I've endured quite enough for one evening," she complained. "I'm willing to submit to many indignities at your behest, but I don't have to have you mauling my unmentionables."

"Really, Helen, you have the most deplorable clothing."

"I do not."

"Why must you attire yourself like such a frump? Didn't your wastrel brother ever give you any cash for necessities?" She was so embarrassed by the question that he was sorry for pressing the issue. "Oh, I see how it was. He spent all his money on himself. What a rat he was to keep you so drab."

"Quit insulting me. My dresses are fine. My undergarments are fine. *I* am fine."

"Don't worry," he advised. "I'll rectify the situation immediately."

"What do you mean?"

"First, I'll arrange an allowance."

"You'll do nothing of the sort."

"There'll be no strings attached. You can fritter it away however you like."

"I won't take money from you!"

"Then, I'll send to London for some new outfits. You'll have them in a few days."

"I don't want anything from you! How would I ever explain such gifts?"

"Why would you have to explain?"

"This is a small place, an established neighborhood. People grow bored, they talk about each other, and what they say isn't always kind."

"You're scared of a little gossip?"

"Yes, and I won't have my relationship with you be the main topic."

He was never concerned with what others thought. In his position, the more terrible the rumors, the better for his grim reputation, so he couldn't fathom why she'd fret.

She ought to tell them all to bugger off, that she'd behave as she damn well pleased, but she never would. There were many rules and conventions in her strange society that he deemed absurd, but they were part and parcel of who she was.

"What if I order a few pieces for you to wear when we're alone?"

"Alone? If you're supposing we'll fraternize on a regular basis, you're insane."

"I'm not insane. I'm being extremely practical. I'll buy gowns in my favorite colors, and you can torment me by looking pretty in them."

She growled in frustration. "You are impossible."

"So are you saying I should go ahead?"

"No, I'm saying you're beyond exasperating."

He took her hand. "Come."

"Where?"

"I'm about to make love to you, and I want to do it lying down."

She dug in her feet, trying to halt his forward progress, so he scooped her up and tossed her over his shoulder. She was hanging upside down, her gorgeous bottom next to his ear, which had her angry as a wildcat, and she pounded on his back.

"Put me down!"

He swatted her on the rear. "You'll wake the dead with all that racket."

"Put me down!" she repeated. "This instant!"

"Your wish is my command."

He dropped her onto the bed, and before she could scurry away, he crawled on top of her and pinned her down. She glared at him, her fury and annoyance clearly evident, and he hated that he made her so miserable.

In his company, women were always cheery and eager. They realized that he wouldn't tolerate a difficult paramour. When there were so many amenable ones available, why would he bother? She was the sole female he'd ever encountered who was unaffected by his advances, and he was seriously irritated that she didn't feel obsessed with pleasing him.

"What is it you want from me?" She sounded so wretched!

"I told you I'd show up at eleven."

"And *I* told you not to."

"Why would I listen when you're being so silly?"

"Has there ever been a woman who *didn't* desire you?"

"Not that I can recall."

"Is that the problem?" she inquired. "You've never been refused, so you don't comprehend what it means when a woman says no?"

"I comprehend; I just don't care."

"Ah . . . the truth comes out."

"I've decided we should be lovers. After I've made up my mind, the rest is easy."

"What about what *I* want?"

"There's the rub, Helen. What do you want?"

She was candid enough to admit, "I don't know."

He'd like to reassure her, but wasn't certain how. If he could figure out what had her so anxious, seduction would be so much simpler.

He untied the belt on her robe, loosening it, the lapels falling away to reveal her soft, worn nightgown. He laid his hand on her breast, massaging the supple mound, and he grabbed the nipple, pinching it between finger and thumb. She moaned with pleasure and arched up.

"Do you know what I think?" he murmured.

"What?"

"You want me, but you're afraid."

"I am not," she bravely insisted.

"I won't hurt you."

"I can't imagine you'll do anything else."

"You're so wrong."

"Am I? What if I allow you to proceed? I'm not one of the trollops you fancy so much."

"No, you're not."

"Will you stay afterward? Will you marry me?"

At the notion, his horror must have been apparent, because she chuckled, but sadly. Her gloom was increasing by the second, and he felt like the worst heel ever.

"No, I would never marry you."

"Well, you see, Luke, in my world, that's what people do. They behave as they oughtn't; then they wed. If I continue with you, what will become of me after you leave?"

"I'd never let anything bad happen."

"But you wouldn't be around to prevent it."

He could have lied to her and offered the falsehoods she was desperate to hear, but he was who he was: a gambler and buccaneer, a con artist, a man on the move. He was determined to establish himself, to obtain the wealth and status that had been denied him because his father was a philandering roué. Of course, the despicable Duke had already had a wife when he'd impregnated Mary Lucas, so he couldn't have married her, but that fact didn't signify.

Luke was driven. Each time he swindled some rich sod, he felt it was his due, his retribution against the contemptible crowd that had persecuted his mother. He'd never remain at Mansfield Abbey and toil away as a gentleman farmer. He had places to go, vengeance to seek, and Helen would play no part in his future.

"I won't be here later," he stated. "But I'm here now. Should we ignore what's between us? Is that what you're asking me? Could you have me depart without learning what it might have been like?"

For a lengthy interval she assessed him; then she shook her head. "No, I couldn't."

Relieved by the remark, he kissed her, and he felt that it had been an eternity since he'd reveled with her, rather than the better share of a day. His fingers went to her nightgown, opening the front, the tiny buttons a nuisance that tried his patience, that urged him on.

When he had several of them free, he slipped under the fabric, and he cupped her breast, the sensation rocking them both.

She broke away and pulled him close, her beautiful face buried at his nape. "You were right, Luke. I'm so frightened."

"Tell me why, Helen. Let me ease your fears."

"I want to be with you so much. It scares me, what I might attempt for you. You won't be satisfied with less than everything. If I say *yes* to you, you'll take all of me. There'll be naught left."

He gazed down at her, affection sweeping through him as he forced himself to admit that she needed a different man—a stable and ordinary man—in her bed. She deserved a husband who cherished her, a home, and children to mother, but he wasn't the person to give her any of those things.

Yet he yearned to be. Deep in his soul, there was a lonely, empty void that had him pining to settle down, to belong, to be important to people who loved him. He'd always been on his own, had had to fend for himself. His survival instincts were strong, and they'd forged him into the stubborn, arrogant creature he'd grown to be, but what would it be like to have someone *he* could lean on for a change?

What if he dared to select another path? What if he abandoned his wanderlust and built a new kind of life? One with ties and connections. The prospect was so tantalizing that it seemed to be precisely what he'd been searching for without his even recognizing that he was.

For the briefest instant, the fabulous possibility washed over him; then he shooed it away.

She inspired the oddest emotions, had him hungering for a reality that could never be. When he was around her, he had to be careful lest he tender pledges he'd regret later on. He never swore oaths he didn't intend to keep, never formed attachments he couldn't bear to sever.

Friendships were fleeting, relationships transitory, human beings unreliable, and with that jaded view he never misjudged or made mistakes.

Yet when she peered up at him with those big, hazel eyes that were so filled with fondness and trust, he teetered on the brink of disaster, eager to utter any wild vow merely to see her smile.

"I can't make you any promises," he told her.

"I know. I hate that about you."

"What if I said I'd stay forever?"

"You'd drive me batty within a week."

"I'm sure I would." He was surprised at how much the truth hurt. "Would you want me to be different?"

"No. I want you just as you are."

He sighed, unable to move beyond the impression that he'd relinquished something wonderful, that he'd had bliss within his grasp but had been too stupid to reach out and grab for it.

"What shall we do now?" he inquired, at a loss as to how he should proceed.

"I don't know what's best. I can't answer."

"Should I go?"

If she ordered him to depart, he wasn't positive how he'd react. He didn't think he could oblige her, but why tarry when his presence was so unwanted and so unnecessary?

She saved him. "No. I'd miss you too much."

"You understand what you're agreeing to, don't you?"

"How could I? I'm a spinster, remember? I haven't the foggiest."

"I'm a lusty man. I won't hold back."

Why was he cautioning her? Was he hoping to dissuade? He was so smitten that after they started in he wouldn't halt. He felt as if he'd been waiting for this moment all his life, as if every choice had been leading him to this very spot. She'd been astute in deducing that he would take all she had to give and still demand more.

His pathetic conscience, which was dormant and never consulted, was warning him to desist, but the voice was very quiet and easy to ignore.

"Do what you will," she valiantly acquiesced, and like a martyr about to be sacrificed, she flung her arms to her sides.

He laughed. "It won't be that bad."

She laughed, too. "I'm certain it will be splendid."

"Aye, it will be. And after we've tried it a time or two, you'll enjoy it so much that you won't be able to resist me. I won't have to ask; you'll come begging."

"Your conceit knows no bounds."

"I've never been humble."

She grinned; then she sobered. "Will you give me your word on something?"

"If I can."

She glanced away. "It's difficult to talk about it."

"It's all right, Helen. When we're together like this, everything is allowed."

"You'll tease me."

"I won't."

"I'm clueless as to what you're planning—"

"I'll show you."

"—but whatever it is, don't leave me with child. I can't end up pregnant."

After witnessing his mother's tribulations, he could never behave so reprehensibly toward a woman. "I won't. There are ways we can . . . things we can do that . . ."

"Swear it to me."

"I swear."

She studied him, probing for deceit or fabrication, but in this he was—for once—being brutally honest.

"I believe you," she said, "and I'm ready to begin."

10

She'd had such grandiose plans.

After fretting for hours, she'd resolved to resist her worst impulses. Instead, she'd hastily abandoned every principle that had ever ruled her life.

When she'd allowed him entry, she'd known what would happen. On some outrageous, decadent level, she'd been hoping to make every bad choice. She hadn't realized she possessed such a scant amount of self-restraint.

There was no path that could lead them back to the moral road. From this point on, there was only sin and pleasure, and she ought to feel guilty or ashamed, but when she was humming with delight it was difficult to muster any remorse.

For once, she had no intention of behaving. She couldn't predict how long he'd stay at Mansfield Abbey, but she was sure it would be for a brief period. He wouldn't forfeit his nomadic, bachelor ways for her, nor would she expect him to. He was a dashing, solitary man who would never change, who would never be a country farmer or a devoted spouse.

He was like a bright, shiny angel who had been dropped from heaven into her gray universe, who'd been sent to make her happy, and she wouldn't reject the opportunity for an adventure.

I'll pretend it's my wedding night, she thought. *I'll pretend he's my beloved husband, who has selected me above all others.*

After she met him, it was clear that she would never have a *real* wedding night, so she would create this false one as a substitute. The memory would sustain her in the weeks and months after his departure.

He sat up and tugged off his shirt. "I'm going to remove my clothes. And yours, too."

"Must we?"

"It's much more pleasant that way."

Without giving the matter any subsequent consideration, she consented. Whatever he wanted to do, whatever he asked, she'd acquiesce. She had to discover how it would be between them. It seemed as if the Earth couldn't possibly keep spinning if she didn't find out.

He pulled off her robe and lowered her nightgown, easing it down so that the fabric was under her breasts; then he dipped down to her nipples, nursing at one while he played with the other. He shifted back and forth until she was dizzy with excitement.

Down below, he was inching up her nightgown, his wandering hand roaming higher and higher. He'd touched her like this before, so she knew his destination, and her womanly core wept with need.

"Oh, hurry, Luke," she embarrassed herself by begging.

"There's no rush, Helen."

"Yes, there is. Don't torture me."

"But suffering is half the fun."

"I don't want *fun*! I want relief!"

"And you shall have it. Very, very soon."

Eventually, he arrived where she was desperate for him to be, his crafty fingers slipping inside to taunt her, but despite how thoroughly he fondled, there was no respite from misery.

"Luke!" she implored.

"Almost there."

"I can't bear much more."

"You won't have to."

His thumb flicked out, jabbing at a spot she'd never noted prior. She was transfixed by the potent sensation centered there. How could she be twenty-five years old and not know the strange cravings of her body? How could *he* know them when she didn't?

He flicked again, again, as he sucked on her nipple. Suddenly she felt as if she'd shattered into tiny pieces and was flying across the sky. She climbed up and up, having no notion of how it would end, or what her condition would be at the conclusion.

Finally—finally!—she reached a peak; then she floated down and landed gently in his arms.

"Oh my," she breathed. "What was that?"

He was very smug. "*That* was a dramatic example of physical passion."

"Can it occur more than once?"

"Most definitely."

"You'll kill me with ecstasy."

"Perhaps."

She chuckled. "You are so wicked."

"I can't deny it."

"I'm a wanton."

"I've never thought a bit of *wantonness* was a bad trait in a female."

"You wouldn't."

"There are worse things."

"I'm beginning to agree with you."

And there *were* worse things, she realized. Like being a spinster. Like never being held by a man. Like never learning of this wonderful bliss.

How could she have deprived herself for so many years? And now that they'd commenced, why would she ever want to stop? Carnal activity was addicting, like a dangerous drug, and she had a humiliating vision of herself, aged and decrepit but continuing to lure him into secluded parlors and demanding he bestow more of the same.

A frustrating prospect dawned on her, and she scowled. "Am I still a virgin?"

"Yes, but you won't be for long."

"So I didn't . . . you didn't . . ."

"No."

Butterflies swarmed in her stomach. "How will I know . . . ?"

"When we're finished, there won't be any doubt."

"You are so exasperating. Will you quit speaking in riddles?"

"If I told you what was about to happen, you wouldn't believe it."

"Try me."

He shook his head. "It's easier to show you."

"So what are you waiting for?"

"I don't know."

He smiled, and they started in again, the spiral swiftly escalating, and she was amazed by how eagerly she joined in. She was rapidly becoming a sexual fiend, so needy and voracious that there was no predicting what she might do to keep his attention.

He freed her from the remainder of her clothes, and he caressed her everywhere. She followed his lead, massaging him with great relish. He was so strong, so masculine, his skin burning hot as if there were a brazier chugging away inside.

She was completely naked, but she didn't flinch or hesitate. She was prepared to let him try whatever he wished, just so he vanquished the terrible ache deep inside.

With each passing minute, he grew more intense, his kisses more intoxicating, and he fumbled with his trousers, loosening them and drawing them off his hips.

"What are you doing?" she managed to ask.

"I plan to make love to you—as a man does to his wife. Give me your hand."

He clasped it and lowered it to his crotch, and he folded her fingers around a firm, pliant shaft. He guided her into a rhythm, her fist stroking him in a fashion he obviously enjoyed. Perspiration beaded on his brow; his pulse accelerated.

"What is this thing?"

"My cock."

"Is it attached to your body?"

"Yes. We're built differently."

She was so naïve! "What is it for?"

"It's for pleasure—and for making babies. Which we won't attempt."

She struggled to move out from under him, to scoot down and look, but he wouldn't let her.

"I want to see," she complained.

"No."

"Luke!"

"When it's over, you can explore."

"I want to do it now."

"Helen," he grumbled, "have you any idea how long and how badly I've desired you?"

"No. How long and how badly?"

"Since the moment I first laid eyes on you."

"Really?"

"I'm in agony."

"I'm sorry."

"It's not your fault." He sounded strained. "Well, a little of it is. If you weren't so damned sexy, I wouldn't be so miserable."

"You think I'm sexy?"

"Yes, and I can't wait another second. Now be silent, so I can mate in peace."

He gripped her thighs and yanked them apart, and he arranged himself between her legs, the odd appendage being wedged in, stretching her in a manner she didn't care for, at all.

"Mate . . . how?"

"I'll enter you."

"Enter!"

"Then I'll flex with my hips."

He shoved the rod in a tad farther, and she squirmed with dismay. "I'm not sure about this."

"You don't need to be *sure*. You just need to relax."

"Relax! Are you mad? It's too big; it will never fit."

Her anatomy rebelled, and she wrestled to escape, but the writhing excited him. "It will fit fine. Trust me."

"I don't," she replied. "I absolutely don't."

He laughed. "The first time is awkward. But only the first. After that, it's wonderful."

"It doesn't feel wonderful."

"It will."

"Luke!" she tried, but he was beyond the point where he could listen, and she was hardly in a position to beg that he cease. She'd given him explicit permission to proceed, yet she was shying away like a frightened ninny.

She was so fickle! Why did he put up with her?

"Let me in," he said quietly. "I want you, Helen. Let me do this with you."

When he spoke like that, so sweetly and so tenaciously, she was powerless to resist. She couldn't tell him *no*. She drew him to her, embracing him with a renewed fervor.

She was terrified, but he wasn't a patient or a verbal man, so he couldn't delay or explain. As if she were on a ship being tossed in stormy seas, she closed her eyes and held on, hoping that he would steer her safely through to the end.

He was sucking on her nipple, his fingers working down below. Without warning, the commotion swept over her again, the second incident even more riveting than the initial one had been.

She was blinded by rapture, and as she wound up and up, he was increasing the pressure at her center. It felt as if her torso would never open to him, that he might rip her in half, when suddenly he burst through a barrier and his body was magically connected to hers.

Keeping himself very still, he murmured, "That's the worst of it."

"It hurts."

"The pain will pass."

A tear dribbled down her cheek, not from discomfort but because of the enormity of what had occurred. She couldn't grasp this new reality. He leaned down and tenderly brushed it away.

"Don't cry," he whispered. "I can't bear it when you're sad."

"I'm not crying," she insisted. "I'm not a virgin any-more, am I?"

"No."

"Do I look different?"

"Only prettier."

How was she to respond to such a dear sentiment?

She cradled him to her, and shortly, as he'd claimed, the ache ebbed, and his invasion didn't seem so abnormal.

He began flexing slowly, his cock pushing in and out. Gradually, his pace escalated, until eventually, he was thrusting with a wild abandon. They stretched and strained, their loins slamming together like the pistons of a huge machine. For a woman who'd never previously participated in a similar endeavor she was especially adept. On some primal level, she knew what to do and when to do it, and she couldn't believe how much she enjoyed the exploit.

With each penetration, she surrendered a bit more of herself, so that ultimately, she forgot that they were two separate people. They were one.

"You're so tight," he muttered.

Deciding this was a compliment, she retorted, "Good."

"It's heaven, being inside you. It's simply heaven. Wrap your legs around me."

"Like this?"

"Yes, just like that."

He pressed into her, his muscles quaking, his cock buried deep. With a growl of anguish, he roared to a conclusion that she couldn't mistake as the end. He retracted himself from her sheath, as something hot and sticky shot across her abdomen; then he collapsed onto her.

She cuddled with him, curious as to what they'd say, how they'd act, and the silent aftermath unnerved her.

Why was he so ponderous? She assumed she'd done well, but how could she be sure? What if she'd failed to entice him?

A horrid vision nagged at her—of the beautiful, sophisticated paramours he'd consorted with in London—and she was certain they all knew how to tantalize him as she never would. If he'd found the encounter distasteful, she'd be dismayed beyond measure, and she yearned to shake him.

It was her first time! How could he expect proficiency? If he told her she was boring or clumsy, she'd die of mortification!

He kissed her on the forehead, and she braced, ready for any awful comment, when he mumbled, "I'm sorry."

"What?"

"I'm sorry." He flashed a wry grin. "And I don't apologize very often, so don't gloat."

"I'll try not to."

"I'd appreciate it."

"Why are you sorry?"

"For being so rough. I can't control myself around you. You arouse me beyond my limits."

"I do?"

"Yes, you minx." He swatted her on the rear. "Are you all right?"

She extended her legs, and her innards protested her new situation with an uncomfortable twinge. "It appears I survived."

"What a stellar endorsement of my amatory skills!" He was laughing, and there was mischief in his eyes. "You're supposed to stroke my vanity and tell me it was the greatest moment of your life and that I'm the most fabulous lover in the entire world."

"Well . . . it was . . . interesting."

"Interesting! Aah!" He flopped onto the pillow. "I must be losing my touch. Perhaps I need more practice."

"Does that mean you'd like to do it again?"

"I'd like to *do it* all night, but I doubt your body could stand it."

Feeling shy, she glanced away. "You liked it?"

"Yes, you silly goose, I liked it. If it had been any more exciting, my heart would have exploded."

"So I . . . I . . . did everything correctly?"

"You were perfect, Helen. I'm very pleased."

He was studying her as if she was a puzzle, as if he couldn't understand his attraction to her, and she was positive he was about to utter a profound remark when he sat up and moved off the bed.

For a frantic instant, she was afraid he was leaving, and like a possessive shrew, she clutched at his hand. "Where are you going?"

"I ought to tidy us up a bit. Is there some water and a towel?"

"There's a pitcher on the dresser."

He walked over to her washbasin, and she watched as he swabbed himself clean, but from her angle, she hadn't a good view of what she was dying to see. When he returned, his trousers were loose around his hips, and she considered slipping her fingers inside to investigate, but she hadn't yet worked up that sort of courage.

He perched on the edge of the mattress, and as he dabbed at the mess on her stomach, she pointed at a white cream that had been emitted during their sexual foray.

"What is this?"

"It's my seed. If I'd spilled it inside you, I could have planted a babe."

"Does it spew out every time?"

"Yes."

"So we must be careful."

"Extremely careful."

She was temporarily diverted by the mention of pregnancy. What they'd done seemed too raucous and physical to result in procreation. It was difficult to fathom how the boisterous event translated into parenthood.

"Would you ever want to have a child?" she inquired.

"No, I never would."

He stared at her, but added nothing further, and she wasn't surprised. He rarely talked about himself, and she knew so little about his past. He'd confessed to having a notorious father, but she hadn't bothered to probe for details about his mother, or how he'd come to be a criminal and pirate.

Shouldn't a woman learn that kind of information before lying down with a man? The fact that she hadn't was more proof of how low she'd fallen, of how strong his influence over her was.

He dipped the cloth and wrung it out; then he pressed it between her legs. The cool moisture soothed her tender places, but when she peeked down she was stunned to note that he was wiping away blood.

"Am I injured?"

"No. The blood indicates that you're not a virgin anymore. There was a piece of skin inside you. It's called your maidenhead. I tore it."

"Will it grow back?"

"No."

"Is it the same for every woman?"

"Yes."

She nodded. "So . . . a husband could guess if his wife had ever . . . ever . . ."

"Yes."

He stared again, his silent message clear: She could

never marry. Her fate as a spinster was sealed, but she wasn't concerned. Luke would forever be her one and only love. After him, how could she have another?

"I'm not sorry," she said.

"Neither am I."

Their gazes locked, a hundred thoughts passing between them that couldn't be spoken of aloud. Helen was overcome by dozens of urges—to chat, to snuggle, to babble about nothing until he was annoyed—but mostly she yearned to have him stretched out on top of her again.

She gestured at his trousers. "Take them off."

"What?"

"I want you naked."

He raised a brow. "You do?"

"I've been undressed from the start. It's only fair that I have you in the same condition."

"If I remove my pants, I'll have to have you again."

"You'd better."

"You're sore, and you probably will be for a day or two. I won't hurt you more than I already have."

"I'm not made of glass."

"No, you're not."

"Take off your trousers," she repeated. "Now."

"Are you positive?"

"You promised I could look after we . . . we . . ."

"So I did, Helen. So I did."

He stood and, without the slightest hesitation, he tugged them off and pitched them away. He posed for her, the rod hardening, extending out, and she was transfixed by the sight.

She scooted over and held him, stroking and petting, and the more she played, the more it reacted. It was a living, breathing—demanding!—organism, with a mind and temper of its own, and she couldn't get over the size and shape. It was so peculiar and intriguing, and it beckoned to an ancient, covetous part of her that had her eager to keep it for her own.

"You are so beautiful." She caressed from base to tip, and he tensed and shuddered.

"Do you think so?"

"I don't want to share you with any other women. I want you all to myself."

"Then I am yours, my dear lady."

She recognized the pledge as a false vow, but they were illicit lovers, embarking on a sinful liaison, so she supposed a few prevarications were allowed.

She leaned forward and kissed the blunt end, licking her tongue across it, and she was amazed at how she focused his attention. He was riveted on her, on her mouth, on her hands.

"You like that, do you?" She licked him again, thrilled when his every muscle went taut.

"I definitely do. I can tell that you and I are going to get along just fine." He grinned. "Let me show you something I suspect you'll enjoy."

She lay back and pulled him down with her.

11

Tell me about your past."

"No." Patricia shifted in the water and grabbed for the soap.

"I don't understand why you're so secretive," Robert protested, though kindly. "I've told you absolutely everything about me."

At thinking of the stories he'd related, she smiled. He tried to make light of his terrible upbringing, and many people might insist that he'd had it easy, that food on the table and a roof over his head negated his right to complain, but she knew better.

Despite his meek mother and cruel father, he had such a tender heart. If the Captain hadn't stumbled on him in the slave market, she couldn't predict what might have happened to him. She'd spent enough time in Arabia, herself, to comprehend the perils that could befall such a handsome man.

What she wouldn't give to bump into his brothers! She'd love to have the bastards at the point of her sword and begging for mercy. Robert wasn't the sort to demand vengeance, but she was.

"How long have you traveled with the Captain?" He was probing for details she wasn't about to share.

"Years."

"You mentioned that he rescued you, as he did me."

"Yes, he did," she answered, supplying nothing further.

She rubbed the bar of soap, working up a lather, and she stroked it across his chest. As it was late at night, it had been many hours since he'd shaved, and whiskers darkened his cheeks, making him appear more dashing and more dangerous than any pirate of her acquaintance.

She never tired of looking at him, and she couldn't explain why he had such a remarkable effect, but it had burgeoned from the first day the Captain had brought him to the ship. He'd been emaciated, sunburned, bruised from shackles, and covered with welts from numerous whippings. The Captain had instructed her to care for Robert, to feed and mend him, which was a chore she hadn't minded.

Through all her ministrations, he'd been so courteous and considerate, and she'd been fascinated. She'd never previously encountered such a cultured gentleman. No one remembered who her parents had been or where she came from. In her earliest clear recollection, at about age four, she was on a merchant ship—but with no kin in evidence. She'd grown up with various crews of sailors, in a world of men who were outcasts and adventurers.

Robert's quiet, respectful habits had called to her

feminine side, had her dreaming of better circumstances. She wanted a home of her own, a family, a peaceful existence that didn't involve pistols or raids.

Reaching down, she took his cock in hand, liking how randy and eager he was. He rippled with bliss and pulled her to him, water sloshing onto the floor. The tub wasn't big enough for two, but she hadn't been able to resist getting into it with him.

It was a treat she missed from her bizarre interlude in Arabia, the sultry baths, the wet skin and naked bodies. In carnal matters, she wasn't a prude and had no ladylike tendencies. She reveled in raucous fornication as well as any man, and she was thrilled with Robert's participation.

She'd never copulated with a virginal male, so she hadn't known how refreshing the act could be. He was so hastily titillated, so keen to try her suggestions, and he joined in with a marvelous amount of passion.

She spread her thighs and mounted him, and she rode him hard, swiftly goading him to the edge and pushing him over. He came with great enthusiasm, being much too loud, and she kissed him, swallowing the sound of his joy lest his cry reverberate throughout the house and alert others to what they were doing.

As sanity returned, he mused, "I was such a modest, subdued fellow before I met you."

She was sprawled across him, her limbs limp from their incessant philandering. "I recognized the beast inside you."

"How could you have?"

"From how you always watched me."

"How was that? If memory serves, I was scared to death of you."

"You shouldn't have been. I was ready to give you what you wanted."

"But how did you know what it was, when I didn't know myself?"

"Your body knew," was her reply.

She wasn't about to provide any hints as to how she'd been schooled in decadent conduct. When she'd begun to change from child to woman, the buccaneer upon whose ship she'd been employed had decided she would cause too many problems with his crew. He'd traded her in Cairo for a pile of gold.

The wealthy Sultan who'd purchased her had been kind in his way, gently training her in carnal affairs until she'd become an expert. He'd deemed her a prized possession, but still, she'd been his concubine slave. He'd proudly shared her with special acquaintances, which had been a shock to Captain Westmoreland when he'd been offered a chance to bed her, only to learn that she was an English captive. He'd felt honor-bound to risk his life in rescuing her.

She'd been the jewel in a harem, but Robert would never understand. He was so typically British, and he would view her as having been a whore. She couldn't bear to dim his affection, so she'd never divulge any pertinent facts of her past.

She couldn't guess how long they'd stay at Mansfield Abbey. Eventually, the Captain would depart, and she and Robert would have to do as he bid them. They'd probably be ordered back to the ship, or—more likely—Robert would be left behind to manage the property. She might never see him again, so she regarded the interval as a precious idyll, where anything was possible, where anything was allowed.

She stood and climbed out onto the rug, and she grabbed a towel and dried herself as he studied her every move. She hadn't a clue how to entice through friendship or conversation. She beguiled by using sex. It's what she'd been taught and who she was. If Robert tired of their physical relationship—as transpired with every man sooner or later—she didn't know what she'd do. For now, she was pretending that they'd go on forever just as they were.

She helped him out and dried him, too; then she led him to her bed in the adjacent alcove. He lay down and drew her down onto him, and as she stretched out, she noted a scar on his chest. She traced a finger across it, remembering how he'd been slashed by a slaver's knife, how she'd stitched the injury with needle and thread.

"I hate that they hurt you," she said.

"I don't mind," he maintained. "It makes me look more menacing and less bookish."

She chuckled. "I'm liking *bookish* more and more."

"Are you?"

"Yes."

Her anger at his brothers was renewed with stunning force. "How could they throw you overboard?"

Their crime was unforgivable, and she couldn't quit obsessing over it. He wasn't irate enough to suit her, so she had to be furious for both of them.

"I told you: I don't believe they intended to abandon me. They were vicious boys who grew to be vicious men. It was a prank, but the wind was in the sails, and I was quickly swept away."

"Why travel with them?"

"They claimed that I was too much of a coward to accompany them. I was out to prove them wrong."

"If I ever run into them, I'll kill them for you. The Captain will let me; he might even volunteer to assist."

"Patricia! You can't go around *killing* people."

"Why not?"

"It's simply not done."

"It is when someone deserves it as badly as they do."

"They don't."

"They do!" she insisted.

He sighed. "Well, perhaps they could use a bit of punishment, but I can handle it myself. I don't need you protecting me."

"That's what you think."

"I can fight my own battles."

"Not very well."

He couldn't wield a sword or fire a pistol. She'd once been with him in a tavern when a brawl broke out, and he'd hid under a table until she'd dragged him to safety. In the violent sphere they traversed with the Captain, Robert was like a quaking puppy.

"I detest that you consider me to be so incompetent," he complained.

"I don't!"

"It certainly sounds like it."

"I feel as if I should . . . should . . ." She couldn't finish the sentence without making him seem even less capable.

"Give it a rest, Pat. Please."

She'd pushed him too far, so she backed off, and she snuggled down, her ear over his heart so she could hear its steady beating. She couldn't confess how much he meant to her, or how afraid she often was for him. If anything happened to him, she'd just die!

They were quiet, lost in thought, when he murmured, "I'll show you that I'm worth it."

"What?" She raised up and frowned.

"If you give me a chance, I'll prove that I can be the man you need."

"You already are."

"No. I've seen the men in your world. I've eaten with them and drunk with them, wagered with them and voyaged with them. I know what you expect."

Why couldn't she keep her mouth shut? When she found him to be so very fine, why denigrate him?

"You're more than enough."

At the remark, he smiled. "You are too good to me."

"And I plan to be even better."

He rolled them so that she was on the bottom, so that he was on top, and his gaze was all hot, focused male. She wondered if he had any idea how fierce he appeared, how determined. He'd taken to debauchery like a fish to water, had rapidly learned how to satisfy a woman, and how to get what he wanted, too. He was so sexy, so handsome, and he was all hers. At least for the time being.

She had no illusions about the sort of female who would eventually catch him. When he'd earned his fortune and was prepared to settle down, he'd choose a wife like Miss Mansfield.

Frequently, Pat spied on them, as they conferred about books they'd read or about articles in the London paper that referred to people they both knew. They were so much alike, and Pat yearned to go to the other woman, to shake her and say, *Let me be one of you so I can keep him! Let me be you!*

She would give anything to stay at Mansfield, to dress and act like a real lady. Once in her life, during her ordeal in Egypt, she'd been beautiful and tempting, and she wanted to be that way again, but she wasn't sure how to accomplish it.

"What do you suppose the Captain will decide about

Mansfield Abbey?" he inquired, daring to broach questions of the future.

"Let's don't talk about it."

"But what if he has you leave and—"

"Hush."

She pressed a finger to his lips. She was superstitious as any sailor, and she wouldn't court bad luck by speaking aloud of grim tidings.

She started kissing him, leading him to the physical realm where they thrived, where there were no annoying doubts, shameful histories, or nagging secrets. He joined in, as anxious as she to avoid discussion of untenable subjects.

He took control of the embrace and entered her with a single thrust.

"I adore being inside you." He flexed with unbridled delight.

"I can tell."

"I assumed I'd lived before, but I hadn't. Not till now. Not till you."

How could she fail to love him? She wanted so much from him, more than he could ever imagine, more than he would ever agree to give.

He pulled out and blazed a trail to her breasts, but he surprised her by continuing on, down her stomach, her abdomen, to her lush center.

He hesitated, curious and eager, but not positive of how to proceed. He knew about this facet of passion— after all, when you served the Captain, you witnessed every salacious behavior—but he hadn't sought to initiate the naughty deed, and she hadn't had the courage to ask.

"I want to taste you," he explained. Politely, he added, "May I?"

"Yes."

"What should I do?"

"Lick me with your tongue."

"Where do you like it best?"

"There."

She spread her nether lips, providing greater access, and she stared at the ceiling, too overwhelmed to peek down. She was suddenly shy when she couldn't deduce why she would be. She'd spied on him at his bath for weeks, had fornicated with him on dozens of occasions. This was simply the next level in a rising tide of ardor.

"Like this?"

"Yes, exactly like that."

His tongue flicked at her, and she arched, attempting to throw him off but lure him closer, too.

"Hold still, my little hellcat."

"I can't. You drive me wild."

"I do?" He was so pleased!

"Yes." She grinned. "I'm insane with desiring you."

"I'm so glad to hear it." He scowled. "You seem to enjoy this immensely."

"I can't deny it."

"Why didn't you have me try it sooner?"

"I didn't know how to suggest it."

"Silly girl. When we're finished, we must have a long chat, so you can inform me of what else you've been hiding."

"Nothing, really. I just . . . just . . ."

"I'm a beginner at this," he reminded her.

"But hardly a novice."

"You can't expect me to figure out everything on my own."

"You're doing fairly well without much guidance."

He raised a brow, licking her again, again. "Should I go faster? Or slower? Which is best?"

"Faster," she urged. "Definitely faster . . . oh . . . and use your fingers to . . . to . . ."

She was too provoked to enlighten him further, but then, words weren't necessary. He grasped what was required, sliding in to taunt and tease, and with scarcely any effort, he goaded her into the inferno.

He pinned her down, tormenting her, riding out the storm, and as she reached the peak, as the ecstasy waned, he was nibbling up her torso to kiss her on the mouth.

She could taste herself on his tongue, and she groaned with pleasure, loving the tang and what it indicated about the new stage of their relationship. He settled himself between her legs, his cock gliding in with no assistance, at all, and he gripped her hips and flexed, penetrating to the hilt. With a wrenching moan, he spilled himself, then collapsed atop her. He was laughing, merry, his erection not having diminished in the slightest.

"How do you do that to me?" he asked.

"You're a man, so you're easy."

"You've turned me into a sexual addict. I can't get enough."

"Good."

He looked so beautiful, so reliable and steady, and she felt something crack and break deep inside. It was her image of herself, of her link to the Captain and the past. She yearned to be more than what she was, to have Robert treasure more about her than the fact that he could sate his lust between her thighs.

They reveled every night, but during the day they carried on as strangers. She wanted so much more. How could she achieve it?

Don't ever leave me, she nearly wailed, and she bit down so she wouldn't blurt out the needy, stupid comment. She couldn't let him ascertain how smitten she was.

She was saved from further embarrassment by a brisk knock on the door. They both jumped. They'd been so wrapped up in their escapade that they hadn't noticed anyone approaching.

"Gad!" Robert whispered. "Who could it be?"

"I haven't a clue," she responded, though she was quite sure she knew the interloper's identity. Before she could inquire, the door burst open, and the Captain strolled in.

"There you are," he said calmly, as though finding them in bed together was an ordinary occurrence. "I've been searching everywhere."

"Oh, my Lord!" Robert breathed.

His phallus withered, and he retreated from her, but he was at a loss as to his next move. Should he leap up and grab for his trousers? Should he conceal himself by keeping himself pressed to her? What was most discreet? The blankets were down around their feet, kicked away in their frantic mating and no help whatsoever.

He was an extremely mōdest individual, unaccustomed to having others view him in a state of dishabille, so he was mortified.

As for herself, the Captain had seen her naked before, as she'd seen him on many occasions. There were few secrets between them. She shifted Robert off and behind her so that she shielded him as much as she was able.

"Did you need me, Captain?" She was as composed as he. She was totally at his service and always would be. If he commanded her to dress and fight, she'd be ready immediately. "Is something wrong?"

"Well, that depends." He studied them, absorbing the debauched details. "What have you to say for yourself, Mr. Smith?"

Robert gulped. "Me? I . . . I . . ."

She was furious. Considering the Captain's constant philandering, he had no right to strut in and interrupt. Robert was terrified of him, deeming him to be much more vicious than he actually was, and the Captain was amused by making him tremble.

Chin up, she declared, "It was all my doing, Captain. I seduced him."

"I'm aware of your numerous charms, Pat, so I'm certain you did."

"He wanted no part of it."

The Captain guffawed, his randy eyes meandering down her womanly form. "And I'm the King of England."

"It's true. I forced him."

Robert piped up, "She did not, Captain. I was the pursuer, and I take full responsibility."

She elbowed him in the ribs. "He was completely innocent."

"Pure as the driven snow, I'll bet," the Captain chided. "Mr. Smith, we'd better talk."

"Now?" Robert's voice squeaked up an octave.

"At the moment, you appear to be busy, so the morning will suffice. I'll break my fast at six. Join me in the small dining parlor." As he turned to go, he warned, "Were I you, I wouldn't be late."

"No, sir, I won't be."

They listened to his fading footsteps, and once it was quiet, Robert shuddered with dread.

"Will he kill me?"

She scoffed. "No. He likes you."

"He does?"

"Of course. And he and I are friends. He'd never hurt you, because it would hurt me."

"How can you be so positive?"

"Because I've known him a long time. Much longer than you." The Captain had an odd sense of justice, but he was basically a fair man.

"What will he do, then? Will he have me flogged? Will he lock me in irons?"

"I really can't say."

"I couldn't bear it if he tossed me in the hold with the rats."

"He won't. Stop worrying."

He flopped onto his back, an arm flung over his face, as he contemplated his fate. Ultimately, he peered over at her. "You don't suppose he'll demand we wed, do you?"

At the prospect his distaste was painfully evident. So . . . this was his genuine opinion. In her mind, she'd realized that he regarded her strictly in a carnal fashion, but her heart and pride had invented other scenarios.

She was such an idiot! When he was so fine, he'd never ally himself with someone so much lower. She was a fool to have presumed otherwise.

She tamped down her distress, her shame, and blandly replied, "He wouldn't order such a silly result. Not over a mere bit of fornication."

"I'm so relieved!"

"He's very practical. He understands how affairs happen between adults."

"Too true."

"Yes, isn't it?"

Obviously, he didn't share her heightened emotions. He craved one thing from her and one thing only. Desperate to mask her wounded feelings with darkness, she leaned over and blew out the candle.

Very likely, the Captain would send him to London, so this might be her last chance to be with him. She wanted him to remember how it had been, to remember—and to never forget—that she had been his first.

She cradled him to her and started in again.

12

It's about time you arrived, Mr. Smith."

"I apologize, Captain."

"I asked you to attend me at six. It's gone past eleven. *Up* late, were you?"

At the sexual innuendo Robert blushed. "I appear to have dozed off. Let me apologize again."

When he'd opened his eyes and discovered the hour, he'd nearly expired with alarm. He'd sneaked out of Patricia's bed, donned his wrinkled, messy clothes, then raced to find the Captain awaiting him in the library. They faced each other across the huge desk—Westmoreland sitting, Robert standing—and he struggled for aplomb, but with his tardiness and disheveled condition it was difficult to muster any composure.

He'd proved himself an immoral sluggard. If the

Captain fired him, it would be the least of the penalties he deserved.

Westmoreland scrutinized Robert's rumpled suit, his unshaven cheeks, and smirked. "Well, let's hear it. What have you to say for yourself?"

"I make no excuses, and I will accept any punishment."

Robert bravely offered himself up for castigation, but inside, he was horridly irked that he had to atone for his indiscretion. To the Captain of all people! The man was the most prolific libertine on earth, and for him to reproach for conduct in which he regularly engaged, himself, was certainly a case of the pot calling the kettle black.

Robert recognized how awfully he'd transgressed, so he didn't need a preachy lecture from the worst of sinners. Should the criticism be acute, Robert wasn't sure he could remain civil.

From his first moment with Patricia, Robert had known that what he was doing was wrong. He'd become little more than a feral beast, his only thought on copulation. With no regard for the consequences, he continually spilled himself in her sheath. Eventually, he would have her pregnant, and then what would he do? He was poverty-stricken, with no income and no family he'd acknowledge, so he couldn't marry her.

More important, if they forged ahead into matrimony, what sort of union would they have? She was accustomed to combative men, who reasoned with their fists. In comparison, he was a frail ninny, and ultimately she would grow to hate him for his failings.

He was disgusted with himself and had to gain control, but he had no idea how. If he was lucky, the Captain would murder him and put him out of his misery.

"So," the Captain mused, "you're thinking you should be punished."

"Yes."

"And what—precisely—would I punish you *for*?"

"Illicit fornication. I admit to every lapse, and despite what Miss Reilly claims, it was all my fault."

Westmoreland rocked on the hind legs of his chair, studying Robert, while Robert squirmed and sweated, and he received the distinct impression that the Captain was enjoying Robert's discomfort.

"I'm amazed, Mr. Smith."

"By what?"

"By your assuming the blame. Perhaps there's hope for you yet."

"Although my recent activities scarcely reflect it, I was raised a gentleman. It's only proper that I own up to what I've done."

Just then, the door banged open, and Patricia stomped in. With a sword dangling from one hip and a pistol strapped to the other, she was a sight, a lithe, tough virago who looked as if she might tear Westmoreland limb from limb.

"Good morning, Reilly," the Captain welcomed. "I'm pleased to see that you could drag your ass out of bed before noon."

Patricia bristled and marched over. In a protective gesture, she stepped in front of Robert, shielding him from Westmoreland's wrath, and Robert was aggravated by the move. He had so few masculine qualities, and he didn't need her reminding the Captain of that pitiful fact.

"Leave Robert alone, Captain," she demanded. "If you have something to say, say it to me."

"I suggest you butt out," Westmoreland responded. "This isn't any of your business."

"If it's not *my* business, then whose would it be?" she asked. "You're not to bully him. I won't allow it."

"You won't?" Westmoreland stared at Robert. "Have you any reply, Mr. Smith?"

Robert was humiliated beyond words. It was bad enough to be braced for a dressing-down, but to have Patricia interfering and pleading his case!

"Patricia!" Robert scolded. "Stop it. You're embarrassing me."

At his sharp rebuke she glanced over her shoulder. "I won't have him badgering you."

"He's not," Robert insisted. There hadn't been time! He nodded toward the hall. "Wait outside. I'll be out in a minute."

"But . . . but . . ."

She was furious with both of them and eager to wreak havoc, but Robert couldn't be further disparaged before Westmoreland.

"Go, Patricia!" he stated more vehemently than he typically would.

To his astonishment, she frowned, then complied. As she arrived at the threshold, she halted and glared at Westmoreland.

"If you harm him," she vowed, "you'll answer to me."

"I'm sure I will," Westmoreland agreed, sounding downright cordial.

She departed, though Robert envisioned her directly outside, her ear pressed to the wood. With minimal provocation, she'd probably rush in again and leap to his defense.

Westmoreland pointed to a chair. "Sit down, Mr. Smith."

He felt like a felon about to meet his executioner. "I prefer to stand."

"And I order you to sit."

So much for defiance! When Westmoreland issued a command, there was no denying him. Robert pulled up a chair, centered it, and perched on the edge.

Westmoreland rose and started toward the sideboard, then detoured to the door. He jerked it open and, as Robert had suspected, Patricia was leaned against it, and she tumbled in.

"Head to your room," Westmoreland said, "and stay there till I send for you."

"I won't," she mutinously declared, daring to be insubordinate. "You can't make me."

"If you don't obey—this very second—it'll be twenty lashes in the yard, with the servants watching. I'll use the cat-o'-nine-tails, and after I'm finished, you won't see your precious Mr. Smith for six months."

She tarried, debating whether to refuse, but she thought better of it and tromped off. Westmoreland dawdled till he was certain she'd left; then he went to the sideboard and poured two whiskeys. He returned, seated himself behind the desk, and passed one to Robert while he sipped his own. Robert gaped at the liquor but didn't reach for it.

"Drink up, Mr. Smith."

"No."

"Drink!" His tone brooked no argument.

"I don't imbibe of hard spirits."

"Maybe you should begin. I'm positive it would have a beneficial effect on your dour character."

Robert was angrier than he'd been in years, and he gripped his chair, restraining himself lest he dive across and pummel Westmoreland. With how the Captain had menaced Patricia, could he actually presume Robert would act as if nothing had happened? Were they to have a friendly beverage and a chuckle? Was the man truly that thick?

"If you lay a hand on her," Robert seethed, "I'll kill you. Not immediately, but someday when you least expect it, I'll . . . I'll . . ."

"You would? Really?"

"Yes."

Not intimidated in the slightest, the Captain waved away the remark. "I'd cut off my arm before I hurt her."

"Then why threaten her with the lash?"

"You haven't had much experience with women, Mr. Smith, especially one as independent as Patricia. Trust me when I tell you that some of them require a firm rein, or they'll run all over you."

"If I ever decide I need your advice on how to deal with a female, I'll let you know."

Westmoreland laughed. "You seem awfully annoyed with me. Why is that? You wouldn't be in love with her, would you?"

"Me?" Robert scoffed. "How could I be? I have no money."

"I've heard that *money* has little to do with the emotional state. It can strike without warning. Has it struck you, Mr. Smith?"

Westmoreland's shrewd assessment dug deep, and Robert felt like an ant trapped under a glass.

"Of course I'm not in love," he maintained. "You're being ludicrous."

"So . . . this is merely a pleasant romp?"

It was so much more than that, but Robert fidgeted and lied, "Yes."

"I have to admit that I'm surprised at you."

"Why?"

"Such reckless spontaneity is so contrary to your nature."

"I guess I can be as impulsive as the next fellow."

"And as randy, it appears." Westmoreland sighed. "You're being extremely irresponsible."

"I am not!" he asserted, though he knew Westmoreland was correct. He'd never behaved so negligently, and he couldn't fathom why rashness suddenly appealed.

"If she winds up pregnant, what are your plans toward her?"

"You're aware of my financial position. How could I have any?"

"How indeed?"

Westmoreland had a way of focusing in, of delving to the crux of the matter. His disappointment was clear, his disapproval excruciating. Under his avid scrutiny, Robert twitched with dismay. He wanted to defend or explain, but there was no rationalizing the unjustifiable.

He took a stout gulp of whiskey, so overcome with regret that he didn't flinch as the searing liquid washed down his throat.

"Are you familiar with her past?" Robert inquired, desperate to change the subject, to urge the conversation away from his personal flaws.

"Yes, I know all about her."

"How did the two of you meet?"

The Captain shrugged. "If she hasn't chosen to inform you, then I don't suppose I ought."

He made it sound sinister, and Robert could barely stifle a shudder of dread. He couldn't bear to imagine what predicament she might have been in when the Captain had stumbled upon her.

"Does she owe you money?"

After being purchased at the slave market, Robert, himself, was in debt to Westmoreland for hundreds of pounds and, barring some windfall, would never earn the amount necessary for reimbursement. If Patricia had to repay him, too, they'd never be free.

"No," Westmoreland answered, "I didn't buy her. I simply rescued her."

"She said it was your idea that she pretend to be a man."

"The Egyptian I stole her from was gravely offended, and he offered a huge reward for her to be murdered. He sent out assassins who'd like to collect it. They still look for her and always will. When she left with me, I vowed to her that I'd never let them find her."

"They're searching for a woman."

"They have been, but they'll figure it out eventually."

A terrible notion dawned on Robert. "Is she safe here at Mansfield?"

"I believe so. England is far from the Mediterranean, and we're in the country rather than on the London docks." He went and refilled his liquor, and he stared out the window. "But I have to tell you, Mr. Smith, that she'll constantly be in danger. She's tough, and she can brawl with the best of them, but she must have a partner who will watch her back."

"Why is this Egyptian gentleman so determined?"

"He has a long memory. There's pride involved over her audacity, you see, as well as a strong need for vengeance. So if I was to give her to someone else—say someone who loved her and wished to marry her—that fellow would have to swear to me that he would protect her with his very life. He'd have to prove himself worthy, that he was capable of fighting to the death for her."

Blue eyes icy with resolve, he spun and faced Robert.

"Do you know of a man who might want her, who might be inclined to that sort of bravery and dedication?"

Obviously, Westmoreland was asking if Robert could be that man, when they both realized he wasn't and never could be. Robert flushed with shame and glanced away.

"No," he muttered, "I don't know anyone like that."

"Just as I suspected," Westmoreland murmured in reply. An awkward silence ensued; then Westmoreland said, "You're excused, Mr. Smith. You may be about your duties."

"Thank you, Captain."

"In the meantime," he added as Robert slithered away, "I recommend that you let the relationship cool a bit."

"Yes, sir, I will."

Feeling numb, he walked into the hall and sneaked to his room.

13

Helen hurried down the stairs. She was late for supper, and the Captain would be irked by her tardiness. He rarely dined in the house, and for once, he would be present and was demanding that she join him.

She'd spent hours consulting with the cook, selecting the menu, fussing with the china and silver, and picking out her dress. She yearned for everything to be perfect so she could illustrate the sort of repast that would be served in London when he met his father. He'd asked for her help in preparing for the grand event, but he'd given her few chances to assist.

If she had a more personal reason for wanting the intimate meal to be a success, she refused to linger on her ulterior motives. Since he'd visited her bedchamber, he hadn't stopped by again. In fact, he'd been notably absent from the premises. Obviously, he was avoiding her, and she was in agony, trying to deduce why.

The evening had been a romantic, splendid experience, and she'd been expecting a similar episode to occur, but he must have found their tryst a tad less interesting. The prospect—that he'd been dissatisfied—was eating away at her.

She'd been informed that he left the property at night. Why? Was he visiting other women in the village? If he was, she had to figure out how to prevent him from straying.

Her pride was now involved, as were her emotions. It galled her to acknowledge the truth, but she was smitten beyond any sane limit, and she was desperate to seduce him so that he'd stay at home where he belonged.

She reached the foyer and increased her pace, racing around the corner when she bumped into Mr. Smith. He and Sergeant Reilly were huddled together and . . . and . . . kissing! Directly on the mouth!

They leapt apart.

Mr. Smith cleared his throat and tugged at his cravat. "Miss Mansfield, if I may explain . . ."

"No, you may not." Helen held up a hand, halting any confession. "Whatever is happening here, I really don't wish to know."

She rushed by them and down the hall without glancing back, and momentarily she was at the door to the salon where Westmoreland awaited. At the thought of being with him she was giddy as a schoolgirl, and she paused, taking several deep breaths to calm her pounding heart; then she entered.

To her dismay, the room was empty—except for the maid Peg, who loitered at the sideboard. Wondering if he'd gone to supper without her, Helen inquired, "Has the Captain arrived?"

"No, miss."

Had he decided not to attend, after all? Was he detained elsewhere?

Crushed by the notion, she sank down on the sofa and was fretting over where he was, over what he might be doing—and with whom!—when she heard him marching down the corridor.

"Mr. Smith," he barked, "don't you have somewhere you need to be?"

"Yes, Captain," Smith replied, though not sounding embarrassed.

"You know," the Captain went on, "when I suggested that you let your relationship cool, this isn't exactly what I had in mind."

Smith grumbled a remark Helen couldn't decipher; then the Captain started toward her. Self-conscious and aflutter, she waved for Peg to pour her some wine.

When he saw her, she wanted to look serene, as if she hadn't been virtually bristling with impatience. She moved to the window, gripping her glass and staring outside as if she'd been there for ages and his appearance was of no consequence whatsoever.

The instant he crossed the threshold, she could tell. She'd planned to ignore him, but she couldn't resist the pull of his gaze. She spun and, on espying him, she inhaled sharply, bobbling her wine and nearly dropping it on the rug.

"Oh my!"

He was wearing one of his new suits, and he was so fashionably attired that she was speechless. The coat was flawlessly tailored, a stunning sapphire that hugged his broad shoulders, his thin waist. His breeches were tan, his boots black, his shirt blinding white. The colors set off the blue of his eyes, the blond of his hair, so that he seemed more majestic and more imposing than she could have imagined possible.

From the first, she'd recognized how handsome he was, but with his hard body and calloused hands it had been in a rough way. Through nefarious methods, he was gradually growing rich, but his affluence was recent, his anatomy still bearing the signs of decades of toil and strife.

The man standing before her wasn't that same person. The fine garments had altered him into someone else entirely. He was . . . was . . .

She couldn't describe what he *was*, but she was unnerved by the transformation. Suddenly she didn't know him at all, and she didn't want him changing. In some silly, possessive, feminine manner, she'd begun to presume that he was hers, that he would always be with her at Mansfield Abbey, but she'd been deluding herself.

He was destined for greatness, for London and the life that would be granted to him as he progressed into his father's realm. He might continue to own Mansfield Abbey, but he would never be part of it. She almost felt as if he was fading into the distance, his magnificent future hovering just over the horizon and luring him away from her.

"Good evening, Helen," he greeted, acting like the most gallant gentleman in the land. "I apologize for being late. I hope I haven't kept you waiting long."

"It's . . . it's quite all right."

"What do you think?" He gestured to his outfit, and he laughed, trying to make light of the question, but he was more anxious than she'd ever witnessed him prior. He was dying to have her praise him, which was easy.

"Very dashing, my dear captain."

"So that crusty old tailor knew his business?"

"Yes, he definitely did."

"What a relief! I'd hate to have to speak with him about any mistakes." He entered, his focus locked on Helen, as he said, "Peg, would you leave us for a few minutes? We're not to be disturbed. I'll notify you when we're ready for supper to be served."

Peg huffed out, shutting the door too loudly, indicating her pique at receiving further evidence of Helen's disreputable fall from grace. The maid would tattle to the staff as to why the meal had been delayed, and the gossip would be atrocious, but Helen didn't care.

His attention was fixed on the swell of her breasts, on the low-cut bodice of her dress. It was the only gown she had that was remotely stylish, and if she hadn't been frantic to entice him, she wouldn't have worn it. Apparently, she'd succeeded in her quest.

He approached until they were toe-to-toe, until he towered over her, and she was dizzy with excitement. Desire sang in her veins, her blood throbbing with lust, and she couldn't believe how fervently she wanted him.

He'd released a veiled, hedonistic side of her character. She was eager to be his sexual pupil, to study and learn every delicious, erotic deed he'd like to teach.

He reached out and traced a finger across her bosom. "Very nice," he murmured. "Very, very nice."

The compliment oozed through bone and pore, making her feel sultry and beautiful. No man had ever looked at her and seen what he did, and she yearned to be the femme fatale he envisioned. If he'd been sneaking off, searching for romance from others, his nocturnal forays had to stop. *She* would be the one to whom he turned when his male ardor was running hot.

"I've missed you," she announced, and boldly she grabbed the lapels of his coat and pulled him to her.

"Have you?"

"Yes."

"How much?"

"Too much."

This wasn't the time to be prudish. Though he hadn't mentioned his father again, his destiny was calling. When the Duke met Lucas Westmoreland, both men's lives would be changed. After all, what father could fail to embrace such a son?

He would be swept into the Duke's world, would be welcomed and flaunted to friends and enemies alike. He would go, and he would never come back to her. She had only these few days or weeks till Fate spirited him away.

She rose on tiptoe, seeking his kiss, and he obliged, dipping down to take her in his arms. He molded his lips to hers, demanding all that she was, all that she was supposed to be.

She reveled, her view of herself rocked by her hunger for him. She wasn't stuffy, boring Helen Mansfield but someone different, someone extraordinary, and she had the power to arouse him, to make him want her.

"Where have you been?" she asked. "You've been hiding from me. Why would you?"

"I tried to stay away," he claimed. "I tried so hard."

"You fool! Don't you know how badly I want you? How badly I need you?"

He nibbled down her nape, to her cleavage, and her body rippled with the urge to have his hands on her, to have his mouth on her.

"I must be mad," he contended. "The only topic I ponder is you—where you are and what you're doing. You've bewitched me."

She was certain it was a lie, that in the hours when he was away he never contemplated her, but she'd act as if it was true, as if he meant every word.

"I've got you under my spell," she agreed, "and I intend to keep you there."

"You'll be the death of me."

"I'll make it quick and painless."

His naughty fingers crept into her dress, to her nipple, and he pinched and squeezed; then he tugged at the fabric, baring the soft mound so that his teeth and tongue could work their dastardly magic. She was draped over his arm, precariously balanced, but she wasn't afraid of falling. He was so strong, so sure in his motions.

There was a writing desk behind her, and he eased her onto it, the jar of pens scattering, the papers flying to the floor. She spread her legs and wrapped them around him, and she was amazed by how swiftly the encounter had descended to decadence.

It was early evening, the sun not having set, the servants rattling around in the next room. Any one of them could walk in. A window was open behind her, the curtains flapping in the breeze, the gardener out in the yard, finishing his chores, yet she proceeded without hesitation.

Lucas was drawing her skirt up her legs, caressing her knees, her thighs. Then . . . his fingers were inside her, stretching her, inflaming her. She was melting, wild for what was coming. He fussed with his trousers, the placard loose, and he centered himself, nudging in the crown, but he wouldn't enter her.

She was shameless, writhing against him, trying to force him to take her, but he wouldn't.

He bent down and sucked on her nipple, the stimulation scorching her until she was weak with lust.

"Tell me you want this," he commanded. "Tell me that you want *me*."

"How could you not know?"

"Tell me that you'll never be sorry."

"Never. I never will be."

"You're mine, Helen. Mine forever."

It was another lie. She would never be his. He was like a stallion she'd seen once in a paddock, kicking and fighting to be free, but still, she gave him the vow he was eager to have.

"I'm yours forever, Luke."

Her pledge seared through him like a brand, riveting him so thoroughly that she had to wonder if she hadn't actually bound herself to him in some significant way. Perhaps she had. Perhaps he was more fond of her than she realized.

How thrilling!

"No going back, Helen."

"No, there isn't."

With a brutal thrust, he penetrated her, his cock filling her to her womb. The incursion was so welcome, so . . . so . . . *needed,* that she was immediately pitched into the uncontrollable spiral of pleasure.

She arched up and cried out, and in some vague portion of her mind she recognized that the servants had probably heard the primal wail, but she wasn't concerned. She was a trollop who was so desperate for him and the ecstasy he rendered that she would stoop to any indiscretion so long as he was the one who instigated it.

As her sheath tightened around him, he reached the end, too, spilling himself far inside, but she didn't pause to worry about future consequences. She was too overwhelmed by the present, and could only surmise that if the staff had had any doubt as to what was occurring, his feral growl of satisfaction confirmed every low opinion that had recently been generated.

He flexed again, again, each invasion intensifying the elation, delaying the conclusion. Small jolts coursed through her, tiny tremors continuing until finally the surge was complete.

He retreated from her and, looking all male, all vain, smug certainty, he preened.

"I absolutely adore fucking you," he whispered.

She shivered. "What does that mean? That word?"

"You know what it means."

He knelt down, and he leaned in and licked his tongue across her privates. She was shocked, but enthralled, too, her body jerking violently, seeking more. Always more. With him, she could never get enough.

In a heartbeat, he had her aroused and ready to begin anew, but he shifted away and kissed a slow path to her mouth.

"I love how you taste," he said.

"Do it again," she begged.

He chuckled. "All in good time, my little beauty."

"Is that a promise or a threat?"

"Definitely a promise. What's between us is about to grow raucous and rough, but I believe that it'll be just your cup of tea."

"What are you implying?"

"Face it, Helen. Deep within, you harbor the passions of a harlot."

"I'm not that bad!"

"Trust me on this: You're an out-and-out slattern, but in my view, that's not a defect."

He stood and straightened his clothes, and he urged her to her feet, but her knees were wobbly, so she kept her bottom balanced on the desk. As if she were a child, he arranged her dress, but her hair was half-down and impossible to repair. For a minute he wrestled with it; then he gave up.

"There's no hope for it." He yanked the last combs away so that the lengthy mass swung down.

"We have to go in to supper," she protested. "I can't have it mussed like this!"

"I like it down. Leave it."

"But . . . but . . . what will the servants think?"

"They'll *think* I tumbled you on the writing desk in the front parlor. And they'll be right!"

"Aah! You're a beast."

"You have no reputation remaining. You might as well flaunt your dissolution." He gestured toward the dining room. "I'm starved. Let's sample this feast you've spent the day preparing. I'm curious to learn whether your *talents* extend beyond the bedchamber."

"You've dined with me before. I didn't hear you complaining."

"I didn't want to hurt your feelings."

"Liar. You devour my food like a hungry wolf. And since I like you a tad more than I used to, I plan to feed you even better."

"You *like* me, do you?"

I love you! The imprudent sentiment swirled by so rapidly and with such vehemence that she scarcely refrained from blurting out the absurd confession.

"Yes, I like you," she admitted, "despite the fact that you're unbearably arrogant."

"Arrogant?" He shrugged. "I've been called worse."

"I'm sure you have."

"Let's stop talking and start eating. I'm going to have you sit on my lap and serve me the choicest morsels. I often have concubines in Arabia do it for me, and I enjoy it very much."

"Am I to be your slave?"

He considered, then grinned. "That's a marvelous suggestion."

She glared, trying to appear annoyed, but he kissed her and caressed her breast.

"I'm tired of avoiding you," he said. "You're an attraction I can't fight, so I've decided to have my way with you whenever the mood strikes me."

"Really?"

"Really. So after we finish our meal, I'm taking you to my room. To my bed. We'll fornicate all night long."

Her pulse pounded with glee as images of the wild hours to come shot through her head. "Then why are we dawdling in here?"

"I haven't a clue."

He clasped her arm and led her to the table.

14

Helen dabbled with her mending, then paused to stare across the parlor at Sergeant Reilly. He sulked by the window, gazing out toward the hills where the road to London meandered north. He was so forlorn that it was painful to watch him.

On the spur of the moment, the Captain had claimed pressing business in the city, and he'd left, dragging a reluctant Mr. Smith with him. He hadn't said how soon he'd return, nor had Helen felt she had any right to ask. Still, she was miserable without him. The house was so quiet, devoid of the energy he'd brought to it, and she jumped at every sound, expecting him to come barreling through the door.

She was so dependent on his presence. Her entire world revolved around him, and with him gone, she was wretched. His short absence painted an agonizing picture of what her life would be like once he went for good.

She stuck her needle through the fabric, but she wasn't paying attention, and she stuck herself.

"Ow!" she complained.

Reilly glanced over. "Have you poked yourself, again?"

"Yes. With how clumsy I've become, perhaps I should give up sewing altogether."

"Let me finish it for you."

Reilly crossed to her and seized the cloth. Helen allowed him to have it; then she furtively spied on him as he settled himself, as he proved himself competent by taking tiny stitches. However, his concentration lasted but a minute or two; then he threw down the work and began to pace.

Reilly made her so uncomfortable that she yearned to flee. Mr. Smith was like an elephant in the middle of the room, needing to be discussed but neither of them able to broach the subject.

Helen decided to switch the direction of their contemplation. Reilly had traveled with Luke for ages, which provided Helen with an opportunity to probe for details about his background.

"How long have you known Captain Westmoreland?" she inquired.

"Years."

"I imagine it's been exciting, sailing with him as you've done."

"On occasion."

Reilly ignored her, and the conversation lagged, the silence stretching to infinity.

"Where is he from originally?"

"England," Reilly said as if Helen were a dolt. "Where would you suppose?"

"I knew that," Helen grumbled. "I meant *where* in England."

"London."

"Oh."

"Although his mother grew up here."

"Here? *Here* as in Mansfield Abbey?"

"Yes," Reilly confirmed. "You seem surprised."

"Very."

"I thought everybody had heard the stories."

"Not me."

"Sorry. I probably shouldn't have mentioned it then."

Wasn't that like lighting the rug on fire? Now that the information had been gleaned, how was she to deal with it? Particularly when the bearer of the tidings was taciturn as a grizzled old soldier?

"Honestly, Sergeant," Helen scolded, "you can't drop a load like that, then swallow your tongue."

"If the Captain had wanted you to know, he'd have told you. It's not my business."

Helen was close to shaking the recalcitrant fellow, but she didn't. She'd spent enough time around both Reilly and Smith to grasp that they wouldn't betray the Captain's confidence. They were loyal to a fault, so she'd have to garner the rest of the tale from the exalted pirate himself, and ooh, when he returned, wouldn't she have a few comments to convey?

His own mother! At Mansfield Abbey! And he'd never uttered a word! So much for assuming they were friends! What could be so terrible that he wouldn't share it?

She was sure the mystery explained why he'd gambled with Archie. She was coming to know Westmoreland very well, and with him, nothing happened by chance. There was always a method to his madness. He'd wagered for a reason, and she felt cheated that he'd kept his motives a secret.

Why couldn't he trust her?

She was so wrapped up in her furious rumination that she didn't realize Reilly was speaking.

"Pardon me, Sergeant. I was woolgathering."

"I said: Might I ask you a question?"

"Certainly."

"It might sound strange." He was so despairing! "Promise you won't laugh."

"I promise. What is it?"

"Would you help me become a woman?"

"A . . . a . . . woman?" Helen shifted uneasily. She'd been quite liberal minded about what she'd seen pass between Reilly and Smith—she hadn't even revealed it to the Captain, though he seemed to be aware of their peculiar association—but this appeal was too much. "Such a thing isn't possible, Sergeant Reilly. You're a man. You should accept the fact and move on."

"I'm not a man!"

"Sergeant—"

"You don't understand." He walked over to her, and he jerked off his cap, his fingers yanking at the strip of leather that tied his hair. He riffled through it, spreading the curly tresses over his shoulders as Helen watched in horrified fascination.

Either he was the prettiest man she'd ever met or . . . he wasn't a man, at all.

"You're not a man," Helen marveled.

"No."

"How long have you been a woman?" she stupidly queried.

"Since I was born, Miss Mansfield. I swear it."

"The Captain knows?"

"Yes."

"And Mr. Smith?"

"Yes."

"Well . . . good."

"I was beautiful once," Mr.—that is, *Miss*—Reilly advised, "and I'm desperate to be that way again. So that Robert will . . . will . . ."

"That's Mr. Smith?"

"I want him to view me differently."

"I'll bet you do."

From the poor woman's pathetic expression, she had to be deeply, miserably in love with Mr. Smith. Was that how Helen looked when she was mooning over Westmoreland? How humiliating!

"I need to learn to dress like you," Miss Reilly declared, "and I have to learn your fussy manners and your fancy habits. Could you teach me, Miss Mansfield? Before he comes back?"

Helen couldn't predict when Smith would show up, so she couldn't guess how much time they had, but as she was rapidly discovering herself, being in love was a pitiful state. How could she refuse to assist? Besides, having Miss Reilly as a project would take Helen's mind off the Captain and how despondent she was over his absence.

"I'll help you, Miss Reilly."

"You will?"

"Of course. Where would you like to start?"

"Maybe with my clothes?"

"A wise choice," Helen agreed.

She stood, gauging that Miss Reilly was taller, thinner, and more muscular than she was. "I have some old gowns up in the attic," Helen said, "but they'll need some work to make them fit. Let's see if you're as proficient with needle and thread as you claim."

❧

Robert wandered down the busy street. Captain Westmoreland was still in the modiste's shop, ordering women's apparel—of all things!—and Robert was weary of fabric hunting. He missed Patricia, and he yearned to return to Mansfield Abbey, but he was growing convinced that the Captain was about to command him to remain on the ship. Robert might never see her again!

He was irritated and distracted when he was grabbed from behind and dragged into an alley by two ruffians. They proceeded to steal his wallet and pound him into the ground, while he did nothing but huddle in a ball in the muck and pray he'd survive the attack.

A wave of ire bubbled up inside him, and if he'd been clutching a pistol—and had had any idea how to use it—he'd have shot them dead.

Suddenly a shadow loomed over his shoulder as the Captain entered the fray. A few swift punches had the pair scurrying away; then Westmoreland lifted Robert to his feet, and he wasn't even winded. Robert flushed with shame. He'd been rescued by Westmoreland—again!—and he speculated as to when he'd be free. With their alliance so lopsided, how could they ever be even?

"I hate them!" Robert murmured, astounded by his vehemence.

"With valid reason, Mr. Smith."

"I've been beat up on my entire life. I never defended myself. Not once."

"W**hy** not?"

"I was so much smaller, and I didn't ever seem to . . . to . . . *want* anything very badly."

"How about now?"

"I'd like to strangle somebody."

"Understandable, but it's come to my attention that bullies focus in on the weakest folks. Someday—when I'm not around—you'll be accosted again. What are you prepared to do about it?"

Fury and bitterness rolled around inside, making him feel reckless and wild.

"I want Patricia," he abruptly proclaimed.

"Well, you can't have her."

"I want her," he repeated. "Teach me how to fight, how to win."

"I've known you awhile now, Robert"—he bestowed a sympathetic, humiliating pat on Robert's shoulder—"and I wish it were otherwise, but I don't think you have it in you."

"Give me a chance to prove I can change."

"You've had dozens of chances."

"Give me one more."

"You're a scholar, Mr. Smith, and there's nothing wrong with that. We can't all be warriors." Though he meant it kindly, it was the cruelest remark he could have uttered. The subject closed, he spun on his heel and marched off.

Raging, indignant, Robert watched him go. He couldn't have it end like this! Not when a future with Patricia hung in the balance. He raced over and grabbed Westmoreland's arm, yanking him to a halt, startling the bigger man with his rough determination.

"In the past, I never had anything to fight for."

"Patricia is worth it; I'll grant you that." Westmoreland assessed him, probing for signs of fortitude, of resolve. Ultimately, he ordered, "Come with me."

"To where?"

"There's a boxing club down the street."

"So?"

"I'm curious to count how many times I can knock you on your ass before you don't get up again."

"I'm going to hit you back."

"We'll see if you can, Mr. Smith. We'll definitely see."

🌺

"You're looking fabulous, Helen."

"Thank you."

"What an interesting transformation. You're positively glowing."

Rippling with anger, Archie gaped at his sister. Adrian's spy had notified them that Westmoreland was away, so they'd hurried to the country, with Archie intent on evaluating Helen's condition. Now that he had, he was more certain than ever that she'd offered herself to the notorious pirate. The two of them had to be plotting to defraud Archie.

How dare she fornicate with Westmoreland! How dare she deceive her own brother! Her only marketable attribute had been her chastity. If she'd furnished it to Westmoreland, with no compensation directed to Archie for the loss, he'd murder her.

With his looming financial crisis, he'd been considering an arranged marriage for her to pox-ridden Lord Fester, who was searching for a sweet virgin to warm his disease-riddled bed. Fester would have paid any price to the fellow willing to sacrifice a daughter or a sister.

Archie had initiated talks, but if Helen's purity was squandered, Fester wouldn't want her. No one would. Who would take Westmoreland's leavings?

"How long are you planning to visit?" she queried. Apparently, she was eager to shoo him out the door.

"Why? Are you too busy to entertain guests?"

"No. I just don't want you to run into Captain West-moreland. The two of you would exchange harsh words, and I hate having you quarrel."

"When will he return?"

"I haven't a clue. He doesn't generally confide in me."

An out-and-out lie, Archie was sure. "Don't worry, Helen. I'll vacate my own home by the stroke of three." He peeked at the clock on the mantle. "You only have to suffer my company for two more hours."

She sighed, acting as if his arrival was a heavy burden. "Oh, Archie, don't let's argue. I haven't seen you in weeks. Can't we have a civil discussion?"

"About what? *I* am the one living in squalor and poverty in London, whilst *you* are managing quite well. Why do you suppose that is, Helen?" He sneered, his malice washing over her. "You haven't clarified for me why Westmoreland let you stay on. What precisely is the reason?"

"I'm advising him about the servants and the tenants."

"Really?"

"Yes, *really*."

"He's too, too kind."

"He has been."

"You wouldn't be assisting him in a more private fashion, would you?"

"What do you mean?" She was silent; then the significance of his insult dawned. "Why, you despicable rat!"

She leapt to her feet, ready to stomp out in a huff, and he rose, too, blocking her exit.

"If I ever find out, dear sister, that you've betrayed me, I'll make you so sorry."

"You were always difficult, Archie, but I'm beginning to believe that you've gone completely round the bend."

She shoved him away. "You may rant all you like, but I don't have to listen."

She waltzed out, and his temper spiked.

Previously, she'd been so docile, easily coerced and led, but suddenly she'd metamorphosed into someone entirely new. If she'd spouted a second head, she couldn't have seemed any more different. What had happened?

The answer was obvious: Westmoreland! He had her putting on airs, deeming herself superior simply because she'd spread her legs for the loudmouthed barbarian.

Well, Archie would show her! Westmoreland wouldn't be at Mansfield forever. Eventually, he'd grow bored and depart, and Helen would be on her own and unprotected. She'd discover—to her peril—that Archie shouldn't be crossed.

He could hurt her in ways that she'd never imagined. Not even in her worst nightmares. Adrian had taught him so many painful games.

"Stupid cow," he muttered. Her days of sassing and disrespecting him were over.

He grinned, envisioning her stripped naked and tied to the bed in the master suite. It would be so exciting to torture her, to taunt and wound and mar. He was counting the hours till Westmoreland left for good. Then . . . then she'd learn her lesson.

He went to the sideboard, poured himself a glass of what used to be his best brandy, and drank it down in a single swallow.

❧

"You've done very well. Now get down on your knees."

"But . . . but . . . you said if I helped, I wouldn't have to do it again."

"There are strings to every bargain, Peg. Haven't you figured that out?"

Adrian stared, intimidating her into compliance. She was so malleable that there wasn't much thrill in her submission. Her swift acquiescence ruined his fun.

She hemmed and hawed, so he placed a firm hand on her shoulder. "If you don't do as I say, I'll speak with Miss Mansfield. I'll tell her you stole a ring out of my portmanteau, and you'll be dismissed. What would become of you then?"

"She'd never fire me!"

"Wouldn't she?" He chuckled. "You have such an elevated opinion of your worth."

"You swore . . . that once Captain Westmoreland leaves . . . you'd have me promoted to housekeeper. You promised."

"I will," he lied, "but there's quite a stretch between now and then, so you have to prove to me that my continued faith in you is warranted. Why would I employ a housekeeper who refuses to obey me?"

He increased the pressure, and ultimately, she went down. She hadn't the will to defy him. At the petty triumph he nearly raised an exultant fist in the air.

He stood, waiting, waiting, as she unbuttoned his trousers, as she pulled his cock free. He did nothing to assist. It was her choice to proceed, and he wanted it to be clear that the shame and debasement were her own fault.

She opened her mouth the tiniest bit, and he entered to the hilt, forcing her against the wall, banging into her over and over. She tried to push him away, but she had no leverage, and the harder she resisted, the longer he kept on. Finally, he took the plunge, his seed pulsing down her throat as she retched and sputtered.

He retreated and adjusted his clothes, and as he studied her, he was more disgusted than ever. He detested weak, greedy women, and he thought that someday he might murder her while he fucked her to death. It would be so easy. Who would miss her? Who would care?

"You're a disgrace," he said. "Straighten yourself; then I'll expect you to be back at your post in five minutes."

He was desperate to locate Archie, and he spun away and sauntered out. Archie could be extremely irascible, and Adrian couldn't have him pestering Helen. Adrian had big plans for Helen, plans that didn't include Archie, and he couldn't have the youngster aggravating her to where her annoyance would be directed at both of them.

With a tug on his stylish coat, he stepped into the hall just as a woman was coming into the house from the verandah. She was very pretty, tall and slender, with a modest but flattering dress.

Obviously, she wasn't a servant, and she looked familiar, but in a vague way. He couldn't remember where he'd seen her before. In a flash, their gazes locked, and it was apparent that *she* knew him, and she was instantly on guard.

"What are you doing here, Bennett?" she asked.

It was a challenge, a warning, and he was amazed that someone so feminine could be so tough. Evidently, the fashionable gown hid many secrets.

He mustered his charm, which was renowned as a substantial amount, and he offered a dazzling smile, but as he strolled toward her, it had no effect.

"I apologize," he started, "but I seem to be at a loss. Have we met?"

"I suppose that snake, Archie Mansfield, is slithering around, too. How could the pair of you sneak in without my noticing?"

"My goodness, Miss . . . Miss . . ." He'd given her an opportunity to supply her identity, but she didn't take it.

"Don't think that because the Captain's away, I'll permit the two of you to run rampant."

So . . . she was a Westmoreland whore, who would tattle about the least indiscretion, and his mind whirred with the prospects for disaster. He couldn't rouse Westmoreland's ire or suspicions. The Captain was a vicious, sly foe, who always came out on top. Adrian wouldn't dare incur his wrath. He'd delay till Westmoreland was gone, then make a move.

"Really, miss, you're upset over nothing. Mr. Mansfield and I were merely passing through the neighborhood, and we stopped to chat with his sister. It's a familial visit and naught more."

She twirled away and muttered, "I'd better ensure that Helen's all right."

Without contemplation, he grabbed her elbow, when, to his astonishment, she whipped around, wielding a very small but very lethal knife.

"You sick pervert," she grumbled. "If you ever touch me again, I'll gut you and feed your innards to the chickens in the yard."

"I say! There's no need for violence."

"Violence?" She shoved the knife under his chin. "You call this violence? You haven't messed with me yet, so you don't know the definition of the word." She yanked out of his grasp. "You and your depraved friend have ten minutes to vacate the premises. Don't make me tell you twice."

She stomped away, headed toward the front parlor where Helen was conversing with Archie. As Adrian watched her exit, his rage boiled over, filling him with revulsion for everything female.

Strong women intrigued him. They were the most difficult to crush, the most satisfying to control, and he hoped that when Westmoreland tired of the property, he'd leave the whore behind. Helen would be the main course. The whore would be dessert.

He grinned and went to find Archie.

15

"*You* wanted to see me, Captain?"

Helen hovered in the hall, but wouldn't step across the threshold. She was nervous, gawking as if he might bite her.

"Yes, I wanted to *see* you. Get your ass in here."

"I really can't speak with you in the master's suite." Even though it was nearly midnight and the household asleep, she was acting as if others might be listening. "If we were caught, what would the servants think?"

"Do I look like I give a shit?"

"If you insist on being crude, I'm leaving."

She turned to depart, and he barked, "Stop right where you are!"

At his sharp tone, she pulled to a halt. "There. Are you happy?"

"Yes, I'm very, very happy."

"Your bellowing is likely to raise the dead. Lower your voice."

"No."

She gestured toward the stairs. "Would you care to go down to the library?"

"I wouldn't."

He rose from his chair, advancing on her like a cobra about to strike. He was so irate that he considered putting her over his knee and whaling on her pretty behind till she couldn't sit down for a week.

She never heeded a word he said! Never followed orders or behaved as he commanded. She didn't comprehend that he was lord, king, and omnipotent ruler of his universe. People were eager to do his bidding. He told them to *jump* and they asked *how high?*

They didn't argue; they didn't countermand; they didn't defy. Helen Mansfield was the sole person he'd met in years who didn't understand this hierarchy and her place in it. Which—currently—was at the bottom.

"I advised you to attend me at seven." He'd sat—hour after infuriating hour—not going to fetch her, but waiting to discover how long she'd dawdle.

"I wasn't about to come up while the servants were finishing their evening chores. I barely have any respectability remaining. I'm not about to have you shred what's left."

"They're *my* servants, not yours, and it doesn't matter to me if they find your conduct indiscreet."

"Oh, I forgot, Mr. High-and-Mighty. They're yours. Silly me, encouraging their good opinion. I've only known most of them my entire life."

Why was he being such a prick? He didn't want to fight with her. He wanted to bed her! Every second he'd been in London, he'd been dreaming about it. He was finally . . . *home*—he couldn't describe Mansfield any other way—and all he could do was bicker. Why couldn't he keep his big mouth shut?

She'd had enough of his obnoxious self, and she spun away to stomp off, but he couldn't let her. He was desperate to wallow in her sweet company. In too short a time, she'd come to mean too much to him, and he couldn't figure out why he'd allowed an attraction to develop. He was a man of action and decisions, and he never permitted his relationships to interfere with his routine or goals. He consorted with women for one purpose, that being satiation of his enormous sexual drive. He fornicated, then he moved on as rapidly as he was able, but Helen had him yearning to stay, and the realization horrified him.

He wouldn't be tied down! Wouldn't be connected to her or her paltry farm, and though his infatuation was his own fault, he was dying to lash out and blame her.

Why couldn't she have been the snippy harridan he'd expected when he first gambled with Archie Mansfield? If she'd been a tad more annoying and a tad less wonderful, everything would have worked out fine!

He grabbed her and yanked her into the room. At being manhandled she was incensed, but her rage was no match for his greater size and irritation. He slammed the door and locked it; then he whipped around and accused, "Your brother was in my house."

"Yes, he was, with his friend Mr. Bennett. For all of three hours."

"What did he want?"

"As far as I could discern, it was to thoroughly insult and aggravate me before traveling on his merry way."

"His opportune appearance seems a bit suspicious. Did you invite him the moment my back was turned?"

"No, I didn't!"

"Then how did he know I was gone?"

"I couldn't begin to guess. Perhaps he has spies in the kitchen." Bored by the spat, she shrugged and glanced around. "Have you any wine? If this interrogation is to continue, I'd like a glass while I endure the tirade."

She noted several bottles of liquor in a cupboard in the corner, and she went over and rummaged around till she found something that suited her. She poured a liberal amount, then snuggled down in a chair to calmly sip the liquid, and her nonchalance had him reeling.

He was livid over her brother's stunt and wouldn't have the cocky rooster tromping within a hundred miles of Mansfield Abbey.

"I don't want him here ever again. Do you hear me?"

"Yes, Luke. I hear you loud and clear. There's no need to shout."

Was he shouting? His lack of restraint was an indication of how unsettled he was around her. The strong, certain man he'd been had vanished, replaced by a weak, smoldering fellow, who was filled with longing and regret. He passed his days hiding from her, and his nights burning with unrelieved ardor, terrified to go to her for fear of being further drawn under her spell.

Out of the blue, she urged, "Tell me about your mother."

"My mother?" He hadn't ceased haranguing over her brother!

"Patricia said she grew up here. Why didn't you confide in me?"

"It wasn't any of your business."

"Really?"

"Yes, really."

The remark was cruel, and it was despicable to utter it. His mother's prior presence at Mansfield Abbey was hardly a secret, so he couldn't deduce why he'd failed to mention the fact.

She leapt up and stormed over. "You've been growling like a bear since I arrived. You're intent on quarreling, and I'm more than willing to oblige."

Her ferocity surprised him, and he couldn't imagine why she'd presume he'd tolerate a display of feminine hysterics. "I'm not about to fight with you. Crawl into bed, and be silent."

"To . . . to bed?" She pronounced the word as if it were an epithet. "If you think I'll lie down with you when you're acting like a lunatic, you're either the stupidest man who ever lived or the most blindly arrogant."

"I didn't notice you complaining the last few times we were together."

"That's because I don't have anybody to compare you to."

"Trust me, honey, it's all downhill from here on out."

"You are impossible, and *I* am leaving."

"You are not."

"Obviously, you're beyond coherent conversation, and I have no idea why. I haven't seen you in three weeks, and in some deluded part of my mind, I thought you might have missed me, but all you can do is nag and pick. Welcome home, Luke!"

She marched to the door, but in her fury, she'd forgotten that it was locked—and that he had the key. She whirled around. "Let me out."

"No."

He didn't understand women, and her tantrum was proof that he'd been wise to spend much of his life on ships, in prison camps and port towns, surrounded by rational, lucid men.

With no regard for his feelings, she had permitted

Archie Mansfield to visit. Why should she be in a snit? Luke was the one who'd been wronged.

"What the hell have you to be angry about?" he demanded.

"Your mother is connected to my past. She's the basis for this mischief with my brother, which means she's overshadowed our every interaction. Yet you claim she's none of my affair?"

"The subject is closed!"

"Closed! Hah! It's barely been opened."

Would he have to gag her to shut her up? For some reason, he couldn't speak to her about his mother. There was an odd shame attached to all of it, as if he, himself, were at fault. He'd been so tiny when she'd died, so it was a ludicrous impression, yet he felt as if he should have saved her.

"Tell me about her!" Helen roared with such vehemence that he lurched away as if he'd been slapped.

Suddenly he was teeming with a deluge of emotions he couldn't control. He was overwhelmed by a resentment and sorrow that was too heavy to carry. How could he have been harboring such a tempest and not know that he was?

"Let it go, Helen," he said quietly. "Please. I can't discuss it with you."

He went to the window and stared out at the stars. He wished he was on his ship and winging across the ocean, with the wind in the sails and the bow smacking at the waves. There was no finer spot, no more beloved freedom.

Without his realizing it, she'd approached, and she draped herself to his back and hugged her arms around his waist.

"It's all right, Luke," she soothed. "We don't have to talk about it."

The entire sordid story was stuck in his craw, tumbling around and eager to spill out. He linked their fingers and pulled her around to his side. Nothing had ever felt better. Nothing had ever felt more fitting.

"I remember that she was so pretty," he murmured without planning to make any comment, at all.

"Was she?"

"When she was here, she was . . . was . . . a girl. Your father was her guardian."

"I suspected as much."

"Your father introduced her to the Duke, and the Duke . . . well . . ."

"He has a pitiful reputation for philandering."

"Doesn't he, though?" It seemed the moment to blurt it out, or he might never have the courage. "When your father learned she was with child, he threw her out without a penny."

"Oh, Luke . . ."

"It was like tossing a lamb to the lions. She didn't have a chance."

"Why didn't the Duke help her?"

"I don't believe she ever asked him." He shrugged. "She was a very proud individual. I'd just turned five when she died. We were scraping by on the streets in London and I . . . I . . ."

There'd been sickness in the city that summer, and he'd tried to hide her body so the Watch wouldn't take her, but they'd found her anyway. He had such a vivid recollection of them hurling her into the wagon, the other corpses ripe and bloated with decay.

After they'd lumbered off, he'd tarried for an eternity, a small boy all alone, with nowhere to go and no one to care what happened to him.

Was it any wonder he'd become such a ruthless, determined man?

"If you don't want to, Luke," she said, "you don't have to meet your father."

"I know."

"He doesn't deserve to have you in his life."

"Probably not."

"You could stay here with me. I wouldn't mind."

I wouldn't, either!

The words rang in his head, but he was too much of a coward to voice them aloud, and he was amazed by how brave she was—so much braver than he.

She was offering him a future, a place to belong and call his own. He craved it more than he'd ever craved anything, but he couldn't grab for it.

He'd always been on his own, and he was tired. Tired of battling for every crumb. Tired of struggling for more than what he'd been given.

What if he dared to accept?

He simply couldn't imagine what it would be like. He was baffled about what he truly wanted and rattled by her urging him to picture himself in a different light. He couldn't fathom who that man would be, and to mask his confusion, he smashed the intimate interlude to pieces.

"If I'm not inside you in the next ten seconds, I can't predict what I'll do."

"You still intend to fornicate? I thought I was clear that I—"

"In ten seconds, Helen."

He lifted her and braced her against the wall. She was off balance and grappling for purchase, and he leaned in, his loins pressed to her center where he needed to feel her most.

This was how he liked her, splayed wide, at his mercy, and ready to satisfy his every carnal desire. They were at their best when they were copulating, and he detested their other exchanges.

He hated talking to her! She had a manner of pestering him until he was morose and unsure and worried that he was making all the wrong decisions. He liked her much more than he ought, and at times, he was terrified that he might . . . might . . . even *love* her. How else could he account for his fixation?

He couldn't abide any evidence that he'd grown too close, so he'd ignore his peculiar yearnings and focus on what he knew and understood.

Until the day that his other life—his *real* life—lured him away, he would dally with her at every opportunity. In fact, if they never left his bedchamber, he'd be tickled to death.

"I don't want to chat anymore."

"Well, I do. You can't—"

He kissed her, cutting off her complaint, as he clasped her dress and ripped it down the middle. Underneath, she wasn't wearing a corset, only a chemise, so he ripped that, too. In a thrice, she was mostly naked, perched on his thighs, her delectable puss open and tempting him to dissolution. He reached down, his fingers slipping in to fondle and stroke.

He'd been celibate for three weeks. Three weeks! He couldn't remember when he'd last endured such a protracted drought, and he refused to admit that he could have broken it in London with many partners but hadn't. Around every corner, there'd been some hussy batting her lashes, but he hadn't followed through on a single solicitation. None of them were Helen, so he hadn't been interested.

Did he require any further proof that she'd driven him completely insane?

She yanked away. "You can't destroy my clothes! I haven't hardly any gowns as it is. You can't be tearing them in half."

"When I was in London, I bought you an entire wardrobe."

She groaned. "Tell me you didn't!"

"All right, I didn't, but deliveries will commence shortly."

"We've been through this. You can't be dressing me."

"I'm not. And in case you didn't notice, I'm *un*dressing you."

"Luke!"

"I'm weary of you walking around like a poverty-stricken hag. You're mine, and I'll attire you accordingly."

"But . . ."

"Be silent! This matters to me. It will make me happy."

"Oh."

"Just bed me; that's all I ask in return." He tried not to sound like he was begging.

"I can do that."

"Thank you!"

He slid her to her feet, and he knelt before her, sampling her breasts; then he continued down, to her stomach, her abdomen, till he was at her woman's hair.

He laved her over and over and, ecstatic at the attention, she hissed out a breath.

"Ooh . . . how can I be angry with you? You're too wicked!"

"I know."

"This is so naughty. Are you sure it's safe?"

"If it's not, let me kill you with pleasure."

He lapped at her sexual nub as his fingers latched onto her nipples, and within seconds orgasm swept over her. She bucked against his mouth, and he rode the storm with her till the tumult waned. Her body went limp, and she glided down to kneel with him.

"I can't believe I allow you to do that to me."

"How could you resist?"

He needed her so badly that his state of arousal scared him. At that instant, he might have done anything to her. He stood and frantically jerked at the buttons on his pants, baring himself so that she was eye-level with his phallus, and she stared greedily.

"My, my"—she grinned—"it appears that you've missed me."

"Take me in your hand," he commanded.

"Like this?"

"Yes, and lick me with your tongue."

She was an avid pupil who'd quickly acclimated to the whore's tricks he'd taught her. She bent in, working from base to tip; then slowly—inch by agonizing inch—she sucked him inside. At being impaled between those lush, ruby lips his balls filled to bursting, and his seed surged with an urgency he could scarcely control.

He staggered away, as she scowled up at him.

"I wasn't finished."

"You can do it again later," he managed to spit out.

He scooped her up and dumped her on the bed. She was half on the mattress, her legs dangling over the edge, with him braced on the floor. With no finesse, no preparation, he spread her thighs, found her center, and penetrated to the hilt.

With a vigorous growl of satisfaction, he thrust and came, flexing to the end and beyond. When the last drop had been spilled, he rolled off her and onto the mattress, too, so that they were both on their backs and gazing up at the ceiling. Perspiring, respirations labored, hearts pounding, they struggled to calm.

"Is this how married couples do it?" she inquired.

He laughed as he hadn't laughed in years, and there was an odd sensation coursing through him that he thought might be joy. "I doubt there's a married man alive who could survive such a coupling."

"Is it always so wild?"

"No."

"Why is that?"

"You're a vixen, and I'm insatiable. It's a combustible combination."

"Do you suppose—just once—that we could try it the normal way?"

"The *normal* way?" Bewildered, he frowned. "And what would that be?"

"Well, you know. We would remove our clothes and crawl under the covers. I imagine there'd be some hugging and kissing, some talking and cuddling."

"Talking?"

"Yes. Talking."

"And cuddling?"

"It wouldn't kill you," she scolded.

He shuddered as if she'd mentioned the plague. He'd never *cuddled* with a woman in his life, but if he had to start, Helen was the perfect partner. Still, he teased, "Do I look like the sort of fellow who would take the time?"

"We can all learn new things, if we make up our minds to change." She arched a brow. "Do you realize that I've never seen you without your trousers?"

"That's because when I'm with you I'm always in such a damned hurry."

"Is that good?"

"Yes, my darling, Helen. That's very, very good."

She chuckled, the sultry sound of it washing over him like cool water. He rose and reached for her hand.

"What?" she asked.

"Stand up."

"I can't. My legs have turned to mush."

Without her assistance, he lifted her and tugged at the blankets; then he laid her down under them.

"What are you doing?" she queried.

"I'm going to show you that I can do it the *normal* way."

"Really?"

"And I can guarantee you'll like it."

"Will it include cuddling and talking?"

"If you're very, very nice to me . . . yes."

She smiled, eloquent and tempting as Eve in the Garden. "I can hardly wait."

He stripped off his pants and stretched out next to her.

16

What happened to your eye?"

"My eye?"

"Don't pretend to be unaware that you have a black eye."

Patricia stomped over to investigate, which Robert knew would be agony, and he flinched away. He was bruised from head to toe, and he couldn't bear the thought of the slightest pressure anywhere on his body.

Captain Westmoreland had made good on his threat to see how many times he could hit Robert before Robert stopped getting up. As it turned out, Robert was much more stubborn than he'd recognized. Over the course of many days at the boxing club, Westmoreland had inflicted a stunning round of punishment, but Robert had absorbed it with a vigor and strength he wouldn't have imagined possible. By the end of their London excursion, he'd figured out how to land a few blows of his own, and he was proud to have delivered them with force sufficient to make the mighty Westmoreland wince.

Still, Robert couldn't explain his activities to Patricia. She'd never understand his desire to be a fighter, so he couldn't allow her to view his chest or back. He looked as if he'd been trampled by a horse, and when they crawled into bed he intended to have the candle blown out and the room dark.

"Don't worry about my eye." He brushed her hand away and gestured at her torso. "What have you done to yourself?"

"I came out of hiding."

"You certainly did."

There was no longer any doubt about her gender. She'd been transformed into a beauty, or perhaps she'd always been prettier than he realized, and her sudden metamorphosis had him unnerved.

Where had his Patricia gone, and how was he to interact with this stranger? She resembled a person he used to know, an old friend's sister or a distant cousin, but not the wild paramour he'd left behind three weeks earlier.

"What do you think?" She twirled in a circle. "And since I haven't worn a dress in years, you'd better say you like it."

"Why did you do this?"

"Do what?"

"Why did you decide to be a woman again?"

"I was a woman from the start! I've been naked for you often enough! You shouldn't be surprised!"

"Yes, but you weren't a . . . a . . . woman like this."

He was being a thick oaf, but he was confused by what had precipitated the alteration, and he had to make sense of it. He'd become someone else, and while he was away, she'd become someone else, too. He couldn't deduce what that meant or why it had to *mean* anything, but she was so fetching that he couldn't envision her keeping him as her lover. She was now the sort of female he frequently saw with Westmoreland, the sort a rich and powerful man flaunted to highlight his position.

Robert didn't stand a chance of retaining her affection, and his spirits plummeted. Why couldn't anything go right?

"What is it, Robert? Are you claiming you don't like how I look?"

"No."

"Then, what's your problem?" Her exasperation was quickly evolving into fury. "Am I not attractive enough to suit you? Is my gown not fashionable? Is my skin not smooth and pale like the simpering girls around whom you were raised?"

"No, it's not that at all."

"Then what the hell is it?"

"You're so different."

Her joy faded. "You don't like it."

So far, his every remark had been wrong, and he stumbled for a reply. "I . . . I . . . I'm very pleased."

She snorted. "You are the worst liar."

"I'm not lying."

She marched toward the door. "Silly me, but I was actually anticipating your arrival from London. I couldn't wait for you to see what I'd done. For you, Robert. I did this for you."

"For me? But why would you?"

"I haven't the vaguest idea."

With how angry she was, his plans for the evening were likely over before they'd begun. In the city, he'd been wretched without her, yet now that he was back, all he could do was quarrel. He hadn't had much experience with women, hadn't spent much time in their company and had spent none in their beds, so he hadn't comprehended that an affair could be so tricky to maneuver.

He merely yearned to fornicate in the easy manner they'd managed previously, without pausing to unravel the perplexing impulses that were driving her.

"Hold it right there, Patricia Reilly!" At his sharp tone he was astonished to note that she heeded him.

She halted and whipped around. "What do you want? And I advise you to be careful lest I simply punch you in the nose."

He approached and walked around her, evaluating the swell of her bosom, the tuck of her waist, the flare of her hips. The fabric of her dress was a dark blue that set off the color of her eyes, the rose in her cheeks. Streams of lace had been added to lengthen the sleeves and the hem, so the garment seemed even more feminine. The bodice had been lowered, thus providing him with a fabulous view of what had always been concealed.

She had on a corset, the contraption shoving her breasts up and out, creating cleavage where none had existed prior. The spectacle had him hungering for her in a whole new way. He felt as if he was about to make love to an unfamiliar woman altogether, and the prospect was thrilling.

"I haven't had my bath," he apprised her once he'd finished his inspection.

"So? What concern is it of mine?"

In the heat of the moment, his worries about her seeing his battered torso had vanished. He was having too much fun telling her what to do and expecting her to obey.

If she objected to his injuries, he'd put her in her place. He was a man, and he had to start acting like it. If he didn't adjust the tenor of their association, Westmoreland would never agree to give her away.

"I will wash, and you will attend me."

"I won't!" she mutinously stated. "Not when you're being a pigheaded prick."

"If it's your intention to be a woman, it's my intention to have you behave as one."

"What do you mean?"

"I *mean* that you'll prepare to bathe me! At once!"

"You think to boss me about? Me?"

"Yes, and I find I rather like it."

"Well, I don't."

"Patricia, we've finally discovered who is to wear the pants in this relationship"—he pointed to her legs, then to his—"and it's not you!"

"Hah! As if you could ever—"

"Be silent!"

With a burst of confidence, he grabbed her and spun her, pressing her against the wall and trapping her with his body. She smelled good, and she felt even better.

He leaned in, his loins flattened to her delightful bottom. Though he'd fondly caressed it on many occasions, under skirt and petticoat it seemed even more curvaceous and alluring.

The ladylike clothes produced an aura of fragility, as if she was pure and innocent, someone whom he'd just met and with whom he oughtn't to trifle. His lusting after her felt forbidden and, therefore, extremely exciting.

He flexed against the cleft of her ass.

"What do you have on under your dress?"

"None of your damned business." She elbowed him in the ribs.

"Now, now, Patricia, I won't allow you to sass me." His fingers went to her breasts, squeezing her nipples,

making her squirm. "Let's try this again: Are you wearing drawers?"

"You'll have to check for yourself."

"You're being very naughty. If you don't stop, I'll
have to punish you." He bit her shoulder, nibbling at her
nape, and goose bumps coursed down her arms. "Drawers, Patricia?"

"Yes." She sighed and tipped her head to give him
more access.

"Are they frilly things, all decorated with lace?"

"Cream colored, with little pink flowers stitched on
the hem."

"You seem taller. Have you found some heels?"

"Yes."

"And a corset?"

"It's so blasted uncomfortable! You'd better tell me
how much you like it."

"Oh, I do, my darling. I definitely do."

He recalled the first prostitute he'd ever witnessed, on
an afternoon as he'd tagged after Westmoreland. The
woman had pranced about in her undergarments, her tiny
feet perched on spiky mules, her breasts pushed up and
over her stays.

Unconcerned that Robert was watching, Westmoreland had gotten his money's worth. In Robert's prim and
proper world, he hadn't known such decadence occurred,
having assumed that the few stories he'd heard at school
were figments of boys' vivid imaginations.

When Westmoreland had finished, he'd offered to pay
the extra coin for Robert to be relieved of his chastity,
but Robert had been too timid to accept. However, in the
months that followed, he'd had many a late-night fantasy,
where the whore had been front and center.

If Patricia shed her clothes and strutted around in corset and heels, Robert would likely perish from ecstasy!

"I want a peek at those pink flowers." He began unbuttoning her dress. The top came loose, then the waist, and he shimmied it down so that it pooled at her feet.

He slithered a hand across her stomach, gliding down to cup and fondle, and he was amazed to ascertain that she'd removed all her womanly hair! Her puss was bare! At the increased depravity his mind whirled with fascination.

He didn't understand why, but the feel of her, all silky and slippery, did something peculiar to his insides. A wave of lust swept over him, one that was so potent he was surprised he didn't faint.

"You've shaved yourself."

"Just for you."

"I like it."

"I thought you might."

How had she guessed that he'd enjoy such wickedness? He hadn't ever suspected a woman would try such an outlandish exploit, and it was clear she knew more about his preferences than he did himself.

The antic was a mystery—a wanton, salacious, wonderful mystery—that hinted at her past life and secrets she would never share. He had no illusions: He wasn't the first man with whom she'd ever lain, and in light of his conduct toward her, he was in no position to moralize or chastise. Yet he couldn't help but be curious as to what other feats she might perform, what other pleasures she might bestow.

With Patricia in his bed, he'd never grow bored!

He grinned. "You're very smooth."

"Think of it as your coming-home present."

"Have you any notion of how hard I am?"

"No, how hard?"

He opened his trousers so that his aching rod was rubbing against her fancy drawers, and the ticklish ruffles were his undoing. He had to rut like a stallion at mating season; he couldn't wait.

"I'm afraid I'm going to have to have you."

"Let me—"

"No."

She tried to shift away so that she could turn and direct the encounter. Of the two of them, she was the experienced lover, the one who knew how to seduce and beguile, but along the way, Robert had been paying close attention. He'd learned a few valuable lessons, especially those about taking what you wanted, about seizing the moment and forging on to a little slice of heaven.

He was so aroused that he had the strength of ten men, and while she frantically grappled for purchase, her palms braced on the plaster, he clutched her to him and invaded her tight, tempting sheath. He reveled like an animal, his balls like rocks, his phallus an insistent, demanding force between her legs.

His concentration was riveted on the point where their bodies were joined. He'd seen couples mating like this before, but he'd never supposed he'd have the temerity to attempt such a degenerate copulation himself. She simply incited him to dissolution beyond his wildest dreams.

He grew more and more frenzied, more and more out of control, his thighs slapping her shapely bottom.

With a merry shout, he came, standing on his feet, with her shoved up against a wall. He'd been rude and selfish, having not considered her gratification or comfort, and he couldn't care less. With scant effort, he was becoming an emboldened cad. How could he not have realized that he harbored such despicable tendencies?

He savored the final thrust, pushing in, holding her;

then he pulled out and collapsed onto her. With his passion spent, his knees were weak, his torso limp, and he was stunned by how much energy he'd expended. He felt as if he'd poured a bit of his soul into the act, as if he'd spilled some of himself and would never get it back.

Which wasn't necessarily bad! He was desperate to fully belong to her, but with no funds and no prospects, and being significantly indebted to the Captain, he'd never have his freedom.

He sighed with resignation, speculating as to how matters could ever be resolved satisfactorily between them, as she wiggled around to face him. She was staring as if she didn't recognize him, and he sympathized with her consternation.

They'd started out as two ordinary people—well, maybe with her being a man they hadn't been *ordinary*— but they'd both metamorphosed in exciting ways. Where would it lead? How would it end?

"My goodness, Robert," she said. "That was . . . was . . . quite rough and randy. It wasn't like you, at all."

"No, it wasn't."

"You were so rigorous. What's come over you?"

"I don't know. I can't describe it, but it feels extremely grand."

"Is this trend likely to continue?"

"Yes."

"So you'll be getting more and more physical?"

"Absolutely."

Her torrid gaze wandered down to his trousers that were barely on, his cock protruding out and half-erect. She took him in hand, and instantly the unruly appendage was stiff and impatient to begin again.

"I believe I'm going to like the new you just fine."

"I believe I am, too."

She stepped away from him, and she sauntered across the room, providing him with a thorough look at her skimpy attire. When he observed her in corset and drawers, her feet on those spiky heels he loved, his phallus wagged like an eager dog.

With how she was vamping, it was almost as if she was aware of his old fantasy, of how often he'd drooled over his memories of Westmoreland's whore. He'd never divulged the incident to her, so perhaps Westmoreland had, but however she'd learned of it, he was thrilled to have the recollection become reality.

She stopped in front of him and inquired, "Do you like my unmentionables?"

"Oh yes, very much."

She hunched forward, teasing him with how her breasts shifted in the stays. "Some men enjoy untying a woman's laces. I wonder if you will?"

"I'm sure of it."

She dropped to her knees. "Let me show you something else you might like."

While in Westmoreland's company, he'd viewed more oral copulation than a moral person ought, so he knew what she intended. But still, at the initial contact, he was unprepared for the jolt of ecstasy.

She ran her tongue over the tip, again and again, quickly and easily spurring him to a rampant edge. As she slipped her ruby lips over the crown, as she sucked him far inside, he decided that he liked the *new* him fairly well, too.

Whatever and whoever he'd been before, that fellow was dead and buried, and Robert wasn't about to permit him to return.

17

Captain, there you are."

Luke tarried by the window as Helen swept into the parlor. He was delighted to note that she'd descended from her snooty high horse and deigned to wear one of the dresses he'd purchased for her in London.

Despite how she'd opposed the gifts, once the garments had been delivered she hadn't been able to refuse them. It had been an eternity since she'd had anything new or pretty, and he'd garnered a substantial amount of satisfaction from how much he'd pleased her.

He'd picked well, having selected the best colors and fabrics. She was a beautiful sight, decked out in an emerald shade that accented her hazel eyes, making them appear more green, her hair more auburn than brown.

The design hugged her curvaceous figure, providing ample indication of how shapely she was, but his favorite part was the bodice. The neckline was cut low to reveal her fabulous bosom, and every time he saw her, his breath hitched in a funny way he didn't understand.

He'd never previously had any money, so he'd only recently accumulated funds that he could waste on frivolities. It was a novel experience, surprising someone with a treat. He'd fussed over his choices, had driven Mr. Smith to distraction at his dithering with seamstresses, but when this was the result, it had been worth every penny.

"You look very fetching." His appreciative gaze roved over her. "Is that a new dress?"

"Why, yes. How sweet of you to notice." She held out a corner of the skirt and twirled in a circle. "I have excellent taste, don't I?"

"You definitely do."

She'd informed the servants that *she* had bought the wardrobe, so no one knew the clothes had come from him. Or if they had suspicions, they kept them to themselves, which was wise. Should he be confronted with demeaning gossip about her, his reaction would be deadly.

"Mr. Smith said you wanted to speak with me."

"I did."

She shut the door and crossed to him, not worrying about the whispers that might be generated by their being sequestered. They were often alone, and the behavior no longer produced the raised brows or condemning glances it once had.

He lifted his arm, and she snuggled under it, pressing herself to his side as casually as if they'd always been together, as if she was his, and oddly, he felt that she was. The summer he'd spent at Mansfield Abbey had been filled with frolic and happiness, and he'd never endured another period where anything similar had transpired.

He peered out, taking in the acres of manicured garden,

the forest and hills beyond. The sun was dropping in the west, the pastures tinted in hues of purple and gold, and he continued to stare, never having believed that it was all his.

Autumn had arrived, and soon the harvest would begin, the weather would turn. The seas would grow vicious, sailing perilous, and an astute fellow would be traveling south, would have the wind at his back.

"You're awfully pensive this evening, Luke," she observed. "Are you all right?"

"I'm fine." He kissed the top of her head.

"You haven't told me what you think of Patricia."

"She's very grand."

"She is, isn't she?"

But of course, he'd known how attractive Patricia was. He'd rescued her from a damned brothel, so he'd espied what was hidden beneath the attire.

"Thank you," he said.

"For what?"

"For helping her."

"I enjoyed it immensely." She nudged him in the ribs. "You might have confided in me about her."

"About what?"

"That she was a woman."

"Well . . ."

"That day I saw her kissing Mr. Smith, I nearly suffered an apoplexy."

He chuckled, pondering Patricia and her dear Robert. What would become of them? Smith claimed to want her, but giving him Patricia would be like giving a hungry lion to a bunny. How would Smith ever manage her?

Smith had been bullied throughout his life and was a prime candidate to be a henpecked husband. When the man had had his share of so much misery Luke wouldn't bring him more.

Then again, he and Smith were secretly sparring every night in the barn. Luke was teaching him to fight, and Smith was learning fast. He was intent on proving that he could handle and protect Patricia, so Luke couldn't say what might happen. Of late, the world had gotten so strange that anything seemed possible.

Suddenly he couldn't abide the stifling confines of the house. Outside, the air was so fresh and cool, the grass so verdant, the sights and smells so tempting. It seemed as if he were looking at a picture in a book, as if he could go out and step into a fairy tale.

"Would you walk with me in the yard?" he asked.

"I'd love to. Let me grab a shawl."

While she went to retrieve it, he waited for her on the verandah. Momentarily she joined him, and he led her down the stairs and onto the path that meandered past the hedges and into the woods.

The farm was quiet, the servants finished with their chores. Suppers were being eaten, children tucked into bed. It felt as if they were the last two people on earth, with only the maid Peg loitering over by the stables and not taking any notice of them.

He had no idea where he was headed, but he'd never strolled with a woman before, and it was a memory he needed very much. In fact, there were many memories he yearned to generate, but there was no time left to produce them.

Though he'd squandered most of the summer in her company, it had been but a brief sojourn. There was so much about her he hadn't discovered. When he was with her, he was so aroused that he couldn't be bothered to talk to her. He'd bump into her, and within minutes he'd be removing her clothes.

They followed the path into the trees, and he stumbled

on a spot that offered a tremendous view of the setting sun. A decrepit bench rested nearby, and he escorted her to it and sat down, pulling her onto his lap. She nestled with him, her back pressed to his front, her lush ass balanced on his thighs. In silence, they watched the sun disappear. As it vanished, he was nipping at her nape, toying with her hair.

"I can't have my hair down," she scolded as she usually did when he trifled with her too publicly. "The servants will assume we've been—"

"Yes, they will, but I don't care."

"Beast!" she grumbled, but she let him proceed.

He tugged at a comb, and the wavy mass swished down as he caressed her breasts, her tummy. He had to imprint her shape in his fingers so that he'd never forget.

"What are you doing?" she inquired as he inched her skirt up her legs.

"I guess I'm going to make love to you."

"Out here? In the forest?"

When he'd fled the house, the notion hadn't occurred to him, but why not? What was to prevent them?

"Haven't you ever been tumbled up against a tree trunk?"

She glared over her shoulder. "You know I haven't been."

Yes, he did, but it was so amusing to tease her. "Then I'm about to broaden your horizons."

"I don't need them expanded quite that much."

"Consider it a new life experience."

"You can't be serious. Are you telling me that couples actually saunter out and . . . and . . ."

"It's done fairly regularly."

"I should pay closer attention," she said. "I can't believe what I've been missing."

"Are you wearing drawers?"

"Of course I am. I'm not a heathen."

He nibbled her earlobe. "Slide them off."

"Right here? Right now?"

"Yes."

"I most certainly will not."

He loosened them himself, and she made a halfhearted attempt to stop him by gripping his wrist, but he was determined to philander, so she couldn't dissuade him. He reached around, his fingers gliding into her sheath, and he fondled her, easing her into passion, her body drifting on the rising tide of pleasure.

"Let me show you something," he murmured.

"What?"

"You'll see."

He clasped the flimsy undergarment and ripped it off, the threads popping, the fabric falling away.

"Luke! Quit acting like a barbarian. You gave those to me. They were special."

On hearing how much she'd cherished the stupid gift, a burst of elation surged through him, but he tamped it down. For pity's sake, they were just a stitched piece of material!

"I'll order you a dozen more, but I'll have them sewn in bright red."

"Bright red? Why would I need red drawers?"

"So I can be titillated whenever I undress you in the woods."

"You're presuming it'll be happening more and more often?"

"Oh yes. Now that we've started, I find I like it very much." He opened his trousers, which was tricky business while keeping her pinned to him, but shortly he had his cock free. "Lean forward."

"Like this?"

"Yes." He shifted, and after some positioning, he located her cleft.

"Lucas Westmoreland! What are you thinking?"

"You know what I'm *thinking*. After all this time, I shouldn't have to explain it all over again."

"But . . . but . . . we're outside!"

"We definitely are, which will make it much more naughty, which will make it much more fun."

"Only in your deluded mind."

"It hasn't failed me yet." He wedged himself in. "Sit back."

Not positive she should participate, she hesitated, but ultimately, she couldn't resist. He clutched her hips, as she giggled and squirmed, and he thrust, careful not to let go of her, not to retreat too far and slip out.

"How do you like it, my little slattern?"

"You are so wicked."

"Stick with me, and there's no telling what else I'll teach you."

"Promise?"

"When your delicious bottom is splayed over me, how can I refuse?"

She wriggled about, trying to force him deeper, trying to get him to move, but he didn't have enough space to maneuver. He'd meant to delay, but she was so tight and hot that he couldn't stand the torment of not being able to flex.

He lifted her off his lap, tossed her shawl on the ground, and lay down on it; then he extended his hand.

"Come here."

She crawled over to straddle him, her skirt billowing around them. He entered her again, and she took all he gave, her anatomy responding with a keen intensity. She was on her knees, working herself across his shaft, and she was so at ease, so confident in her decadence. He'd never seen a sight so exquisite as her perched above him, the indigo sky darkening behind her.

He rolled them so that she was beneath him, so that he could smile down at her. She wrapped her legs around him, her feet locked to hold him close. She cradled his face and pulled him to her for a gentle kiss.

"I'm so glad I met you." Her words surprised him; she rarely mentioned anything personal.

"Are you?"

"You changed me in so many ways."

"For better or worse?"

She laughed. "I won't stroke your vanity by saying it's all been for the better."

There were numerous replies he could have made to confess how much he'd treasured their association, too. She brought him an odd sense of joy, and when he was with her he suffered such peculiar exhilaration, but he couldn't verbalize his sentiments.

He wasn't adept at declaring himself, at discussing his emotions or proclaiming his happiness. He wasn't even sure *why* he was happy, had no clue as to what had created the unusual situation or how he should deal with it. He only knew that when he was around her he felt like a different man, a superior man to the one he'd been prior to their crossing paths.

"My vanity doesn't need stroking," he joked, "but some other parts do."

"You're insatiable."

"For you, Helen. I burn for you every second."

He took slow, leisurely penetrations, intruding all the way, withdrawing to the tip, then intruding again. It was so magnificent to have her like this, to tarry and revel without rushing to the conclusion.

She simply pushed him to all manner of abnormal behavior. If he stayed six months, if he stayed a year, who and what would he become? She'd have him so altered that he wouldn't recognize himself in the mirror.

"Tell me that you're crazy about me," he demanded.

"No."

"Then tell me that you're wild for me."

"Well, maybe."

"Tell me that I'm the best lover you've ever had."

"You're the *only* lover I've ever had—as you well know."

Though it was pathetic, he was dying to hear that he mattered to her, that if he went away she'd be devastated. He thought she was infatuated, that perhaps she even loved him, and he was desperate to have her divulge it. Pitifully, he was despairing over their future—rather their lack of one—and he couldn't imagine how he'd get along without her, which was idiotic in the extreme.

He'd move on with no trouble, at all. He was certain of it. Still, his feelings for her were so conflicted, so raw and unsettled. If he left Mansfield with some hint as to the depth of her regard, he'd be more content—though how her elevated esteem would keep him warm on cold winter nights was a mystery.

Not that he needed her with him on winter nights. There would be other women. Plenty of other women.

He scowled, stunned to realize that the notion of having other paramours was distasteful. Gad! She had turned him into a eunuch! He was aghast.

"Why are you frowning?" She ran a finger over his brow to smooth away the creases.

He shook himself out of his shocked stupor. "Because you won't admit how fabulous I am."

"My dearest, Luke"—she chortled with delight—"don't ever change. Swear to me that you'll remain just as you are this very moment."

"And how is that?"

"Arrogant and impossible and so unbearably sweet."

"Me? Sweet?"

"Yes."

She kissed him again, and she nestled next to his ear and whispered, "I love you."

He stiffened with alarm and amazement, and he knew he should provide a response, but he couldn't figure out what it should be. He had to swallow twice before he could say, "Oh, Helen . . ."

"Wherever you go, whatever happens, remember, will you? There's someone in the world who loves you, someone who will always love you."

He'd assumed he was a brave man, but in reality, he was too much of a coward to disclose any heightened sentiment. He wasn't positive what the appropriate words meant. If *love* was this all-consuming, blazing obsession, then maybe he loved her, after all.

But so what? Where did that leave them? He would never stay at Mansfield, and she would never run off with him. How could she? Would she live on his ship and sail the Seven Seas, fighting off storms, other pirates, and native savages?

The prospect was ludicrous.

"I'm so glad that you do," he murmured, which was as much as he could offer.

"So am I."

He began to truly make love to her then, perhaps for the very first time. He was exact and deliberate, yearning to savor every sensation and detail, so that he'd never forget how it had been.

He linked their fingers, pinning them on either side of her head. Their desire rose, their torsos straining. She was so near to the edge, and she arched up, her eyelids drifting shut.

"Keep your eyes open, Helen. Watch me to the end."

She was taut as a bow, ready to explode. The tremors started in her womb, her muscles tightening around him, the fever more intense than it had ever been previously.

"Oh, oh, Luke," she moaned.

"Give yourself to me, Helen, as you never will to another."

"I'm yours, Luke. Yours forever."

"Yes, you are."

His own orgasm commenced, and he joined her in ecstasy. They spiraled up together, reached the top, then floated down, their pleasure matched, their joy complete. It was the most special, most magical, experience of his life.

He remained in her, buried deep, until his erection waned. Then, he pulled away, and they shifted onto their sides, their feet and legs tangled. They were silent, recognizing that any conversation would shatter the enchantment.

Finally, she asked, "Are you leaving me, Luke?"

He wasn't sure how she'd guessed, but then, she was adept at reading his mind.

"Yes."

"When?"

"Tomorrow morning."

"So this was merely your way of saying good-bye?"

"Better than not saying it, at all, I suppose."

At the curt remark she studied him, then nodded, her

disappointment in him painfully clear. "It's for real, isn't it?"

"What is?"

"You're never coming back, are you?"

"No, I'm not."

"Why now? I thought you were happy here."

He sat up and made a great show of straightening his clothes. "I heard from my father."

"What did he want?"

"He's decided he'd like to be introduced to me."

She sat up, too, and adjusted her dress, but she wouldn't look at him.

"I realize you're searching for something, but you won't find it with him."

"I'm certain you're correct."

"I know him, Luke. I've met him."

"Well, I haven't, and I need to."

"He's not the sort of man you're hoping. He'll break your heart."

He shrugged, unable to explain the impulse that was driving him. It was like a rampaging monster shouting at him, and he couldn't get it to cease its harangue.

"I have to do this, Helen."

"I understand that, and after the two of you have become chums"—he couldn't miss her sarcasm—"then what?"

"If I pass muster, I'm to be knighted. By the Prince of Wales." Apparently, the Prince had ordered the Duke to proceed with the interview, then provide a report as to Luke's suitability, which was the sole reason the Duke had deigned to fraternize.

Luke smiled, making light of the honor, though he was so greedy to receive it. "It's silly, I know."

"You're a very courageous man, Luke. You did a

courageous deed. You're a hero. If anyone deserves such a distinction, it's you."

"Thank you."

"Will you live in London after the ceremony?"

"I'm debating. I have my ship and crew to consider, but there are rumors that property and money might be awarded to me."

"You're constantly yearning for more than what you have."

He was irked by her statement. She acted as if ambition were a bad thing. It seemed as if she was reminding him that she was from a different world, that she was superior to him and always would be, no matter how hard he scraped and fought.

"That's because I started out with nothing and I grasp how quickly I could land myself back in the same kind of desperate spot. If you'd ever wanted for anything, if you'd ever been hungry once in your privileged life, you might be entitled to chastise me for my choices."

She stared and stared, trying to figure him out, as if she was just ascertaining that maybe she'd never really known him. "What about me?"

"What about you?" he rudely replied.

"What if I'm with child?"

"What if you are?"

They were very likely the cruelest words he'd ever uttered to another person, and he couldn't believe that he'd said them to her. He viewed her as so extraordinary, but he had no idea what he'd do if she was pregnant, and the notion panicked him.

He had no concept of how to be a parent, and he didn't wish to learn. He wouldn't be tied down. Didn't she realize that about him? Didn't she fathom how it was?

"Precisely," she mused. "What if I am? I suppose I

should ask how many children you've sired. Have you a woman in every port? Are your progeny scattered around the globe?"

"I have none," he truthfully claimed.

He'd never dallied with the abandon he'd displayed to her. He comprehended—better than anyone—the consequences of illicit fornication. As a result, he dabbled with whores who used their mouths. Helen had been the only one he'd treated so recklessly. Why had he risked so much for her?

"Would you at least send me money? So that we wouldn't starve?"

"Helen!"

"Would you?"

He blushed with shame. "Yes, I would. I'll leave an address. If there's a babe, you can write to me. I'll have funds delivered."

"You're too, too generous, Captain Westmoreland."

"What do you want me to say?"

"Nothing. Your position is very clear."

Tears flooded her eyes. They pricked at his conscience, making him feel like the churl he was.

She stood to go, and he couldn't bear to have these acrimonious, harsh comments be the last they ever spoke. He slipped his hand into hers.

"Don't fret, Helen. Everything will work out for the best."

"Yes, it will."

"I'll take care of you, and . . . and . . . a babe—if there is one. You're needn't worry."

"I'm not *worried*," she declared. "In fact, I'm quite sure that I'll never need anything from you ever again."

"Helen . . ."

"Good-bye."

She yanked away and walked off, and he dawdled in the quiet forest, watching her disappear down the path toward the house till the evening shadows swallowed her up.

Her ripped drawers were draped across the bench, her shawl wadded under him. He pulled the two items onto his lap, running his palm across them, pondering her and the future without her.

Dammit! He was right in going to the city. He was! He wouldn't let her spoil his moment of triumph with her doubts and her castigations. His connection to the Duke was his heritage, and he would seize what was his, what should have been his long ago.

Still, as she vanished, and the dark night crept in, the most terrible melancholia swept over him. He'd never been so alone or so isolated.

With a heavy heart, he rose and followed her, the gilt of London bitter as brass.

18

You're leaving when?"

"First thing in the morning."

Unable to believe her ears, Patricia gaped at Robert. "Is it for good this time? It's not just another trip to the city?"

"That's what the Captain says. He's buying the house he was renting in London, and we'll tarry for a few months. After that, I haven't a clue as to what will occur. Depending on how matters resolve with his father, he may muster the crew and sail to the Mediterranean."

Recalling her hard life on board the ship, she tamped down a shudder. "When will he come back to Mansfield Abbey? I mean, he has to check in, to keep track of the servants and the farm."

"I don't think he ever intends to return."

"But he was so happy. What happened?"

Robert walked over and took her hand. "You know he doesn't confide in me."

No, the Captain wouldn't. When it involved his personal affairs, he was silent as a marble statue. With a snap of his fingers he'd totally disrupted many people's lives, but he hadn't paused to consider the consequences for any of them.

"What has he told you about me?"

"We didn't discuss many details, so I'm not positive what he expects."

"Are you going?"

"How could I not?"

At the distressing reply she pulled away and went to the window to gaze out at the black night.

From the beginning, she'd understood that the Captain would go eventually, that he had other, more pressing responsibilities, but she'd convinced herself that their idyll in the country would continue forever. She was existing in a bubble, where nothing was real, where she could maintain the fantasy as long as it suited her, and she didn't want anything to change.

She liked her routine with Miss Mansfield, how the days slipped by so gracefully from one to the next. There were no battles where death was always a possibility, no strutting and huffing with the Captain and his men as they proved how tough they were. She had plenty of food to eat, clean sheets on her bed, warm blankets and fires on cool evenings.

It was a magical, precious interlude that had altered her view of the world and her place in it. What was she to do?

She couldn't bear to join the Captain. In the locales he was known to haunt, she'd be thrust into peril, with the constant prospect that some fanatical Arab would jump out of a crowd and kill her to collect the Sultan's reward.

And what about her liaison with Robert? The ship was too small to hide a carnal relationship. Where would they meet? How would they dally?

She pined for more than furtive couplings in secluded alcoves, and she yearned for peace of mind and contentment. Was that too much to ask?

"I want to stay here," she blurted out. "I don't want to ever leave. I'll speak with Miss Mansfield. If she agrees, I'm sure the Captain will allow it."

"I'm sure he will," Robert said from behind her. He was very glum. "What about us?"

She whipped around. "Stay with me."

"You know I can't."

"I know nothing of the sort. Miss Mansfield likes you; she'd be glad to have you."

"You're talking crazy, Pat."

"Why? Because I want to be happy? Because I want more for myself than fighting and destruction?"

"It's not that."

"Then what is it?"

She was being deliberately obtuse. The Captain had plopped down a fortune to buy Robert at the slave market, and Robert was determined to repay the debt, plus he was so accursedly loyal. He'd stand by the Captain through thick and thin, would never desert him. Not for Patricia. Not even if she demanded. Not even if she begged.

He crossed to her and quietly catalogued her features. The thorough assessment was more horrid than any indignity she'd endured so far. It underscored how much was already settled.

"Stay with me," she pleaded. "Marry me."

He was aghast. "Marry you?"

"Yes."

"How could I?"

"How would you suppose? We'd march down to the vicar and have him call the banns."

"Don't be flip. I can't support you. Where would we live? How would we get on?"

"I'll ask the Captain to have you serve as his land agent. You can run the farm and oversee the accounts. You'd earn a salary. He likes you. He'll be generous."

"I'm not certain he's keeping the property."

"What? But that's absurd! He loves this place."

"Not really. He coveted it because it belonged to Archibald Mansfield. You remember how it was."

Yes, she did. All too well. When the Captain had gambled with Archie Mansfield, he'd been like a child with a new toy, but now that the estate was his, the excitement had faded. It was the same with his paramours. He'd seduce a woman but would move on as soon as the thrill of the chase was concluded.

She'd assumed that this time was different, that he felt the same sense of home and connection that Pat felt herself. Neither of them had ever had anything of their own. They'd been orphans, cast to the vagaries of Fate. He'd been so satisfied with Mansfield Abbey, had taken such a fancy to Miss Mansfield. What had transpired? How could it have fallen apart so quickly?

"You have to stay with me." She was starting to sound hysterical, but she couldn't stop herself.

"I can't, and I won't."

"And that's to be the end of it?"

"Yes."

"What about what I want? What about what I need?"

He shrugged. "How can it signify?"

"Do I mean anything to you?"

She braced for the worst, ready to finally hear his true opinion. He liked crawling into her bed and was tickled by the sexual acts she'd shown him, but any experienced woman could have behaved similarly.

He'd never hinted at a deep attachment, had never provided the smallest inkling of his feelings for her, so it was very probable that his esteem didn't extend past the four walls of the tiny room where she slept.

"Of course you *mean* something to me," he replied.

"What, then? Tell me, and please be very precise, because I've suddenly realized that I haven't a clue."

"I . . . I . . ."

He stumbled and hesitated, and she couldn't deduce why it was so difficult for him to answer. Was it because he was a male and professions of emotion beyond him? Or—more likely—had he no genuine sentiment to convey?

Her heart sank. She'd been raised in the company of men, but she actually understood very little about them. She'd persuaded herself that if she was sufficiently intimate with him, she could win his abiding affection.

She knew better. She really, really did. If she'd learned one lesson in her travels, it was that men were lying dogs. He'd seemed more honorable than others she'd met, but apparently, she'd been tricked by the impressive clothes and the prissy manners.

"Just go, Robert."

Desperate for the hideous scene to be over, she waved to the door, but he tried to pull her into a hug, which she wasn't about to permit.

"Pat, don't be this way."

"What *way*?"

"I don't know what to say."

"How about that you love me, and you can't live without me? That you'll do whatever it takes for us to be together?"

"But how could it become a reality?"

"How indeed?"

"There are a few steps between wanting something and having it."

"If two people are in love, they can make it work." She hadn't grasped that she harbored such impractical tendencies, so she was surprised to have uttered the romantic statement.

He slumped against the wall, his arms sullenly crossed over his chest, as he silently studied her. A gulf stretched between them, a crevasse as wide as an ocean that couldn't be breached.

Ultimately, he shook his head. "I'm not the man you need, Patricia."

"I thought you were. My mistake."

"You spent your life around brigands."

"And I hated every moment of it."

"No, you didn't. I'm merely someone different from the norm, and you're attracted to me because of it, but I could never care for you in the fashion you deserve. Even the Captain said so."

"What the hell does he know about it?"

"He *knows* that you should have a tough man by your side, a man who can protect and defend you."

She scoffed. "I don't need protecting."

"Every woman does, and every man has to feel that he's up to the challenge."

"And you're claiming you're not?"

"I'm not *claiming* it. It's true."

He looked so dejected, so young and out of his element, and a day earlier—even an hour earlier—she'd have comforted him. *She* would have been the strong one, the resolute one, who would have fixed every problem, but the last few minutes had altered their connection. In fact, the last few minutes had dissolved it entirely.

If he was sad, if he was hurting, it was none of her concern.

"Good-bye, Robert."

"It doesn't have to be good-bye!"

"It must be."

Was he mad? Why couldn't he perceive the future as clearly as she did? Eventually, he'd have the funds to buy his freedom and to marry. He'd establish himself in the society he'd left behind when his brothers had tried to murder him. His bride would be educated and refined, elegant and sophisticated. Someone like . . . like . . . Miss Mansfield. Patricia would be a fond memory, a youthful indiscretion.

She had been the whore. Another woman would be the wife.

"Listen," he said. "I've been talking with the Captain. He's training me."

"Training you to what?"

"To fight. To guard you."

Her temper spiked. "You fool, I never wanted you to be a brawler. I wanted you just as you were."

"Well, I'm tired of being the whipping boy for every bully who strolls by. I'm ready to strike back for a change."

"There are more important things than battling for every scrap."

"Not to me."

"If that's what you believe, you've become as deranged as the Captain."

She had turned to go when he implored, "Will you wait for me, Patricia?"

"What?"

"I plan to work hard, to save my money. When I have enough, I'll send for you. I'm begging you to tell me that you'll wait for me."

He held out his hand, beseeching her to take it and consent, but she couldn't. She had this ridiculous vision, of herself as a wrinkled old woman, tottering through the halls at Mansfield Abbey.

He'll be coming for me any day now, she imagined herself croaking to Miss Mansfield. *Any day! Just see if he doesn't!*

"No, Robert, I won't wait for you. You're determined to walk this path that has you so enthralled, so have at it. I wish you happy."

Actually, she didn't wish him happy, at all. She hoped he was miserable without her, that he married a harpy and regretted it throughout a long and wretched life.

She spun and stomped out.

❧

"I've been very pleased during my sojourn at Mansfield Abbey."

"Have you?"

Helen stared across the desk at Captain Westmoreland. He was attired in an exquisite suit that Mr. Haversham had sewn for him, and she was curious as to why he'd worn it. It hung like a mantle of his new prestige and status, a beacon announcing that he wasn't the lowly bandit he'd been when he'd first arrived. In the dark blue coat, the stylish tan trousers, the white shirt with its frilly cravat, he looked like a prince, like a god-come-to-earth, like someone she'd never known.

He was a stranger, and she tried to match him with the exotic, adamant man who'd stolen her heart, but she couldn't find that fellow anywhere.

It was obvious that, in his mind, he'd moved on, that any link he'd had to Mansfield—and thus to her—had been severed. His destiny had called, and he'd answered. She knew him so well, and she could sense his distraction, his thoughts so preoccupied with departure that it seemed as if he was scarcely in the room.

She couldn't blame him for going, for making the only possible choice, but oh, how it wounded her to ascertain that everything in his world had been more important to him than her.

She felt frozen, as if ice flowed in her veins. Her fingers were cold, her smile brittle.

"I've given the issue a good deal of consideration," he advised, "and I've reached a decision."

"How nice."

She couldn't figure out why he was dawdling. Why couldn't he just go? Didn't he appreciate that every second of delay was torture? Each word, each glance, pricked like the blade of a sharp knife.

Mr. Smith had sought her out to explain that they were about to leave and that the Captain had to speak with her. She'd come as he'd commanded—for who could defy him?—but what could he still have to communicate?

Hadn't every remark of any consequence been uttered the prior night?

He peered over at Mr. Smith. "Have you the papers?"

"Yes, Captain." Smith laid some documents on the desk, and he shoved over a bottle of quills and a jar of ink.

"Mansfield Abbey is your home," Westmoreland started, "and I'm aware of how much you cherish it." He paused. "So I'm giving it to you."

She cocked her head, not sure she'd heard the last phrase correctly. "What did you say?"

"I'm giving you Mansfield Abbey."

"Thank you for thinking of me, but I don't want it."

Why would a refusal pop out of her mouth? Was she

insane? According to the terms of their agreement, she was due to reside at Mansfield through the following spring, and then she'd be deposited back in her original predicament of having no options and nowhere to go.

His gifting her with the estate solved every problem and settled her future. She ought to have grabbed onto the suggestion like a magnet to metal, but the offer seemed extremely sordid, as if he was paying her for services rendered. Perhaps he reimbursed all his paramours when he finished with them and the fact that he'd tender such a valuable property indicated that she'd performed better than most, but the realization was scant comfort.

"The deed is done, Helen," he quietly informed her. "When I was in London over the summer, I had the solicitors draw up the papers. Mr. Smith had them appropriately signed and sealed. The estate is yours."

So . . . the bastard had been planning his escape for ages. While she'd been alone in the country and missing him every minute, he'd been conferring with his lawyers as to how he could be shed of her most expediently.

She felt as if the air had rushed out of her body. If she stood, her legs wouldn't support her.

She shrugged with resignation. "As you wish."

"There's one condition."

"And that is . . . ?"

"Patricia would like to remain with you."

"She doesn't want to return to the ship?"

"No."

An understandable decision. Helen scowled at Smith. "What are your feelings in this, Mr. Smith?"

At her question Smith appeared stricken, but he hastily shielded any reaction. "I have no opinion, Miss Mansfield. The Captain needs me, and I'm happy to do whatever he asks."

How could he abandon Patricia? How could he walk away simply because Westmoreland demanded it? Hadn't either man an ounce of sense? Of shame? To what was the world coming? Didn't integrity matter anymore? Not obligation? Or duty? Or devotion? Or fidelity?

"You're the Captain's man, through and through, Mr. Smith," she needled. "We wouldn't want you to upset him, would we?" At her sarcasm they both bristled, but she ignored them. She was beyond caring about them and their idiotic male sensibilities. "The *condition,* Captain, is easy to accept. Patricia may stay as long as she likes . . ."

She glared at Smith, letting him read her mind as she finished her thought. . . . *if it will help to keep her away from you.*

With no difficulty, he received her message, and she was elated to see him flush with humiliation.

"Will there be anything else, Captain?" she inquired.

Suddenly his cravat seemed to be choking him, and he tugged at it and cleared his throat. "I don't believe so."

"Then may I be excused?"

He didn't respond, but stared and stared, his discomfort plain. He recognized how badly he'd mucked up the situation, but there was no way to mend their rift. His greatest fault—or virtue, depending on one's point of view—was his absolute veracity. He was excruciatingly blunt, and he never said what he didn't mean.

He was through with her, and if she had troubles later on, he couldn't be bothered over them. She wondered if he fathomed how very much like his father he was. He and the Duke were two peas in a pod, which was so very sad. How apropos that Captain Westmoreland would pick the Duke over herself.

She blandly matched his stare, her face blank and not

exhibiting a hint of emotion, even though she was dying inside.

Don't go! Don't leave me! she yearned to shout, but she said nothing. She did nothing. He'd made his bed. He could lie in it with his precious father.

"Well?" she pressed.

His cheeks reddened, and she might have detected a touch of regret, but she was positive it was a trick of the light.

"If there's any news to share—"

Egad! The blasted oaf wouldn't mention their affair in front of Smith, would he? Could he be that crass? If he uttered a single word, she would march over to the fancy weaponry displayed on the wall, would grab a pistol and shoot him right through the middle of his black heart.

"There won't be any news."

"But if you need me, and I—"

"Trust me, Captain Westmoreland, should I ever require assistance, you would be the last person I would ask." She rose. "Have a pleasant journey."

Despite her rebuff, he persisted. "Helen, you must promise you'll contact me. I'll come straightaway."

"I'd sooner jump off a cliff than have you back here. Good-bye."

Regal as any queen, she strode out, but once she was far enough away that he couldn't hear, she raced up the stairs to her room. Numb, bereft, she lay down and gazed up at the ceiling, pondering how quiet the house would be without him.

How would she bear it? How would she carry on?

Noise erupted in the yard as horses were brought out. Orders were given, banter exchanged with the grooms. His voice was easy to discern, and he sounded so calm, so eager to be away.

She couldn't resist creeping to the window to watch him ride off. She huddled behind the curtains as he checked his saddle, as Smith mounted, then he mounted, himself. He jerked on the reins and kicked his horse into a canter. Within seconds, he was disappearing down the lane and just a tiny speck on the horizon.

She'd assumed he would pause to take a final glance around, that he might smile fondly or wave in farewell, but he never looked back.

🌿

"You're certain?"

"Yes."

"Dammit! The bitch!"

Adrian observed as Archie snatched up a perfectly decent decanter of brandy and smashed it against the wall. Shards of glass flew everywhere, and amber liquid spewed down the plaster and onto the priceless rug.

"Let me see the letter," Archie said.

Adrian surrendered it, as he decided that the annoying maid, Peg, had outlived her usefulness. There was no reason for her to continue on at Mansfield. When he returned there, he'd have to ensure that she vanished.

"The bloody thing is a scrawl," Archie complained. "Was it written by an illiterate?"

"Yes, but at least it *was* written, or we wouldn't have known what happened."

"I can't read this . . . this scribbling." Archie tossed the letter on the floor. "Tell me again what it says."

"Westmoreland has departed."

"But not before deeding the estate to Helen!"

"Apparently so."

"Why would he?"

"I haven't the vaguest idea."

"I should have killed her years ago."

"You still could," Adrian goaded, loving to push the younger man.

"That property is mine!" Archie seethed. "The house, the stables, the fields, the woods. All of it—every blade of grass, every pebble in the dirt—is mine!"

"Then you must wrest it from her. How will you go about it? She can be terribly stubborn."

"I'll bend her to my will! I'll force her to obey me!"

Archie started pacing and, not yet bored by the tantrum, Adrian went to the bed and reclined. Occasionally, it was entertaining to have Archie strut and fret. With his brown hair and puppy-dog hazel eyes he was so desperately attractive, which was why Adrian had tolerated him for so long. Luckily, Adrian's days—and nights!—of putting up with Archie were about to conclude, which was a vast relief. Adrian was so tired of feigning desire for the little prig.

"Do you want the details, Archie?"

Archie stopped and whipped around. "What details?"

"The dashing Captain and your plain elder sister were lovers."

"So you've claimed before. I don't believe you."

"It's true. Their antics were often quite wild, and she enjoyed their sexual romping very much."

"Helen? Helen enjoyed it?"

"Yes."

"She couldn't have. She's too much of a prude."

"Westmoreland had her screaming in ecstasy."

Archie shuddered with distaste. "My Lord, when I think of all the times *I* could have had her but didn't! I never realized she was such a slut at heart. I'd give anything to have her now." He gestured crudely over his cock. "I'd show her the penalty for deceiving me."

"How were you deceived?"

"She was supposed to fuck him for a month. That's all she had to do. She wasn't supposed to carve out her own arrangement. I'll murder her for this. If it takes the rest of my life, I'll make her pay."

Adrian chuckled, curious as to whether Archie had any genuine courage regarding his sister. It was amusing to consider, titillating to envision. If Archie ever dared to ravage her, Adrian would definitely assist. Adrian already knew how to control Archie, but it would be so satisfying to break Helen to his will. She had no reference point that would carry her through the ordeal with any level of sanity.

After he finished, Helen would be totally at his mercy. What an appealing picture to ponder!

"Archie, you rant and rave, but you never act."

"Honestly, Adrian, if you can't discern how angry I am, or how determined to avenge this treachery, there's no explaining it to you."

"Well then, I should see about you getting your big chance."

"As if you could orchestrate it!"

"Archie, darling, as opposed to you, *I* have a plan."

"What? What is it?"

"The Captain was imprudent in his copulations, and according to my spy, your sister may need a husband. Very, very soon."

"A husband!" Archie groaned. "I can't marry her. The church would never allow it!"

"No, you can't." Adrian smirked. "But I can."

"You? Marry Helen?" Archie threw up his hands in disgust. "What good would that do me?"

"Once I'm her husband, her property will be *my* property. I'll own everything that's hers, and I can manage it however I wish."

"Gad, yes!" Archie breathed. "It's the perfect solution."

"You know how much I love you, Archie."

"Yes."

"I'd do anything for you," Adrian lied.

"As you rightly should."

"What's mine will be yours."

"You'll give the estate to me?"

"I will," he lied again.

"Swear it!"

"I swear."

Archie grinned, looking like the spoiled child he'd always been, and Adrian grinned, too, content to have him laboring under such an idiotic misconception.

Adrian's gambit was working out much better than he'd expected. He'd have Helen to manipulate and command. He'd have a fine, though small, estate that would propel him into a new tier of affluence in society. What he wouldn't have was Archie Mansfield, who was no longer worth the bother.

Poor Archie! When he tried, he could be such a dear boy. Unfortunately for him, he could also be such a stupid ass. Could he actually believe that Adrian would share? Helen, yes. Money and property? No.

What a fool Archie was!

Adrian stifled his glee and stood. Archie had just bathed, the tub of water was still warm in the adjoining dressing room, and Adrian was eager to wallow in sensorial exhilaration.

"Come," he said to Archie. Lust and power had Adrian's cock swelling, and he began unbuttoning his trousers.

"To where?"

"All this talk has left me aching with desire. You'll wash me, then tend to my carnal needs."

"I can't dabble with you now," Archie protested. "I'm absolutely aflutter over your scheme. I must spend some time in quiet contemplation."

Adrian's irritation sparked. "You will not refuse me."

"I will," Archie insisted.

Adrian rippled with malice. He liked it when Archie was petulant, when he was rebellious and defiant. Adrian went to the wardrobe and fetched a belt he kept for this very purpose.

"You will not refuse me," he repeated.

He pointed to his waiting bath, excited to learn what Archie would do and hoping he would disobey.

19

He was taller than his father.

It was a bizarre detail upon which to dwell, but Luke couldn't get it out of his head. They stared at each other across an ornate desk, the cumbersome interlude stretching to infinity.

They were both blond and blue-eyed, though age had faded the Duke's hair to silver. With the same strong nose and brow, cheekbones and mouth, broad shoulders and long legs, they were similar enough to be . . . well . . . father and son.

Luke was gaping like an imbecile, but he was stunned to realize that the grand and imposing Duke of Roswell wasn't old and decrepit but an extremely handsome and charming man who was probably in his late forties. For some reason, Luke had always envisioned Roswell as an elderly pervert who'd enjoyed a salacious life of seducing young girls against their will.

He'd pictured his mother as a sweet, chaste maiden, who'd been lured to her doom by a crafty roué, but now, Luke was forced to admit that his father had been only sixteen or seventeen when he'd had his brief affair with Luke's mother. At the discovery Luke was greatly unsettled, feeling as though his past had come unraveled and he had no history that was true.

The Duke was silent, examining Luke as if he were an odd insect, and Luke couldn't decide if he was checking for signs of paternity, if he was shocked at meeting a thirty-year-old son, or if he was simply too overwhelmed to speak.

Luke hoped it was a combination of trepidation and amazement and not a repudiation of his mother. If the Duke contested Mary Lucas's assertion that the Duke was Luke's father, Luke would beat him to a pulp. Duke or no, Luke wouldn't have his mother slandered.

"My son, eh?" the exalted swine finally muttered, one brow raised in question.

Mimicking stance and expression, Luke raised an identical brow. "They say it's a wise man who recognizes his own children."

Roswell scrutinized Luke's clothes, a suit Mr. Haversham had sewn. "At least you know how to dress yourself."

At the Duke's insulting tone Luke bristled. "I'm not such a dunce that I can't figure out how to hire a competent tailor."

Roswell barked out a laugh. "I was told you have a smart mouth. Don't use it around me. I won't brook any insolence."

The caustic opening volley shook Luke out of his stupor. He'd been loitering like a fool, pacing for over three hours, with Roswell rudely late for their scheduled appointment. Had it been any other person in the land, Luke would have left after fifteen minutes or so. Instead, he'd waited and waited, anxiety gnawing at him till he'd nearly gone mad from the suspense.

He turned and walked to a sideboard, grabbed a bottle of liquor, and gestured with it.

"I'm dying for a brandy, and you're rich enough to afford the best, so this ought to be pretty good."

"I haven't granted you permission to proceed."

"Like I give a shit." Luke filled a glass to the rim and took a hefty swig. The crudity and disrespect had the Duke so aghast that Luke wondered if he might faint.

"What . . . what did you say to me?"

"You can drop the bluster. I'm a master at it, myself, so it doesn't work on me." He picked up a second glass and held it out. "Would you like one?"

"I only drink with peers." If the Duke's nose had been stuck up any higher in the air, he'd have floated away.

"Your loss, then."

Luke gulped the remaining contents as he acknowledged that Helen had been correct: Roswell was a certifiable ass. If Luke had listened to her, he'd have saved himself a load of grief. Why had he raced to London? He was as crazy as Roswell, but then, they were direct kin. What had he expected?

Merely to aggravate the lofty man, Luke poured a bit more liquor, and he swilled it down, then he started toward the door.

"This has been . . . interesting and enlightening," he said, "but I've heard all I need to. The brandy's excellent, by the way. Thanks."

He'd reached the threshold when the Duke demanded, "Where do you think you're going?"

Luke looked over his shoulder. "It's clear that this was a mistake, and we'll chalk it up to experience. No hard feelings."

He spun away, and the Duke snapped, "Captain, get in here—at once!—lest I shout for the footmen and have them drag you back."

"I've seen your servants, Roswell. You don't have any who are big enough to *drag* me anywhere."

"All right . . . all right. . . ." The Duke was flustered, his polished exterior slipping for a moment. "Let's try this again. Close the door and . . . and . . . sit."

There was a chair by the desk, and—against his better judgment—Luke marched over to it.

Roswell was rattled. He plopped down in his own chair and confessed, "I guess maybe I could use a brandy. Would you . . . ?"

"Are you sure you can lower yourself?"

"Just fetch the damned liquor!"

Luke went over and poured them both a glass. As the Duke downed his serving, Luke chided, "All better?"

Roswell glared. "Have you any notion of how disturbing this encounter is for me?"

"No. How disturbing?"

"Have you any children, Captain?"

"Why? Are you worried you're a grandfather?"

Roswell blushed. "No, I was making a point."

"That being . . . ?"

"This is a strange circumstance."

"No stranger than many others I've endured."

"It's awkward."

"Since I haven't any progeny," Luke replied, "I wouldn't know about that. I'm more cautious in my philandering than some of my male relatives."

Roswell didn't take the sarcasm very well. "You're obnoxious, Captain."

"So are you, Roswell. Like father, like son, I suppose."

"Call me *Your Grace*."

"Not bloody likely."

Luke stood and started out again. He was angry and disillusioned and speculating as to why he'd invested the situation with so much importance.

An image flashed of that terrible day when he'd been a tiny boy and the grave diggers had pitched his mother's corpse into their wagon. Even after all these years, the vision had the power to sadden, to wound, and the Duke had been responsible for it.

Why had Luke presumed he could change the memory? Why had he persuaded himself that he could erase the past? The old sensations of loss and heartache could never be wiped away.

"You can't leave yet," Roswell huffed. "We've barely begun our conversation."

"I have other engagements," Luke lied.

"Cancel them."

"I don't wish to."

"But . . . but . . ." Obviously, no one had ever walked out on the Duke before, and he couldn't conceive of how to force Luke to stay. "We have details to discuss, matters to attend to."

"Write to my secretary, Mr. Smith, in care of my ship. He'll handle whatever you need."

"There are parties planned in your honor. Festivities and balls have been arranged."

"So apprise Mr. Smith of when and where, and I'll be there when required."

Roswell scowled, pulling himself up to his full height,

and with his expensive clothes and bejeweled fingers he was an intimidating sight. No doubt, his minions trembled at viewing his disdain. Unfortunately for Roswell, he didn't understand that Luke was skilled at the art of intimidation, too, that he could bully and coerce better than anyone, so the Duke's arrogant sneer had no effect.

"I command you to remain until our business is concluded," Roswell ordered.

"And I don't choose to obey."

"You will do as I say. I am your father."

Luke scoffed. "No, you're not. You're simply a deceitful dog who had sex with my mother, but that doesn't make you anything to me, at all."

He stomped out.

"Captain!" Luke kept on, and the Duke cried, "William! Lucas!"

Luke halted and frowned at him. "The next time we're scheduled to meet and you're late, I won't wait for you."

He departed, hoping Mr. Smith was out in the mews with their horses and that he wouldn't have to search for him before they could head out.

🙟

Robert strolled down the busy street, and he passed by a narrow alley when he was once again yanked into the shadows. Wouldn't you just know it? He was by himself, with no one to watch his back. The Captain had been right: The first moment he could be cornered, he had been.

As he wiggled free and whipped around, he wasn't surprised to confront one of the brigands who'd previously assaulted him, and the man snickered.

"It seems your precious Captain Westmoreland has left you all alone."

"I don't need a champion to defend me anymore."

Robert rolled his shoulders and flexed his fingers, glad that he'd discarded his suit for the flowing shirt and loose trousers favored by the crew on the ship. He was still small and trim, but after his sparring with Westmoreland he wasn't skinny but whipcord lean, his arms and legs lined with muscle.

The man lunged, but before he could attack, Robert delivered several nasty blows to his face. There was a loud crack, blood squirted everywhere, and the criminal fell to his knees in a stunned heap.

"My nothe! My nothe!" he wailed. "You broke my nothe!"

Robert punched him in the stomach, then clasped him by his jacket and shoved him against the wall. A knife magically appeared from Robert's boot, and he dangled it before the man's terrified eyes. "If you ever come near me again," he threatened, "I'll cut your balls off."

He let go, and the knave wet himself and slid to the cobbles to wallow in the muck and stench, but he managed to hurl, "Bastard!"

"Aren't I though?"

Robert grinned and strutted off, quite sure he'd never fear anyone ever again.

❧

"Might I ask you a question?"

"Certainly."

Patricia glanced up from her stitching, relieved to have Helen interrupt the quiet. Since the morning that Robert and the Captain had ridden away, the place had been as glum as a mortician's on funeral day. It was enough to have her wishing she'd put on a pair of trousers, strapped on a pistol, and gone with them.

No! As swiftly as the absurd notion took root, she pushed it away. This serene rural existence had been her dream, and she'd made it her reality. She wouldn't be sorry.

Robert had chosen duty and money over her, so the hell with him! He could fritter away to eternity searching for his perfect situation. In the meantime, she'd be *living* hers.

Helen mumbled, "Oh, this is so embarrassing."

"What is?"

Helen was very distressed, and she tried to hide it by going to the window and staring out into the yard. "My mother died when I was very young, so I never had a confidante who could enlighten me on various topics."

"Such as?"

"Well . . . female issues."

"Aah . . ."

"I hate to bother you, but I have no one else with whom I can discuss it."

Having grown up on ships and in port towns, Patricia wasn't much of an expert, herself, but she probably knew more than Helen ever would. Plus, she'd had her stint in the Sultan's harem, where feminine complaints were daily fare.

Delicately, she probed, "What is it that has you upset?"

When Helen cleared her throat and turned, there were tears in her eyes, and Patricia braced for the worst.

"Have you any idea," Helen inquired, "of how a woman could tell if she's . . . she's . . . if she's pregnant?"

"Are you worried that the Captain left a little bundle behind?"

"I believe he might have."

As her suspicions about Helen and the Captain were confirmed, Patricia's spirits plummeted. The Captain was no different from any other man. Once his cock was involved, there was no dissuading him. He'd take what he wanted, though he was always so cautious about not siring any children.

How had this occurred? Why had he done it? To Helen, of all people!

"Damn him," Patricia muttered. "Damn him straight to hell."

"My thoughts exactly."

"He won't come back," Patricia felt it important to mention. "Not even if you beg."

"I realize that."

"You could write to him, though. He might send money or—"

"No," Helen interjected. "I pestered him before he went—about the possibility of a babe—and he was quite blunt. He couldn't care less. I won't humiliate myself by contacting him."

"I wouldn't, either, but what will you do?"

"I can't decide, but I have to think of a solution—and fast."

Which was a definite understatement. In Helen's world, an illegitimate pregnancy was an unpardonable sin. Her life as it had passed up till now was over, and she had meager, degrading options. She could move far away, establish herself in a new village, and pretend to be a tragic widow. She could go off on *holiday,* have the baby, and abandon it at a church or orphanage. And, of course, there could be an ominous trip to the barber.

Most likely, she would have to seduce some poor sod, marry immediately, then claim the child was born early—while hoping her husband was an idiot who never learned otherwise and murdered her for her betrayal.

On pondering the terrible jam Westmoreland had

created, Pat was shaking with fury. At that moment, if he'd been standing in front of her, it would have been pistols at dawn.

Helen had no one to speak for her, except her spoiled, queer brother, which was the same as having no one. Patricia knew about being alone, and it grieved her, having Helen reduced to such a pitiful circumstance. She was too fine for the likes of Westmoreland, too fine to be deserted and facing calamity.

Well, the Captain might have totted off, but Patricia wouldn't.

"Don't fret, Helen." Patricia rose and walked over to her. "I'll be here with you. We'll figure it out."

"You'll stay? Despite what I've done?"

"It's not as if you killed someone. You're simply having a baby."

"Yes, I am." She appeared frightened and thunderstruck.

"I'll stay, Helen. I'll stay as long as you need me."

And longer than that, Patricia mused. *Much longer than that.*

❧

"She's pregnant!"

"You're positive?"

"I was listening through the keyhole. I heard them talking."

"My, my, Peg, aren't you a marvelous spy."

Under Mr. Bennett's approval, Peg preened with satisfaction. She'd been scared about traveling to London on her own, but obviously, she'd made the proper choice.

"Look what I have." As she drew out her prize, she

rippled with excitement. "It's a letter Miss Mansfield penned to Captain Westmoreland!"

Mr. Bennett was suitably impressed. "How did you come by it?"

"She wrote it when the other one, that Miss Patricia, was out. She asked me to post it for her in secret."

Mr. Bennett took the letter and read it over and over. "She sounds desperate."

"She is! They're whispering constantly, trying to devise a method for hiding the scandal."

"As well they should. What have they planned?"

"They can't determine what's best, although I'm sure Miss Mansfield is assuming the Captain will receive her message and rescue her."

Mr. Bennett stuck the letter inside his coat. "We both know that won't happen, don't we?"

Successful conspirators, they grinned in unison.

A frigid wind whipped at her cloak, and she pulled it tighter. She was cold and hungry and wished Mr. Bennett would invite her inside. The bastard!

It was growing dark, the rain falling harder. She'd spent her small cache of savings to purchase her seat on the mail coach, so she hadn't any coins to rent lodging or buy a hot meal. She was cranky and frozen and ready for a grand reward, but with their conversation concluded, she was seriously questioning whether compensation would be forthcoming.

If he didn't reimburse her—and generously—it would be the last bloody time she ever assisted him!

"You've been extremely helpful, Peg." He patted her on the shoulder, and he smiled the slick, nauseating smile that used to be handsome and endearing but that now only made her want to go home.

She shouldn't have come to London. What had she
been thinking?

"I'd better be off," she murmured. "Could I have some
money for the coach back to Mansfield?"

"Of course," he said without hesitation, which surprised her. "You should have a little extra, too, for deliv-
ering such intriguing news."

"Yes, I should." She was unable to keep the petulance
out of her voice.

"I must retrieve my purse. Why don't you wait in the
stable while I fetch it?"

"I will."

She turned toward the building, relieved to have a
chance to get out of the rain. After he paid her, she might
sneak in and sleep there, might snuggle down in the hay
and tiptoe out at dawn. No one would be the wiser.

She'd stepped to the door when she was hit on the
head, numerous ferocious blows landing in quick succes-
sion. The force knocked her to the ground and had her so
disoriented that she couldn't react. She struggled to
stand, but her arms and legs wouldn't work.

"Thank you, Peg, for all you've done," he eerily
soothed, "but I have no further need of your services."

She tried to call out, but as he bound her wrists and
stuffed a kerchief in her mouth her brain was scrambled,
and she couldn't form any words.

"I have to move you away from the house." He was
dragging her down the alley. "When your body is located, we can't have any connection traced to us. You'll
merely be another poor, unfortunate girl who's met with
a bad end."

He peered down at her, his face barely visible in the
dim light, but he was evil personified, as if the Devil
had entered him.

"You won't be missed, Peg. You realize that, don't you? No one will search. No one will care."

You're so right.

She'd left Mansfield without giving notice. She had no family in London to anticipate her arrival. She was an anonymous servant, her appearance already forgotten by those who'd seen her. Any catastrophe could transpire.

The depressing thoughts flowed through her mind, but she couldn't concentrate, so they didn't bother her overly much. She could sense water nearby—was it the river?— but she didn't comprehend the significance.

"Let's hurry and finish this," Mr. Bennett said. "I must pack my bags so I can proceed to the country with all due haste. I'm about to be married."

Was he? She couldn't recollect hearing any such gossip. With his perverted tastes and habits, what woman would have him?

He was pulling up her skirt, his cock between her legs, and suddenly he was thrusting with a viciousness that should have been painful, but she felt so peculiar, as if she were floating in the air, so it didn't hurt.

He produced another cord and tied it around her neck. As his lust spiraled, he was squeezing it tighter, tighter. She couldn't breathe, but it didn't seem to matter. There was a splash, and it occurred to her that he'd vanished, that she was in the water, though she couldn't deduce how it had happened.

She meant to kick her feet, to flail her arms, but they were fettered. Not that it would have done her any good, for she'd never learned to swim.

She sank to the bottom, and then, she felt nothing, at all.

20

Helen, are you all right?"

Helen saw Adrian approaching on the path from the house, and she fought down a groan. She wanted to be alone, but of late, solitude had become a tricky commodity.

Without invitation, her brother had arrived, with Adrian in tow, and Archie had swiftly established himself in his old suite as if he'd never been gone. He'd been awkwardly solicitous, and she had the sinking feeling that he expected her to give Mansfield Abbey to him. In his convoluted mind, it would seem the only appropriate course, but she refused to be at his mercy ever again, so she couldn't do it.

At any moment, he was likely to broach the subject of ownership. Then there would be fighting and rancor, and in her delicate condition she couldn't abide any quarreling.

She'd considered speaking with Adrian, convincing him to remove Archie from the premises. She was positive Adrian would assist her, but due to Patricia's strong opinions in the matter, she'd hesitated. Patricia kept warning her not to trust Adrian, and Patricia disliked him for reasons she wouldn't clarify, merely saying over and over that Captain Westmoreland didn't like him, either. Westmoreland's views no longer held sway with Helen, and she found Patricia's dire predictions about Adrian to be silly.

Patricia was also pressuring her to kick Archie out the door, and Helen knew she should demand his departure, but he was her sole kin, and she'd always felt such a heavy sense of responsibility toward him. He'd proved repeatedly that he was incapable of caring for himself, so she had shouldered the obligation. As far as she could see, in the interval that he'd been away nothing had changed between them, except that he was penniless and in desperate need of an allowance and a place to stay.

"Hello, Adrian," she welcomed as he neared. "What brings you out in the cold?"

"I was worried about you."

"Me? Whatever for?"

"Since we came home, you've been so . . . so . . . sad."

"I have?"

"Yes, and I was wondering if there's anything I can do."

To her shock and horror, tears welled into her eyes. His concern was a soothing balm, a bracing tonic. It had been an eternity since anyone had fretted over her, and suddenly it was just what she needed. There was a bench next to her, and she sank down onto it.

"Could you take Archie away from here?" she asked.

"Why, yes," Adrian agreed without hesitation, and he joined her on the bench. "Has he upset you? You should have mentioned it sooner. We'd have gone immediately."

"I'm such an ingrate. What sort of sister doesn't want her brother to visit?"

"He's difficult at the best of times, but it's clear that this is a particularly distressing period for you. I'll persuade him to leave tomorrow."

"Would you? Oh, Adrian, thank you."

"I'm your friend, Helen, and I love you like a sister—as much as Archie does himself. You know that. I'd do anything for you."

"You've been so kind to me, when I've done so little to deserve it."

As usually happened anymore, she was swamped by emotion. The tears that had threatened dripped down her cheeks. She couldn't stop them.

"Helen, what is it? You must tell me."

"I can't . . . I can't . . ."

"Surely you can confide in me. Perhaps I can help. I'm not without experiences that might permit me to provide guidance."

"It's so futile."

She collapsed into a humiliating torrent of weeping that he tackled with his typical aplomb, patting her wrist in commiseration and murmuring softly as he discreetly passed her a kerchief. It wasn't a pretty picture, no diplomatic cry over spilt milk but a full-on deluge that was mortifying in its lack of restraint.

She wept for the loss of her innocence, for the loss of Captain Westmoreland. He'd blazed into her life like a wildfire and had left scorched earth in his wake. Her world was so quiet without him, and she didn't know how to carry on.

Up until that instant, she'd believed that he would return, that her letter would have had him rushing to her side. Though she'd told Patricia she wouldn't contact him and had pleaded with Pat not to contact him, either, panic had caused her to relent. In impatient anguish, she'd watched for the mail to be delivered, her pulse racing whenever a horse went by out on the lane. Her certainty—that he wouldn't fail her—had prevented her from making decisions that had to be made.

How long did she intend to wait? How long could she keep hope alive?

He wasn't coming back. Not today. Not ever. She'd tarried—week after agonizing week—but she'd been fooling herself. He hadn't truly cared for her, and she couldn't continue to dawdle while her stomach grew and rumor festered.

She was sick every morning, and the maids studied her with perceptive glances. They would be speculating among themselves, and the scandal would spread quickly. As she was a prominent female landowner, her behavior had to be above reproach, but her first act had been to shame herself. A bastard would never be accepted by her neighbors. *She* wouldn't be allowed to remain in their midst to flaunt her disgrace. She'd be shunned, her child ostracized.

The new vicar was an agitator who saw sin lurking behind every tree and stone. He might have her charged with illicit fornication, might demand she be whipped in the village square, then jailed, and the prospect was petrifying.

"I've done a terrible thing," she confessed.

"You?" Adrian scoffed. "What could be so bad as all that?"

"You must promise not to judge me harshly. Please."

"I never could. Tell me what it is."

Out on the horizon, the road wound through the hills toward London, where Captain Westmoreland was being feted as England's hero. Did he ever think of her? Did he ever miss her?

"I'm going to have a baby."

"A baby! Well . . ." There was a strained silence; then he inquired, "May I ask . . . ask . . . who is the . . ." As if to cancel the query, he waved a hand. "It doesn't matter. It's none of my affair. What is it you wish to do?"

"I don't know."

"You must marry."

She laughed, but it was a wrenching, painful sound. "There are so many candidates who are dying to be my husband."

"Have you talked to the man who . . . who . . ."

"He has no interest in the situation. He was very definite."

"The bounder! Would you like me to speak to him for you? I could confer with Archie. He's your brother, and we could—"

"No, no! You mustn't breathe a word to Archie." That was all she needed! To have her brother strut and chastise! The scenario didn't bear contemplating.

Adrian scrutinized her, then vowed, "All right, I won't, but where does this leave you? You can't hide your condition forever." He peeked at her tummy, checking for a condemning bulge.

They were silent again, lost in thought, when he cleared his throat.

"Might I propose a solution?"

"I'm open to any suggestion."

"Swear that you'll hear me out. Don't automatically dismiss my idea."

"Of course I'll hear you out."

"What if you were to marry me?"

"You?"

"Yes."

"I could never saddle you with such a burden."

"It wouldn't be a burden."

"But I don't . . . don't love you." In light of her predicament, the remark was ridiculous. People frequently wed without love. Who was she to be choosey? She was drowning, and he was throwing her a rope.

"But I believe you feel some affection for me. We're friends, with many likes and dislikes in common, and we could build on that strong connection. Many marriages have started with much less."

"Yes, but I could never . . . never . . ."

She simply couldn't discuss physical intimacy with him, and he saved her by jumping in.

"Nor would I expect you to."

"Nonsense. You're a healthy adult male. You should have a real marriage."

"Helen, my dear . . ." He sighed and blushed. "This is so embarrassing."

"What is?"

"I love your brother."

"I know you do, but—"

"No . . . no . . . you misunderstand." He hemmed and hawed and finally blurted out, "I *love* your brother, as a man loves his wife."

"I guess I'm confused."

"I don't doubt that you are. My tendencies are so revolting; they're beyond a moral person's comprehension."

A glint of awareness dawned, the outrageous possibility taking shape. How could she have failed to suspect? "Are you claiming that . . . ? Are the two of you . . . ?"

"Yes. I'll always love him. I'm just *different* that way. Can you forgive me?"

At the admission he was so stricken, and she was so stunned, that she couldn't seem to do anything but murmur, "Yes, I forgive you."

"So you see, you'd never have to perform any wifely duties."

"We'd have a marriage in name only?"

"Except I imagine I ought to stay here occasionally—so that our union appears legitimate—but I'd keep Archie away. We can't have him underfoot and upsetting you."

She assessed him, trying to figure out his motives. "This is such a sacrifice on your part. Why would you do it?"

"I told you: I love your brother. You're his sister. How could I not offer to assist you in your hour of need?"

He was such a beautiful man, his blue eyes so frank and trusting, his smile so genuine, and she was so desperate. At that moment, she couldn't conjure any reason not to assent. Still, she hedged. "If I agree—and I'm not saying I am—how would we accomplish it?"

"It probably ought to be right away. I don't think there's time to call the banns."

"We'd elope?"

"Or we could inquire about a Special License, which would finish the process in a few days."

"A Special License . . . hmm . . ."

It was the obvious solution, but it seemed so wrong, so calculated and dishonest. Could any good ever come from such a sad, fraudulent beginning?

She gazed out at the hills again, at the road meandering so peacefully to London.

Damn you, Luke Westmoreland, she thought. *How could you do this to me?*

"Let me reflect on it overnight, would you?"

"You certainly should. It's a huge step."

"We'll talk in the morning."

"I'm looking forward to it," Adrian said. "You go on to the house now, and try to rest. Everything will be fine, and I'll stand by you whatever you elect to do. Remember: You have one true friend."

He helped her to her feet, and she wandered away, her mind racing with questions that couldn't be answered, with dread that couldn't be erased.

❧

"She swallowed the bait."

"And . . . ?"

"We wait to see if she's hooked," Adrian declared.

Archie bit down on the oaths he yearned to hurl. He hated loitering behind the scenes while Adrian forged the ending. With so much riding in the balance, Archie was a nervous wreck.

"When will you know her decision?"

"She's to apprise me in the morning."

"So . . . you could be wed in two or three days."

"Yes."

Archie grinned, almost able to see the infusion of funds swelling his bank account. "After the ceremony, what treat shall we purchase first? Shall we take a trip? Shall we both have new wardrobes sewn? Perhaps we should pick out that gig we've been wanting."

"Whatever you wish, Archie." Adrian was showing a deference he rarely displayed. "I'm content with whatever you select for us."

Archie smirked. It was about time that Adrian learned his place. Archie was a man of destiny, of wealth and power, and he had a brilliant future that he was more than happy to share with Adrian. Together they would enjoy a life of affluence and debauchery the likes of which High Society had never witnessed.

Still, an irksome worry nagged at Archie. "What if Westmoreland finds out about the letter you burned? Or about the babe? What if he comes here?"

"What if he does?" Adrian shrugged, unconcerned about the brawny, dangerous villain. "Once I've consummated the marriage, there's not a man in the kingdom who can gainsay me."

"I suppose you're correct."

"I am! I can do whatever I want to her, and in the eyes of God and the law, the child will be mine. How could Westmoreland claim otherwise? He'll have no business poking around."

Considering Westmoreland's violent propensities, Archie judged Adrian as having a tad too much bravado, but he didn't mention his qualms. Adrian always knew best, and his schemes worked to Archie's advantage, so Archie wouldn't second-guess.

Yet, deep down, he was afraid of Westmoreland—and with valid reason. The criminal had wreaked havoc. "But what if—"

"The man's a convicted felon, Archie. He spent years in the penal colonies. Stop imbuing him with more importance than is warranted."

Adrian stood as if to exit, and though there was a possessive whine in his voice, Archie challenged, "Where are you off to now?"

"I must have some privacy while I ponder the fate of Miss Reilly."

"Why would you waste your energy on her?"

"She's an annoying busybody, and I don't care for her close relationship with Helen."

"She has a smart attitude."

"Which I abhor in a female."

"As do I," Archie concurred. "A woman ought to be wary of wagging such a sharp tongue."

"Yes, she should, and Miss Reilly must be taught to use that mouth of hers for something besides sassing."

"I agree."

"Then she needs to leave and never return." Adrian started out. "I simply have to determine when and how she's to go."

※

"Is it true what I heard?"

"Is what *true*?"

Patricia rushed into Helen's bedchamber and skidded to a halt. "Are you planning to marry Mr. Bennett?"

Helen's hair was arranged in a concoction of braids and curls, with flowers woven through the strands, and she was wearing a blue gown that was much too fancy for eleven o'clock on a Friday morning.

Helen dithered, then admitted, "Yes, very shortly as a matter of fact."

Patricia was aghast. "Why didn't you tell me?"

"I couldn't let you talk me out of it."

"Oh, Helen, don't do this. I'm begging you."

"Patricia, please . . ."

"This is a terrible mistake. You can't go through with it. I won't permit it."

"It's not up to you."

Patricia was frantic and overstepping her bounds, but she couldn't be silent.

"Mr. Bennett is a sodomite," she bluntly explained. "Do you comprehend what that means?"

"Yes."

"He won't be a real husband to you."

"No, he won't. He doesn't love me, Pat. He loves my brother."

"In a sick fashion, though! Don't you see how they are?"

"My brother has always been difficult and demanding, but I've never witnessed any discourtesy from Mr. Bennett."

"He'll hurt and degrade you; he'll . . . he'll . . ."

"Mr. Bennett is my friend."

Helen's comment had an air of finality, but Patricia couldn't give up. "Have you advised Captain Westmoreland?"

"About the wedding or the babe?"

"Either one."

"Why would I?"

"Don't you think he deserves to know?"

"Actually, I don't."

"Then I'll notify him for you. Postpone the ceremony. I'll ride to London immediately, and I'll bring him back with me."

"To do what?"

"To . . . to . . ."

Helen's expression was filled with pity and exasperation. "Pat, I never told you this, but when I first learned I was pregnant, I wrote to Captain Westmoreland."

"You did?"

"He couldn't be bothered to answer, and I can't keep waiting for him to rescue me. I have to rescue myself."

The Captain hadn't answered?

Patricia was stunned. He had many faults, but he never ignored a plea from someone in distress. Something bad must have transpired. She wondered if he was dead or perhaps he'd left England and she hadn't been informed. She had a vision of Helen's letter, trailing after him, from seaport to seaport, a tiny appeal for assistance floating across a world of large oceans.

"Well, if he won't help you, I will. Let me," Patricia implored. "We'll go away from here, where no one knows who you are or what you've done. We'll start over. We'll build a new life."

"But Mansfield Abbey is my home."

"I'm a hard worker," Patricia insisted. "I'll find a job, and I'll work for both of us so that you can—"

Helen sighed with resignation. "It's not possible for me to leave."

"But . . . why?"

"I'm not like you. I'm not some free, unattached person who can flit off whenever she likes. I'm connected to this place and these people, but I can't remain without a husband. The scandal would destroy me."

"The hell with these people!" Patricia crudely replied. "I don't care two figs for their opinion. I care about *you* and what will happen to you."

Helen smiled sadly. "You're sweet to worry, but you needn't. It will turn out for the best. Mr. Bennett said that—"

"He must want something. What is it?"

"He doesn't *want* anything. He's merely being kind."

"You're wrong, Helen. He hasn't a kind bone in his body." She glanced around at the ornate furniture. "It has to be the estate. He and your brother must be plotting to wrest it away from you."

"They won't be able to," Helen naïvely claimed. "We discussed it. My solicitor is drawing up papers."

"Are they're signed yet?"

"No, but they will be."

"He'll toss you out. You'll be abandoned and destitute—if he doesn't simply kill you and be done with it."

"Kill me! Honestly, Patricia, you're beginning to sound deranged."

"He's a monster!" she shouted. "Can't you see? Can't you tell?"

"Desist with this nonsense," Helen calmly urged. "I'm very distressed as it is, and your tirade is only making me more anxious."

"Good!" She grabbed Helen by the arms and shook her. "Don't do this!"

"I have to, Pat. Try to appreciate my dire position."

Carriage wheels crunched on the gravel in the drive, and Patricia's heart pounded as she vainly hoped it was the Captain, even though she knew he'd have arrived on horseback.

"It's the vicar," Helen explained, "come for the wedding. Will you go down to the parlor with me, Pat? Will you stand by my side?"

"I can't, Helen." She'd never felt more terrible. If Helen could see it through to the bitter end, why couldn't Patricia? What sort of fair-weather friend was she? "I can't watch. Don't ask it of me."

"I won't, then."

"I'm sorry."

"It's all right."

"I'd better go, so you can . . . can . . ."

Too overcome for words, she hurried out.

She had to travel to London, had to locate the Captain, and, her thoughts in turmoil, she fled to her room. She raced in and had shut the door when a voice stopped her in her tracks.

"Well, well, if it isn't Miss Reilly."

Pat whirled around. "What are you doing in here, Bennett?"

"I'm checking out my new property."

"Get out."

"I'm not ready to depart. Not yet anyway."

"Get out!" she repeated.

"You're much too bossy for a female. I don't like it. You should be taught a lesson."

"Hah! As if you could teach me anything."

"We'll see, won't we?"

Instinctively, she reached for the knife she usually carried in a pocket she'd sewn into her skirt, but with her leisurely existence she'd grown lax, and it wasn't there. She was unarmed but unconcerned. She'd whipped bigger asses than his.

He stepped toward her, trying to intimidate with his maleness, with his greater size.

"I'm not afraid of you," she said, and she really wasn't.

"You should be."

He lunged, and she leapt away, but her skirt tangled around her legs, making it difficult to fight as she'd done so competently when wearing trousers. She swung at him, but the fabric became more snarled around her ankles.

He raised a fist and coldcocked her alongside the head. Her last clear memory was of how hard she smacked into the floor when she hit it.

21

Luke tarried in the corner of the ballroom in his father's mistress's house. He scrutinized the waltzing couples, and he wondered what it would be like to join them. Since his entire life had been occupied with survival, he'd never tried to dance, and it looked amusing. Perhaps he'd have dancing be his next project, like learning to wear fancy cravats or use the correct silver at the supper table.

He could picture himself walking over to Helen, bowing politely, and . . .

Abruptly he pushed the vision out of his mind. Why keep ruminating over her? His fixation was driving him batty.

He'd been right to leave her—he had!—and he wouldn't rue or regret! Still, he couldn't get over the niggling suspicion that she needed him, that she was in trouble or in danger, which was silly. He'd left her hale and hearty, with the income from a prosperous farm. What woman had ever had a more profitable alteration of circumstance?

Yet he fretted. What if she was pregnant? That last, horrid day, he'd said all the wrong things and made all the wrong moves. If she was increasing, she'd never contact him, and suddenly he was fuming over the possibility. What if she was with child but kept it a secret? As swiftly as the absurd thought arose, he shoved it away.

Helen wouldn't hide her condition. Even though she was furious with him, she'd write, which was why he constantly checked the post, certain he'd hear from her, but he hadn't. Obviously, she was getting on just fine without him. He had to accept the fact and stop obsessing over her.

Across the way, he noticed Robert—it no longer seemed appropriate to refer to him as Mr. Smith—slipping in from the verandah. He was dressed in his sailor's clothes again, having completely forsaken his business suits and polished shoes. Luke watched him cut through the crowd, as tongues wagged over his unsuitable attire.

Of late, Robert was so transformed that Luke scarcely recognized him. He wasn't the toughest man Luke had ever met but probably the most stubborn. In a fight, Luke would now be more than happy to have Robert guarding his back.

Luke was glad for the changes, but frequently he missed the old Mr. Smith, the courteous and studious fellow who was so fussy in his habits and so adept with letters and numbers. What benefit was there to having an accountant who couldn't be bothered to add or subtract?

"There you are," Robert greeted as he approached. "I've searched through every accursed party in London."

The Prince Regent had requested that the Duke have

Luke introduced and feted, and there had been so many celebrations. His social schedule was so full that not even the competent Mr. Smith could track it all.

"What did you need?"

Robert held out an envelope, and Luke peeked inside, amazed to see a substantial quantity of cash.

"What's this?"

"A thousand pounds, plus some interest. The extra is meant to cover my room and board."

The amount was the approximate equivalent of what Luke had forked over to buy Robert from the slavers. It had cost a pretty penny to win the bidding, and to square the debt it had taken every ounce of gold Luke had had stowed on his ship, plus several rings, six pistols, Pat's sword, and the diamond in his ear.

Robert had insisted that he'd reimburse Luke some-day, and Luke had humored him by agreeing that he should, but he'd never actually expected it to happen. He was extremely suspicious as to the money's origin, and with how Robert had recently been acting, there was no telling where he'd acquired such a large sum.

"I think it's a fair defrayal," Robert protested, as if Luke had disputed his calculations.

"Where'd you get it? You weren't gambling, were you?" Gaming would be the final straw for Luke, and he'd have to intervene in Robert's odd plunge into ab-normality. If Robert had stooped to wagering, he'd gone too far round the bend.

"No. My brothers sent it."

"Your brothers?"

"I filed a lawsuit against them. For damages regarding my misadventure in the Mediterranean."

"You did?"

"I had your solicitors draft legal papers for me, demanding a settlement."

"You rascal! You never told me."

"You don't have to know everything," Robert claimed.

"I don't see why not."

"Then I went to visit them, and I threatened bodily harm if they didn't compensate me."

Luke was so proud! "I wish I'd been there to witness it."

"I guess I scared the hell out of them. They couldn't predict what I'd do next, so they allotted me some funds from the family coffers—to shut me up."

"I hope you're keeping it."

"Damn straight! They gave me several thousand more than what I passed on to you, so I have a nest egg." He grinned like the village idiot. "So . . . you're repaid, I'm free, and I'm leaving. Thank you for all you've done. I've enjoyed working for you." As if he planned to stomp out that very second, he spun away.

"Whoa! Whoa!" Luke reached out and yanked him around. "You skipped the middle section of this story. What are you doing?"

"I quit."

"You can't quit."

"Of course I can."

"But . . . but how will I carry on without you?"

His dismay couldn't be concealed. He'd grown so accustomed to Robert's company, considered him a true friend, and trusted him implicitly. Luke needed Robert in more ways than he could count and couldn't imagine his absence.

"You'll have to hire somebody else, Captain."

"I don't want anybody else."

"I'm sorry," he said, "but I miss Patricia, and I have to be with her. I feel terrible about how it ended between us, and now, with this windfall, I can make it right—if she'll let me."

This was about Patricia? "So go see her, romp a bit, then get your ass back here."

"You don't understand. She wants me to build a life with her."

"She's a woman. She should be happy to do whatever you tell her."

Robert stared, then muttered, "You can be such a prick."

Luke was stunned. It was the only impolite remark Robert had ever uttered in his presence. "I'm a prick, am I? When did you arrive at this conclusion?"

"If you must know, I've always thought so." He took a step away. "And on that final note, I'll be off."

"Wait just a damned minute! I won't allow you to insult me, then saunter out."

"What will you do? Pummel me?"

"Maybe."

"If we start brawling, you'll rip your fancy coat, and all your pompous acquaintances will be shocked."

"More insults! What's come over you?"

Robert sighed with exasperation. "Look: I merely want to be with Patricia. Is that too much to ask?"

"Yes," Luke selfishly answered.

Robert pointed around him, derisively indicating the ostentatious affair. "I don't belong here. I assumed I did, but I've changed too much. I can't abide these people, with their affluence and their sloth and their pretensions. I just want to go home."

"You don't have a *home*," Luke viciously reminded him.

"Yes, I do. It's wherever Patricia is. I had to travel to London to realize that."

Luke had hunted for *home* forever, and Robert made it seem so simple to find. What if he, Luke, chucked it all and left, too? What if he let Helen be the choice? It was such a thrilling notion—to flee London for her—but there was nothing for him at Mansfield. Nothing at all. What would Helen do with him if she had him? She'd likely murder him before the first week was out.

"If Patricia takes you in—and you're being overly optimistic about how stubborn she can be—what will you do?"

"I haven't a clue, but we'll figure it out. I'll seek employment; that's for certain. I won't twiddle my thumbs like these lazy bastards." He glanced at the bejeweled crowd; then his astute gaze landed on Luke. "Come with me, Captain."

"I'm having the time of my life." A lie. "Why would I depart?"

"You don't belong here, either." Robert laid a hand on Luke's arm, a comforting gesture intended to soften a blow. "I hear them gossiping about you. They'll never let you breach the walls and become one of them. Run away with me. Don't give them a chance to hurt you with their rejection."

"*Hurt* me? For heaven's sake, you talk as if I'm a swooning schoolgirl."

"I can sense how much this matters to you, but whatever dream you wish would come true, it isn't going to occur. Your father is a horse's ass—"

"You don't have to convince me. I discovered it on my own."

"His peers say you're a criminal, putting on airs. They don't care about your valor, or your assistance to the Royal

Navy, or anything else. There's a nasty undercurrent of complaint about the Prince's scheme to honor you. They're claiming it shouldn't be done, and they're his lords. In the end, he'll listen to them."

"Their posturing doesn't bother me in the slightest."

"Yes, it does. Leave with me. Please!" he implored. "Helen would welcome you back. You were a beast to her, though, so you'd probably have to beg."

"Helen?" he mused as if he didn't know who she was. "You mean Miss Mansfield?"

"Don't pretend with me. You love her. I can see it in your eyes."

Luke gasped. "Me? *Love* Miss Mansfield? If that's what you believe, you've tipped off your rocker."

"Have I?" More quietly, he urged, "Fix this, Luke. For her and for yourself."

Luke was confounded by how he should respond. Robert was correct: He would never be granted a knighthood, wouldn't spend the rest of his days hobnobbing with his father's conceited associates.

Luke had always grasped that the rich closed ranks and excluded inferiors like himself, so deep down he had no illusions. Yet he couldn't relinquish the possibility that something more could transpire, that he might *belong,* after all. His yearning was like that for a feast that was just out of reach, and he couldn't stop trying to sit at the table.

"I have to stay." He shrugged, unable to explain further.

"And I have to go," Robert replied. "I'm sure it sounds strange, but I have this eerie feeling that Pat's in trouble, that she needs me."

The hairs prickled on Luke's neck. Hadn't he been having the same premonitions of dread? How was it that Robert had become the sort of man who would act on them, while Luke was content to gad about, sipping champagne?

"I understand," Luke offered. "It's been a pleasure, Robert."

"Yes, it has."

"If you change your mind and decide to return, I'd be glad to have you."

"That's good to know. Thank you again, Captain. For everything."

As if he'd done nothing worth mentioning, he waved off Robert's praise. Robert studied him, cataloguing his features; then, without a farewell, he spun and left.

Luke observed him as he meandered through the crowd, and as he vanished, whispers drifted into the void caused by his exit. The snobs were angry that Robert had dared to attend, angry that Luke was among them and they were forced to socialize with him.

One fellow was especially incensed. "Filthy pirates!" he huffed. "Who does Roswell think he is, bringing his bastard into our midst?"

Their comments rolled off, like water over a waterfall, but the glimmer of the evening had worn away. He was surrounded by hundreds of revelers, yet he was so alone, and the isolation was killing him. His infatuation for Helen reared up, choking him with his inexplicable desire to be with her, and he slipped out into an empty hall, seeking a secluded parlor and a fortifying glass of brandy.

With ease, he located a deserted salon and he entered, only to stumble on his father, kissing a fetching girl who was young enough to be his granddaughter. The Duke had a wife—his duchess—safely tucked away at home. His mistress was in the ballroom entertaining his guests, and he was off cavorting.

The man was a dog!

"I trust I'm not interrupting anything," Luke said as he strolled in.

The two lovers jumped apart, the girl frantic, the Duke nonchalant.

The situation was rather comical, but Luke failed to see the humor. His own mother had once been an innocent maiden like this one, until she'd started sneaking off with the handsome Duke. The notion made Luke incredibly irate and—to his surprise—incredibly sad.

"Hello, Luke," the Duke greeted a tad too jovially. "I was wondering where you'd gotten to. I haven't seen you all night."

Luke scowled at the girl. "Your nanny is searching for you, so you'd better be off. If she finds you in here, there'll be the devil to pay."

She scurried out, as the Duke sighed and murmured, "So many women, so little time."

"Can't you keep your trousers buttoned?"

"Why should I?"

"Maybe because your actions are . . . are . . ." He nearly said *wrong,* but in light of his own sexual misbehavior, it was hardly the appropriate word. Instead he settled on, "Because there are consequences for the women you select."

"I don't *select* them," the Duke indignantly maintained. "They throw themselves at me. They always have. Why would I refuse what's freely bestowed?"

"Why indeed?" Luke went to the sideboard and poured them each a hefty drink.

"I've heard of some of your antics," the Duke needled, "so don't be sanctimonious. You know how it is."

"I definitely do."

"Like father, like son, eh?"

How pathetic! How awful to be included in such a despicable duo!

"Have you ever worried about any of them?" Luke queried.

The Duke looked confused. "About who? My paramours? Why would I?"

"Some of them have babies, you fool!"

"Not lately. I made my mistakes when I was a boy. As I matured, I learned to be more careful."

"Bully for you."

At being pitched into a basket with the Duke's other castoffs Luke was extremely irked. He speculated as to his other half siblings. Were there dozens? Hundreds? Perhaps there were thousands of the Duke's offspring scattered across England and suffering the stain of the Roswell paternity.

"How many children have you sired?"

"Two legitimate ones," the Duke answered, "but I suppose you're inquiring about the bastards."

"Yes." Luke rolled his eyes. "How many?"

"I haven't any idea. I've had a few come forward recently with their hands out." He peered at Luke and hastily added, "Not you, of course. You haven't asked me for anything. Yet."

"That's because I don't want anything."

The Duke shrugged. "You all want something."

"Not me."

Luke assessed his father and had to acknowledge that he'd never gotten to know the man. They'd fraternized extensively, but there was a clear barrier between them that the Duke wouldn't permit Luke to cross.

The Duke had a son and heir who was also named William, the two boys conceived less than a year apart, but Luke would never be allowed to meet his half brother. Nor would Luke ever set foot in the Duke's home. The galas the Duke had arranged were hosted by his mistress at the house the Duke had purchased for her. The male guests brought their paramours—not their wives—with the general consensus being that Luke was too disgraceful to be presented to a respectable female.

Luke had tolerated the slights, but why? In any prior circumstance, he wouldn't have brooked any discourtesy. He kept on so that he could be with the Duke, but when he didn't appear to have any redeeming qualities, was it worth the bother it took to continue a connection?

"Do you ever think about my mother?" Luke wasn't certain why he'd raised the indiscreet topic, but suddenly the Duke's reply mattered very much.

"Oh . . . aah . . ." The Duke was flustered by the question. "Yes, I reflect on her occasionally—as I do on all of the women with whom I've dallied. I love women. Don't you?"

"I don't have many memories of her. She died when I was five."

"Really?"

"When her guardian discovered that she was pregnant, he tossed her out without a penny."

"I wasn't aware of that."

"I was left on the streets of London, to fend for myself. I've always been curious if she came to you for help."

"It was so long ago, Luke." He casually sipped his liquor. "I'd have to check my records."

"If she'd asked, you'd have assisted her. Wouldn't you?"

"Why . . . why . . . yes, I assume I would have."

The tepid assurance embarrassed them both.

"It was difficult for me," Luke admitted. "I was too little to be abandoned. I missed her; I needed her."

"You've done quite well, though," the Duke blandly responded, "despite your rough beginning."

"I recollect that she had the prettiest brown hair and the biggest green eyes. That's what I remember most about her. How about you?"

"Oh yes, she had the most beautiful brown hair I'd ever seen."

Luke sat very still; then he laughed miserably. He was such an idiot! Such a pitiable, stupid idiot! Why was he wasting his energy on this harsh, callous oaf? Why was he lingering—day after bloody day—hoping the exalted prick would throw him a bone?

Luke downed his brandy and stood. "Well, Harold"—since it would annoy and offend, he used the Duke's given name—"I'll concede that it's been interesting, but not much more than that."

"What do you mean?"

"I've had enough of you, and I've had enough of this."

The Duke stood, too. "Quit speaking in riddles. I have no idea what you're saying."

"My mother had blond hair and blue eyes. Just like you. Just like me."

"Oh . . . hmm . . ." The Duke had the decency to blush.

"You don't have the faintest notion of who she was, do you?"

The Duke hesitated, then confessed, "I'm sorry, Luke. There've been so many over the years."

It was probably the only genuine moment they would ever share, the only chance he'd have for the real Harold Westmoreland to peek through the bluster of the Duke of Roswell.

"It's all right," Luke said. "I'm a good judge of character. When I first met you, I decided you were an ass, and you've merely confirmed that I was correct."

He moved toward the door.

"Where are you going?" the Duke demanded.

"I'm not sure."

"When will you return?"

"I won't."

"You can't be serious."

"I persuaded myself that this was the life I wanted"—he gestured around the ornate chamber—"but it's not. I was happy with how things were before."

"What a perfectly ludicrous remark. We have soirees scheduled for the next month, while the Prince ponders whether to receive you or not. If he takes a fancy to you, there'll be money and property involved."

"It will never happen, so you can advise your fussy friends that they don't have to worry."

"About what?"

"About me joining their ranks. I'd rather poke my eye out with a sharp stick than become one of you."

At the slur the Duke bristled. "There's no need for insults."

Luke spun round and was almost through the door when the Duke called, "Luke, wait!"

Luke stopped. "What?"

"Will I . . . will I ever see you again?"

There was a melancholy note in the Duke's voice, as if he actually wanted to know, as if he'd liked Luke more than he'd let on. With how aloof he'd been, why would he seek a subsequent encounter?

"If I'm ever in London again—which I doubt I will be—I'll look you up." He wasn't positive if he would or not.

"You're leaving the country?"

"Perhaps."

"Well . . . write . . . or something."

"I'm an orphan who had no schooling. I never learned how to write." It was a cheap parting shot, but he couldn't resist taking it. "And give the Prince a message for me, would you?"

"What is it?"

"Tell him I thank him for considering the knighthood, but—"

"Don't be a damned fool! I won't allow you to decline such an honor. If it's offered, you'll accept it."

"No, I won't. I don't want his snooty award. But inform him that I was proud to help out, and if I ever stumble on any of his sailors drowning again, I'll rescue them. I don't mind."

He whirled away and strolled down the hall and out of the mansion, and as he reached the front steps, he was close to breaking down and blubbering like a babe. He'd always fantasized about his father, but it had been a boy's dream, fueled on cold, rainy nights when he was desperately hungry and alone.

When had he grown to be so sentimental?

He loitered on the walk, the orchestra playing inside, the candles blazing in the chandeliers, the carriages lined up for blocks.

Where should he go? What should he do?

The large, gaudy house he'd bought was a few blocks away. It was still mostly unfurnished, and the dim, empty rooms held no appeal whatsoever, so his ship was his likely destination. It was moored in the harbor. He could muster the crew; then he'd set off to . . . to . . .

Where?

With a start, he realized that he couldn't bear to go away.

As long as he was in London, his feet firmly planted on English soil, he could jump on his horse and head to Mansfield Abbey. If he hoisted the sails and left, each cut through the waves would fling him farther and farther from where he truly yearned to be.

A horse's hooves clopped toward him, and he peered through the darkness to see Robert approaching. He was dressed and ready for his trip to Mansfield.

Luke moved out to the street as Robert reined in.

"What are you doing out here?" Robert asked. "Shouldn't you be inside with your father?"

"He and I have had all the chats we'll ever have."

"Good. He was an awful man."

"Not *awful*." Luke felt the word was too disloyal. "Just different from us."

"Yes, very different from us."

"Return to my house."

"No, I must be off at once."

"Just do it, Robert. I'll meet you there."

"I can't dawdle!"

"I'm going to change my clothes and pack," Luke surprised him by saying. "Then I'm coming with you."

"Have you had a sudden attack of conscience?"

"Yes."

"Maybe there's hope for you yet."

"Maybe there is," Luke concurred. "Now, be off. You mentioned that you were fretting over Patricia. Well, for weeks my intuition has been pestering me about Helen."

Robert stiffened with alarm. "Why didn't you say anything?"

"I thought it would sound crazy."

"It's not crazy. I can feel in my bones that something's happened."

"So can I." Luke studied the starry sky. "The moon's up and full. We can travel all night."

"My plan exactly."

Luke took off at a dead run, Robert loping along beside him.

22

What a day!"

"I'm exhausted."

"So am I."

Helen pushed back from the dining table and tried her best to smile at Adrian, but it was difficult to feign merriment when she was so unhappy. It was his wedding day, and though it wasn't a *real* marriage, she wanted it to be as special as she could make it. After all, how many times did a man marry in his life?

Carriage wheels sounded in the drive, and Adrian peeked out to see the vicar pulling away.

"I'm glad he's gone," Adrian said.

"I have to agree."

"Did he seem a tad zealous to you?" He gave a mock shudder.

"He takes his duties very seriously."

"I've always hated men like that."

They both chuckled, though Helen's voice was strained. She'd never felt more isolated. Westmoreland had abandoned her. Patricia had fled, having declined to stay for the ceremony. With Archie's reappearance, most of the servants had quit, so many walking out that Helen had barely been able to get her wedding dinner served. Those who'd remained had the rest of the day and evening off as a bribe to persuade them to keep on at their posts.

Even the maid Peg had left, and it was a sorry statement on Helen's situation that she missed the dour, slothful girl. At that very moment, if Peg had strolled in, she would have been a welcome sight.

"It's so quiet," Helen murmured.

"We're all alone."

"Except for my brother. Where is he?"

Archie had attended the brief ceremony. Looking glum and resolute, he'd dawdled at the rear of the library and had signed as a witness, but she hadn't seen him since. He'd refused her invitation to dine, which had actually been a relief.

"I believe he's chatting with your friend Patricia."

"Patricia? I thought she was on her way to London."

"She tried to go, but she was detained."

At Adrian's peculiar tone she glanced up, and she was surprised to find him assessing her strangely. She couldn't pin down the expression—it might have been rage or annoyance—but it frightened her, and she shivered, which was silly.

She'd been acquainted with Adrian for ages and got on with him so well. If she was perceiving unusual characteristics, it was likely caused by fatigue and stress.

"If I'd known she was still here"—she attempted another smile—"I'd have had her join us for the meal."

"I'm afraid that wouldn't have been possible." He stood, and he held out his hand in a fashion that demanded she take it. "Come with me."

There was no mistaking his demeanor. He was furious, when she couldn't figure out why he would be.

"To where?"

"Don't quibble. Just come."

"You seem distraught. What's wrong?"

"Get up!"

"Honestly, Adrian. What's the matter?"

He grabbed her arm and yanked her to her feet. "I am now your husband, Helen. You must obey me without hesitation."

She strove to wrest away, but he dug his fingers in tightly enough to leave bruises. "Let go! You're hurting me."

"You don't know the definition of *hurt,* my dear, but you're about to learn."

He started toward the door, lugging her along, and she struggled to stop him. She wasn't certain what he intended, but she wasn't about to follow like a lamb to the slaughter. She was a rational person. If he wanted something from her, he only had to ask. He didn't have to act like a bully.

"You're scaring me," she complained.

"Am I? Good."

They were in the hall and heading toward the stairs.

"What do you want? Tell me!"

"Can't you guess?"

"No."

"I'm eager for my wedding night to commence."

"Your . . . your wedding night?"

"We have to consummate the union."

"You swore I wouldn't have to."

"You didn't buy all that drivel, did you?"

"But you said you love Archie, that we'd have a white marriage!"

He chuckled. "I lied."

They were at the staircase, and he paused at the banister and pushed her against it. His crotch was pressed to her side, and she could feel his erection. He was excited by their skirmishing!

The idea of cohabiting with him was repulsive, and she couldn't do it. Surely he understood her qualms. He couldn't mean to force her!

She gazed up, hoping to reason with him, but the face that stared back belonged to someone she didn't recognize. He appeared quite mad, and with a sinking heart, she realized that she didn't know him, at all.

"Adrian, please," she begged. "You don't want to do this."

"Yes, I do. I want to very, very much."

"I'm with child! You could harm the babe."

"You think I care about Westmoreland's brat?" He began climbing, dragging her with him. "You should pray you lose it over the next few months, for if it's born alive, I'll drown it."

She laid a protective hand over her stomach. "You're insane!"

"Why would you say so? I merely decline to expend a farthing of my newly acquired wealth raising Westmoreland's bastard."

"You knew I was increasing! I confessed everything!"

"Yes, but I plan to inform others that you tricked me, that you were in dire need of a husband and I was the dunce who fell victim to your scheme." He flashed a look that was all innocence, that anyone would presume was genuine. "I was never apprised that you were pregnant; I swear it! I thought you were a virgin, and . . . oh . . . the horror of being deceived! I'll be able to divorce you. I'll have your money and your property, but I won't have to have you—or your foul little monster."

"You'll never get the estate. It's mine."

"No, Helen, we haven't signed the papers yet, remember?" They'd made it to the hall at the top of the stairs, and he explained his ploy as he hauled her on. "They're still being drawn up. You were in such a hurry that you couldn't wait to obtain my signature. You're my wife, and what was yours is mine—as soon as we copulate, which will happen very shortly."

"I trusted you," she stupidly cried.

"In that regard, you're as foolish as your brother. Neither of you has a lick of sense."

She hit him as hard as she could, but she wasn't a brawler, so the blow was weak and off balance. The swipe startled him, though, and his grip momentarily lessened. While he regrouped, she wiggled away and ran, screaming.

He caught her from behind, tackling her so that she toppled to the floor with a loud thud. He pinned her down and hissed, "You may screech all you like. There's no one to hear you, except Patricia, but she's in no condition to come to your aid." He rose and pulled her up. "When the servants return on the morrow, you'll be beyond help."

"What have you done to Patricia?" she demanded.

"The same thing I'm going to do to you."

He continued down the corridor, and she should have fought him, but she was dazed by the violence. He was a fiend, and he'd trapped her like a rabbit in a snare. Her spirits flagged. Couldn't she do anything right? Why did she keep landing herself in one disaster after the next?

I have to guard the babe, she reminded herself. It was the only part of himself that Luke had deigned to share.

She'd loved him so desperately, and if she had to kill Adrian for the child to be safe, then that's what she would do.

He brought her into the master's suite and heaved her onto the bed, and she was stunned to note that he'd already been in the room and prepared it for whatever atrocities he envisioned. There were cords secured to the bedposts, and in a thrice, he had them tied around her wrists.

"Perfect," he murmured, as he studied her predicament. "I'm told this is where Westmoreland used to fuck you. Is it?"

"Go choke on a crow, you deranged maniac."

"Now, now, you must learn to curb your tongue, lest I simply cut it out of your mouth." He leaned down to painfully squeeze her breasts, making her wince, making her squirm in fear. "Where is your dashing captain, Helen?"

"I haven't any idea," she truthfully said. "I was nothing to him. He didn't care about me."

"You're correct," Adrian concurred. "Shall I torment you with stories of his antics in London? Should I tell you about his beautiful paramours and wild orgies? Do you imagine he's spent a single second mooning over you?"

"I'm certain he hasn't."

He laughed. "God, how I've been waiting for this day!"

"How could you have been? What is it you want?"

"Don't you know? Really?"

"I haven't a clue."

"I want it all!" he preened. "I want the house, and the farm, and the status that goes with them. And you! Most of all, I want you—submissive and groveling."

"But . . . but what did I ever do to you?"

"Nothing. Nothing, at all."

He grabbed her dress and ripped it down the center to expose her chest. Her bosom was covered by corset and chemise, but it was only a matter of time before she would be naked and at his mercy.

"You have small tits," he said. "I'm glad. I hate it when a woman looks like a damned cow. I wish I hadn't agreed to share you with Archie."

"What did you say?"

"Oh, have I forgotten to mention Archie?" He was glimmering with a demented sort of lust. "I promised to let him have you—while I watch, of course. I'm sure I'll find it very arousing."

"Archie wouldn't . . . wouldn't . . ."

"He's often pondered it."

"You're lying!"

"Am I? He's considered raping you for years, but he was too much of a coward. I've urged him to move beyond his inhibitions. He's not so timid as he used to be. In fact, he's quite abandoned all restraint."

"He would never hurt me!" she loyally asserted, though it was bluster. She'd never understood Archie, had never particularly liked or trusted him, and if Adrian was egging him on, he might commit any evil deed.

"Wouldn't he? You're so naïve."

He reached to the table by the bed and retrieved a knife he'd placed there. On seeing it, her eyes widened with alarm, and he grinned.

"You're afraid. Marvelous."

"I'm not scared of you," she contended.

"Yes, you are, as you should be. Give in to the terror, Helen. If you do, our night will be so much more enjoyable."

With a flick of his wrist, he sliced through corset and

chemise to bare her breasts. Luckily, he hadn't nicked her, but eventually, he would. What was best? To resist? To humor him and survive? To succumb without argument?

She would probably be murdered despite what she did or didn't do, and she chose to go out fighting. She wouldn't stop till she drew her last breath!

Attempting to throw him off, she bucked with her hips, but she hadn't any leverage. And she screamed and screamed, so loudly that she felt her lungs might burst.

"I like it when you try to be tough," he growled. "When I finally break you to my will, the end is so much more satisfying. Now, let's amuse ourselves before Archie arrives. I'm eager to determine if your precious captain taught you any worthwhile tricks, though I have to confess that his tastes—and mine—are a tad different."

"Who is making all that racket?" Archie scowled and halted.

"Who do you think? It's your sister."

He glanced down to where Miss Reilly was strapped to the bed. "My sister? She's caterwauling like a banshee. What could be so dire?"

"She's crying for help. What would you suppose?"

"*Help* from what?"

"Your degenerate friend has started in on her. From the sound of it, she's not too thrilled with how her wedding night is progressing."

"But Adrian said he'd wait till I finished with you. He promised!"

Archie was livid. Adrian had sent Archie to Miss Reilly's bedchamber, advising Archie to do whatever he liked to her but keep out of sight. He'd claimed he had to

lure Helen upstairs without Archie getting her riled.
Archie hadn't wanted to miss the fun of seeing Helen's
expression when she realized that she'd been duped,
but Adrian had insisted, and like the puppet he was in
Adrian's hands, he'd scurried off.

Clearly, Adrian intended to ravage Helen first, without
letting Archie assist, and the notion that he'd been deceived was galling.

He crawled off the mattress and went to peek out the
door. Down the hall, he could hear Helen wailing and
cursing. There was some scuffling, followed by a sting-
ing slap, but Helen's tirade wasn't silenced. If anything,
it grew in intensity.

He was anxious to join them but tantalized by Miss
Reilly's quandary, too. He could treat her however he
wished, and the exciting prospect was difficult to ignore.

"I'll be back shortly," he ultimately told her. "Don't
go anywhere."

As if she could! Hah! Adrian had done his work well,
having bound her while she was unconscious and unable
to defend herself. Her face was battered, an eye puffy
and turning black-and-blue.

"Where are you off to, you disgusting prick?"

Archie whipped around. "What did you call me?"

"Are you deaf?" she mocked. "I called you a disgusting prick."

"You will not disrespect me! Not in my own home!"

"Last I checked, this wasn't your *home,* and even if it
was, I'd talk to you however I please."

At her impertinence Archie was aghast, and he stomped
over to her. "Shut your mouth!"

"Or what? Will you shut it for me?"

"Yes, you presumptuous hussy. How dare you offend
me!"

She rattled the ropes on her wrists. "Once I'm loose, I'll do more than *offend* your sorry ass. I'll kill you."

"That's a grand speech from a woman who's completely under my control."

"I won't always be fettered. I'll figure out how to free myself. When I do, you'd best beware."

"Of what?"

"I can hit a man with a knife from thirty paces. Someday when you least expect it, I'll simply slip out of a crowd, toss my blade, then vanish, and no one will have any idea who threw it."

"You'd actually have me believe that you'd commit cold-blooded murder?"

"In a thrice, Archie old boy. In a frigging thrice. Better be saying your prayers."

At the threats Archie was appalled. Had Adrian thought through this portion of their adventure? How could they ever release her? They'd have to . . . to . . . do away with her to keep her quiet.

"I'm weary of listening to you."

He searched for a gag to stuff in her mouth and found a stocking hanging out of a dresser drawer. All the while, Helen was clamoring on and on, the keening howl grating on his nerves. He had to cram the stocking between Miss Reilly's lips, but he wasn't sure how. In her angry state, she resembled a rabid dog, and he was terrified that she'd bite off his finger.

"Your friend hasn't let up on Helen," she chided. "Don't you feel any sympathy for her?"

"No."

"No twinge of brotherly concern?"

"Helen is reaping her just reward."

"For what?"

"For betraying me with Westmoreland."

"You think she *betrayed* you?" Miss Reilly seemed astounded by the possibility.

"I'm positive she did. She deserves whatever happens."

"That's rich. You know, Arch, you make me glad I never had any siblings."

"I told you to shut up!"

"What's it like, taking it in the butt for that pervert, Adrian? I've always wondered how you could stand it."

A hot flush coursed across his cheeks. No one knew how he behaved with Adrian when they were alone. No one! How had she guessed?

"What did you say?"

"Does he hold you down and force you? Or are you willing?"

A wave of rage swept over him. He'd never been so furious. "I'll kill you for uttering such a dastardly insinuation."

"You don't have the courage, you sick fuck."

"We'll see about that, won't we, Miss Reilly."

He went to the wardrobe, riffled around till he located a belt, and when he returned with it, he was more aroused than he'd ever been.

❦

"It's too quiet."

Robert reined in his horse and studied the deserted yard.

"Very strange," the Captain mused.

"Something's wrong."

"I agree."

"The house looks empty."

No boys emerged from the stable; no gardeners raked

leaves; no footman tarried on the stoop. Spookiest of all, the front door was wide open. It made the entire place seem as if everyone had picked up and moved away.

"Helen was so fussy about appearances," the Captain mentioned. "She'd never have let visitors arrive without a servant to greet them."

"No, she wouldn't."

Robert's pulse pounded. "What should we do?"

"Is your pistol loaded?" the Captain asked.

"Yes, and I'm carrying both my knives, but I have to tell you that if anybody has harmed Patricia, I won't need a weapon. I'll slay them with my bare hands."

"Good man." The Captain nodded. "I've taught you well."

He had urged his horse forward when a scream rent the air.

"Did you hear that?" Robert knew the sound had been real, but he couldn't quite process it. The noise was too incompatible with the bucolic surroundings.

"Let's go"—Westmoreland kicked his horse into a gallop—"and be ready for anything."

They raced up the drive, and the Captain leapt to the ground and ran into the foyer. Robert hurried after him, and they both paused long enough to determine that the ruckus was coming from upstairs. They rushed to the second floor, then the third. Pistols drawn, they marched down the hall, searching through one bedchamber, then the next. Westmoreland was a step ahead, with Robert bringing up the rear.

The Captain shoved at a door and froze. Then he muttered, "Sweet friggin' Jesu!"

"Westmoreland!" a male voice squeaked. "What are you doing here?"

"Captain," Patricia shouted over the man, "that deranged bastard Adrian Bennett has Helen. They're in the master's suite. You've got to help her!"

Robert was still out in the corridor and unable to see. The Captain spun around, his expression more deadly than it had ever been.

"Take care of this." He gestured to whatever was occurring inside. "I must find Helen."

"I couldn't stop him!" Patricia called. "I tried. I'm sorry."

Robert entered, and initially, his brain couldn't make sense of the shocking scene. Patricia was bruised and battered, shackled to the bedposts as if she'd been tortured— or was about to be. Archie Mansfield hovered over her.

On espying Robert, fully armed and brimming with wrath, Mansfield gulped with dismay and frantically calculated routes of escape.

"So, Mr. Mansfield," Robert seethed, "we meet again."

"Who the hell are you?" Mansfield clamored off the mattress.

"Surely you remember me," Robert said. "I'm Mr. Smith."

Mansfield scrutinized him, and as recognition dawned, he laughed. "The accountant? I'm quaking in my boots."

"Robert, is that you?" Patricia bellowed.

"Yes, darling. Are you all right?"

"Bennett took me by surprise, but this puppy hasn't laid a finger on me. He's all talk."

"I've always thought so," Robert concurred.

"Release me," Patricia pleaded. "You can hold him down while I beat the living daylights out of him."

"Yes, I'll release you," Robert replied, "but you won't need to bother with him. I shall be more than happy to assume the task."

"Robert!" she complained.

He could feel anger seeping into him, commencing at his feet and surging up his legs, his genitals, his belly. His heart seemed to enlarge to twice its usual size, his torso to strengthen and expand, as he came toe-to-toe with Mansfield.

All bluster, Mansfield sneered, "Don't you have some numbers to add or something?"

Robert chuckled. "I'm going to enjoy this so much."

"Enjoy what?" Mansfield taunted.

"Whipping your stupid ass."

Mansfield was clutching a belt, and he raised it and tried to strike Robert with it, but Robert jerked it away.

With his only weapon lost to him, Mansfield ran, but Robert tripped him as he passed, and he sprawled onto the rug. In a flash, Robert was on him, as Mansfield screeched like a girl and covered his face.

Robert pummeled him repeatedly, relishing how bone smacked flesh. It was over so swiftly that he was almost disappointed at how easy it had been. He rose, looming over the sniveling oaf, and was thrilled to note that he wasn't even breathing hard. Blood oozed from Mansfield's nose and teeth, his eyes were swelling shut, and he was crying like a baby.

"You contemptible swine," Robert growled. "How dare you hurt Patricia! How dare you hurt any woman!"

Robert kicked Mansfield in the ribs, then went to Patricia and sliced through the ropes that bound her.

He'd imagined she'd hug him, but instead, she jumped up and stomped over to kick Mansfield several more times, landing her blows with much more vehemence and glee—and much less mercy—than Robert had shown. She grabbed what was left of the cords Robert had cut, and she wrenched Mansfield's wrists behind his back and tied them securely, which caused a renewed wave of squealing.

"My arm!" Mansfield shrieked. "You broke my arm!"

"You wimpy little coward," Patricia fumed. "Before I'm through with you, you'll be lucky if that's all I break!"

She stood over him, fierce as any Viking goddess; then she turned to Robert and—to his utter astonishment—she burst into tears. He pulled her to him and cradled her to his chest.

"You came for me!" she said. "I can't believe it."

"Of course I came for you," he soothed.

"I was certain he'd murder me."

"I know you were."

"I thought I was all alone."

"You're not alone," Robert comforted. "You'll never be alone again."

"Promise you won't leave me."

"No, Pat. I won't leave you. I'm here to stay."

23

"We're not so tough now, are we, Mrs. Bennett?"

"I'll never be your *Mrs.* Anything," Helen claimed.

"Really?"

"I'm tougher than you realize."

Laughing at her helpless state, he checked the knots on the ropes that affixed her to the bed. "Such boasting! How long do you suppose it will last?"

"Quite a while, I'd guess. I'm perfectly capable of enduring, while you won't be able to continue. You're too crazy for words."

"Crazy? No, Helen, that's where you're wrong. I've never been more lucid."

He laid his knife on her cheek. "You're very pretty, so I don't believe I'll mar your face. As to the remainder of your body"—he drew the blade down her torso, enjoying each flinch as it passed—"I'm not overly partial to it, so there's no telling what marks I'll make under your clothes."

The threat rattled her, and she screamed again. The racket was beginning to irritate him, and he was weary of listening to her. He wanted her begging for her life, which would occur soon, and in the meantime, he wanted silence.

He went to the adjoining dressing room and found a robe. He retrieved the belt from it and returned to her. He wrapped it around her neck, and as he pulled at the ends, obstructing her air, her screeching stopped.

"Very good." He nodded with approval. "You catch on quickly."

"I'm a fast learner."

"Yes, you are. Let's see how much more I can teach you."

He tugged on the belt, and he was delighted to have surprised her. She'd assumed that a cessation of shrieking would keep the suffocation at bay, but she'd been wrong. There was nothing she could do—or not do, for that matter—that would have any effect on him, at all.

"My Lord, but you're sick!" She was gasping, trying to fill her lungs before he started in again.

"Not sick, Mrs. Bennett. I'm excited to have you raising a fuss, but let's have it be from real terror."

"No, you're sick. Call it whatever you like, but you're stark-raving mad."

His temper spiked. He was tired of her bravado. By now, she should have been pleading for mercy. "Be quiet or I'll gag you."

"Gag me. Don't. You can slice out my tongue for all I care."

Why did she insist on mocking him? Why persist with challenging his authority? What was it going to take for her to recognize that she had to yield?

Her clamor recommenced, the shrill timbre echoing off the high ceiling, and his patience was exhausted.

"I told you to be silent!"

"Well, I don't choose to obey!"

"Shut up!" He tossed his knife on the floor, and he slapped her, but she was too stupid to cease, so he administered another blow. "You must heed me!"

There was a note of hysteria in his tone, and he couldn't ever remember being so angry, not even when he'd strangled that fat whore Peg. Would he have to do the same to Helen? Would she be dead before the wedding night was through?

He'd just lifted his fist for a more vicious strike when a male voice bellowed from behind him.

"If you touch her again, I'll cut off your hand."

He paused, in his frenzy, not able to fathom how he'd been disrupted. He was master of the estate. Who would dare? Who would have the gall to barge in?

He glanced over his shoulder as Helen breathed, "Luke!"

"Get off the bed, you scurvy dog," Westmoreland growled. "When I murder you, I want you standing on your feet."

Adrian was unnerved by the Captain's inopportune appearance but wasn't afraid. Helen was his wife, had married him of her own volition, and he could treat her however he wished. It was none of Westmoreland's affair.

Adrian scoffed, concealing any trepidation, and he climbed off the mattress, acting as if it was what he'd meant to do, rather than what Westmoreland had commanded.

"Why are you in my home, Westmoreland?"

"Your home?"

"I'm quite sure no one let you in, so you've entered without invitation. You're not welcome. Go at once."

"Luke, don't leave," Helen implored. "Please help me."

"You know I will, Helen."

Westmoreland walked toward her, ignoring Adrian as thoroughly as if he were invisible, and Adrian blocked his path. Westmoreland was taller and broader and renowned as a brawler, but in truth, he was little more than a savage, Adrian thought. No doubt, he'd be easily cowed by Adrian's superior intellect and aplomb.

"Can't you hear me, Westmoreland? Depart! Or I shall summon the law and have you arrested for trespassing."

"You'll never have the chance."

Westmoreland swatted Adrian away like a bothersome fly, then extracted a knife and slashed through Helen's bindings. She rolled to the opposite side of the bed and scrambled onto the floor, but her knees were weak and she had to brace herself against the wall to remain upright.

Westmoreland studied her reddened cheek. "He hit you?"

"Yes."

"Did he do any worse?"

"He hasn't had time."

He turned to Adrian, his mouth a grim line, his eyes blazing with fury, and Adrian had to admit Westmoreland was a sight when riled. No wonder villains cringed in his presence. Adrian, however, was made of sterner stuff.

"This melodrama is over, Westmoreland," Adrian taunted.

"Is that so?"

"Helen has neglected to mention an important detail."

"That being . . . ?"

"She and I were wed this morning." He'd hoped for a

reaction, for some sign of dismay or disbelief, but there wasn't a flicker of response, which was so annoying. "This is our wedding night, so I suggest you tot off so we can continue with our celebrating."

"You married her?"

"Yes." Adrian smiled in triumph as he waited for a wail of anguish or despair, but still, none was forthcoming. By all accounts, Westmoreland had doted on her. Why wasn't he raging?

Westmoreland gazed at Helen. "Is it true?"

"Yes."

She blushed with shame, conduct for which Adrian would punish her later.

"So, you see"—Adrian preened—"you have no business here. Begone."

"I don't think so."

"Are you deaf? Stupid? What? She's my wife, and I'll—"

"Not for long," Westmoreland interrupted.

"What?" Adrian barked.

"She won't be your wife for long."

"Of course she will be. The vows were exchanged but a few hours ago. The vicar presided, and witnesses attended. It was recorded all neat and proper. There's nothing you can do."

Westmoreland chuckled, and it was such a severe sound that Adrian felt the initial frisson of alarm slither down his spine.

"She may be married to you," Westmoreland pointed out, "but you're about to die, so very shortly, she'll be your widow."

"*I* am about to die?"

"Yes. By my hand." Westmoreland was calm as could be. "Right here. Right now, and good riddance. I should have killed you the day I met you. It would have saved me the trouble of doing it in front of Helen." He glanced over at her. "Although maybe she'll be happy to observe your demise. What say you, Helen? Would you like to watch?"

"No."

"Go out in the hall, then." He was much more gentle than Adrian might have predicted. "Mr. Smith is there. Stay with him till I come out."

Clutching at her tattered dress, she took a faltering step, then another, and once she'd rounded the bed, she ran past them as if she worried that Westmoreland was an apparition.

They tarried till she'd exited; then Westmoreland leaned in. They were toe-to-toe, and it was an incredible sensation for Adrian to have so much raw power focused on him. Westmoreland's wrath was plainly evident, and Adrian supposed that he should have been scared, but he wasn't. A man wasn't attacked in his own bedroom. Not even a barbarian like Westmoreland would risk it.

"Aren't you curious as to why she agreed?" Adrian goaded.

"Yes, actually, I am."

"She has a little bun in the oven, a gift you left behind." He glittered with malice. "In the eyes of the church, and the law, your child will be mine. Can you imagine it living to see its first birthday?"

Westmoreland hit him so hard that several teeth were knocked out. Adrian had been hit before in his life, but until that moment, he hadn't really comprehended how deadly a human fist could be. He fell like a stone, his head smacking the floor, and he was completely discombobulated. Blood oozed from his mouth and nose, but strangely, he was invigorated by the pain.

A wave of indignation swept through him, an energy growing deep inside. Who was Westmoreland to presume he could stroll in and assault Adrian? Who was Westmoreland to presume he could behave however he pleased?

The knave obviously had no clue as to Adrian's lack of fear. Prepared to defend himself, Adrian moved up on his knees, but before he could rise any farther, Westmoreland punched him again, a staggering blow that had Adrian's ears ringing and his vision dimming. Reeling from the ambush, he huddled in a ball, hating Westmoreland more than he'd ever hated anyone.

Westmoreland chided, "Didn't your mother ever tell you not to beat a woman?"

"I didn't have a mother," Adrian spit out, a loosened tooth plopping out on the rug.

"That I can believe," Westmoreland concurred. "You're likely the spawn of Satan, himself."

"Perhaps, I am."

"Now get up and face your death like a man."

Adrian felt giddy, out of his body, as if the battering were happening to someone else. He wanted to oblige the Captain, but he couldn't manage. He lay there, trying to concentrate, when he realized that the knife he'd used to terrorize Helen was right next to him. Apparently, Westmoreland hadn't noticed it!

"Get up, you filthy swine!" Westmoreland hissed. "Get up so I can kill you."

As Westmoreland grabbed Adrian's arm and yanked him to his feet, Adrian curled his fingers around the pearly handle. He came up, braced himself, and with all his might, he stabbed Westmoreland, whipping out the knife before Westmoreland had a second to grasp what he intended.

With ease, the blade sunk all the way to the hilt.

Adrian lurched away, grinning with amazement to see it dangling from the Captain's stomach.

"Fuck you, Westmoreland," Adrian sneered. "Why don't you crawl away to perish in a rat's hole? I have pressing business to conclude with my bride."

As if naught were amiss, as if he were stabbed every day, Westmoreland casually peered down at his belly. "If you're determined to kill me, Bennett, you need a bigger knife."

With a quick jerk, he pulled it out, and he didn't so much as flinch. Blood squirted everywhere, proof of how grievously he'd been wounded, but the injury didn't slow him. If anything, it gave him greater strength. Bent on mayhem, burning with plans of homicide, he approached.

"Die, damn you!" Adrian commanded, but Westmoreland kept advancing.

"Maybe tomorrow," Westmoreland replied. "Just now, I'm busy."

Like a pair of dancers, they moved across the room until Adrian's back was against the wall and he could go no farther. Westmoreland was clutching the knife, and though he'd taunted as to its small size, in his skilled hand it looked large and lethal.

"Are you a religious man?" Westmoreland asked, sweat popping out on his brow, blood staining his shirt and trousers.

Adrian couldn't quit staring at the knife. "What?"

"Would you like prayers read at your funeral?"

Adrian refused to be slain in a common brawl with a felonious miscreant, and he haughtily claimed, "I'm not going to die."

"Yes, you are."

Westmoreland clasped him by the throat, as Adrian kicked at his shins and pried at his fingers, but to no avail.

The man was strong as an ox, solid as marble, and Adrian couldn't budge him.

"Westmoreland! Let's discuss this rationally. You can't . . . can't . . . murder me! Not in my own bedchamber!"

"Yes, I can."

"My God, man. It simply isn't done!"

"Yes, it is. It's done all the time."

Without warning, without debate, Westmoreland plunged the knife into Adrian's lung. There was an odd whooshing sound, and Adrian didn't know if it was air speeding out of his body or if it was horror ringing in his mind.

You stabbed me! You stabbed me! He bellowed the phrase over and over, though no words emerged from his mouth. There was a nasty spittle spewing from his lips that prevented him from speaking.

Westmoreland filled his line of vision, seeming to grow bigger and bigger, until Adrian could see nothing else, not the plush bed, not the ornate furniture or the picturesque farm outside the window. It had all been his for such a short while.

Help me! he wailed inside his head, but there was no one in the entire world who would come to his aid.

Where was Archie? Couldn't he have been bothered? Couldn't he have pretended to care? At least in the end? Adrian was about to expire alone, with only Westmoreland for company. How morbidly pathetic!

Westmoreland leaned in. Closer. Closer.

"I love Helen," he whispered, "more than my life. What were you thinking, harming her? Didn't you understand that I'd have to kill you for it?"

He extracted the knife and thrust it in again, the second jab piercing the center of Adrian's chest. To Adrian's surprise, the new wound didn't hurt. He was detached from his torso, drifting above it and observing from afar. He couldn't feel anything, couldn't cry out or weep in agony. His gaze was glued to Westmoreland's, his sight fading.

Good-bye, he attempted to say. Then, *I'm cold.*

A final shudder wracked him; then his eyes fluttered shut.

❧

Luke watched dispassionately as Adrian Bennett slipped away, though he didn't suppose Bennett would be winging *up.* His destination was straight down to the fires below.

"Rot in hell, you disgusting bastard."

It was as much of a eulogy as Bennett deserved.

With the battle concluded and the soul having departed, Luke had spent the stamina necessary to hold Bennett. His own life was in poor condition, his gash painful and his blood loss dangerous. He was dizzy, disoriented, and drained of the energy required to remain conscious.

He released Bennett, and the prig dropped like a rock, his corpse falling with a muted thud.

Luke swayed, bracing his palms on the wall, as Robert rushed in.

"Oh shit!" Robert muttered.

He grabbed Luke around the waist, taking his weight.

"Did you have to murder him?" Robert asked.

"Yes, as a matter of fact, I did."

"Well, the deed's done. No use complaining."

Luke managed a chuckle, though it was difficult to breathe, difficult to talk. "Where's Helen?"

"I'm here, Luke." She snuggled herself to his other side.

"Are you all right?"

"Don't worry about me."

At her reassurance, his waning strength evaporated. His knees buckled, and Robert and Helen had to fully support him. Patricia raced up from behind, a third pair of arms to keep him steady.

"Let's put him on the bed," Patricia said, her no-nononsense attitude making it seem as if all would be fine.

He didn't want to lie down, but he couldn't force himself to protest. He opened his eyes, and he was stretched out on the mattress, though he couldn't recollect how he'd gotten prone.

"There's so much blood," Robert murmured, as Luke's shirt and trousers were ripped away. "Oh, God! Look at that!"

"Press a cloth to it. Don't let up!"

"I'll fetch the sewing box. And the medicinals."

Their conversation was indistinct and fuzzy, and Luke wondered if he'd gone deaf. He reached out, but his limbs were heavy as lead, and he groped like a blind man.

"Helen . . . ?"

Suddenly she was there, hovering over him.

"What is it, Luke?"

She'd been crying, though he couldn't remember why she was sad. It was so hard to concentrate.

"Are you married to Bennett?"

"We'll discuss it later."

He stared into her beautiful face, and he was so happy to have her with him.

"Are you having my baby?"

"Yes, Luke, I am."

"Is it a boy?"

"I don't know. I hope so. I hope he's just like you."

"So do I."

He meant to say something else, but the comment eluded him, and he dozed.

"Luke!"

There was a panic in her tone that he didn't comprehend. He was in a very lovely place that was quiet and serene, and he felt more at peace than he'd ever been. The ache from his injury had vanished, and he wasn't lonely anymore.

"Keep him awake," someone nagged. "Don't allow him to drift off."

"Luke!" Helen called, pestering him like a buzzing gnat. He should have answered, but he couldn't. He didn't *want* to answer. The spot where he'd gone was so tranquil, so welcoming and familiar.

"Lucas! William Lucas Westmoreland! Speak to me! Captain Westmoreland! You must stay here! Are you listening?"

She was so frantic, and he should have told her not to fret, but she was so far away, and he was so tired. There was a woman off in the distance—his mother?—beckoning to him. She was standing in a shower of light, and he walked toward it.

"Luke!" Helen called again.

He smiled, glad her voice was the last he heard.

24

But . . . but . . . you can't mean to leave me here."

"Actually, I do," Mr. Smith replied.

Archie peeked out the carriage window, studying the moonlit cove with barely concealed terror. A smuggler's ship loomed in the distance, looking large and menacing. The gangplank was down, and men were unloading cargo onto a dilapidated hidden wharf.

He suffered a surge of panic that swiftly metamorphosed into rage, and he struggled against the rope at his wrists. How dare Smith attempt this! How dare he treat Archie like a common criminal!

"I won't stay!" Archie declared. "You can't make me!"

"Would you rather I killed you?" Mr. Smith blandly inquired. "I could, you know, without blinking an eye."

"You haven't the courage."

"Haven't I?" Smith chuckled and extracted a knife,

flicking a finger across the sharp tip. "I'm not certain where I'd start. Most likely, I'd stab you in the belly and—while you writhed and moaned—I'd cut off your cock and stuff it in your mouth so you choked on it. Then, I'd dump you in the bay and let the bottom fish pick your bones clean."

Archie's heart pounded. "You're just saying that to frighten me."

"Am I? I've traveled across Arabia. Those Mussuelmen are awfully harsh to their enemies, and I paid close attention to their violent methods. You have no idea of the things I've seen and done."

Archie scrutinized him, wondering how much was bluster and how much was fact. Anymore, he couldn't decide what to make of Mr. Smith. With his rough clothes and shaggy hair, the gold earring in his ear, there was nothing remaining of the scholarly fellow Archie had met during that stupid card game with Westmoreland. Smith appeared every inch the brutal villain he claimed to be, and Archie had to accept that his threats were probably genuine.

It was obvious—with his hands bound—that he couldn't fight Smith, so he had to reason with him. But how was he to talk himself out of his predicament? How could he sway Smith to mercy?

"Where is Adrian?" he asked as he had numerous times already. "I demand to confer with him."

"I told you: The Captain murdered him, and I secretly buried him out in the woods in an unmarked grave."

"You did not!"

"I did. He's vanished, and you will, too. No one knows where either of you went, though the entire country is searching. Even as we speak, your pathetic face is being plastered on every fence post and in every tavern from

Cornwall to Edinburgh. If you're caught, Helen, Patricia, and I will lie about your involvement in Adrian's scheme, and you'll be hanged."

"Helen would never behave so despicably toward me!"

"If that's what you think, then you don't know her very well. She'll get an annulment from Adrian, she'll inherit all your worldly possessions, and she'll be free of you forever." Smith chuckled, the sound sending chills down Archie's spine. "I realize it's difficult for your enormous ego to grasp, Archie, but you'll never be missed. Not by anyone."

The carriage door was opened, and Smith hopped out, and he was much too enthused for Archie's liking. Archie shrank into the squab, but he couldn't avoid the fate Smith had arranged. Smith reached in and dragged him out but did nothing to ensure Archie's safe landing. With Archie being fettered, he was off balance, and he thumped to the ground and bounced in the dirt.

He whimpered in agony but bit down, not wanting his cry of distress to be detected by the sailors swarming around the dark ship. They would be titillated by a show of weakness, so he had to mask his fear.

He curled into a ball as a man approached, and Archie recognized that he should stand and present himself as competent and composed, but he was trembling and worried that his bowels might let go.

"Are you Captain Morrow?" Smith queried.

"Yes, and you're Smith?"

"I am."

The two men shook hands; then Smith leaned down and lifted Archie to his feet.

"This is no one of any consequence, at all," Smith said.

Archie huffed with offense and pulled himself up to his full height. "I am Archibald Mansfield! This miscreant"—he gestured at Smith with his chin—"has assaulted and kidnapped me, and I solicit your assistance. I'm a rich and important gentleman. If you help me, there'll be a hefty reward in it for you."

Captain Morrow was a grubby, disgusting oaf who stunk to high heaven, and he laughed to Smith. "He's a conceited little snot, isn't he?"

"Yes, he is."

"I'm sorry about Captain Westmoreland. My condolences."

"Thank you."

"This sniveling bastard had a part in it?"

"Hard to believe, isn't it?"

"Yes, it is." Morrow assessed Archie so keenly that Archie felt as if he were the main course at supper. "I always thought the Captain was a fine man, and I owe him several favors. I'm happy to do this for you."

"I'm much obliged." Smith slipped him a bag filled with coins. "I don't care how long you keep him, though five years wouldn't be too much. I don't envision your being able to tolerate him for such a lengthy period, but please try."

"Will do. For Westmoreland."

"For Westmoreland," Smith echoed as though raising a toast. "Once you're through with him, it's up to you where you leave him, but I'd appreciate it if you make sure he hasn't the means to return to England."

"It will be my pleasure." Morrow spun away and issued commands that had his crew hurrying to complete their tasks.

Smith grinned and rubbed his palms together as if

dusting them off after a job well done. "Good-bye, Archie. And good luck! You'll need it."

He moved to climb into the coach, and Archie leapt over to block his path.

"Mr. Smith," he begged, "if you have any decency remaining, you'll not abandon me to these barbarians."

"I used to be *decent,*" Smith reflected, "but my honorable tendencies fled when you tied Patricia to those bedposts."

"So I'll apologize. I'll reform. I'll . . . I'll . . ." He couldn't deduce what to add that might convince Smith to relent. It was tricky business, pretending remorse when he didn't feel any. "Give me another chance."

"I don't wish to. I want you to suffer and suffer. I hope your misery never ends."

"I did nothing to your precious Patricia! I didn't even administer the black eye. Adrian is the culprit. Why blame me?"

"Why *blame* you?" Smith snorted with derision. "It's time to grow up, Archie. You have to learn to accept responsibility for your actions. Perhaps this adventure will imbue some of the maturity you so clearly lack."

Archie's temper spiked, and he vowed, "I'll see you hanged for this. The moment I'm free, I'll come looking for you."

"Oh, Archie. . . ." Smith sighed. "You don't understand what's transpired, do you?"

"No, what?"

"You've been sold into slavery."

Archie gasped. Was Smith **mad**? This was modern-day England! Archie was a citizen of the Crown! He couldn't be . . . be . . . bartered like an African savage!

"I won't abide such an outrage." His panic and his

voice were rising, and he stomped his foot. "I won't! I won't!"

"Be silent down there!" a sailor growled from the deck of the ship.

If the smugglers were concerned about noise, then there had to be others nearby who might hear and rush to his aid. He drew a deep breath, eager to let out a blood-curdling scream, when Smith brandished a pistol and coldcocked Archie alongside the head. Archie dropped like a stone and lay on his back, wheezing and shivering with despair. Smith bent down and stuffed a kerchief into his mouth, preventing any subsequent outburst.

"I suppose I should warn you," Smith counseled in a whisper.

What? What? Archie's frantic question mutely flitted between them.

"Captain Morrow is a pirate in the truest sense of the word, which is why I picked his ship rather than another." Archie frowned, not comprehending, and Smith explained, "He's a renowned sodomite, and his crew regularly practices buggery—as most pirates are presumed to do. I'm positive you'll be very popular with your new companions."

No! No! Archie pleaded with his eyes. Smith couldn't think he had perverted inclinations! Yes, he'd occasionally dabbled with Adrian, but still . . .

"A sailing vessel requires many hands to keep it functioning," Smith went on. "During the day, they'll work you to death; then at night, they'll have other *duties* for you to perform." He patted Archie on the cheek. "You're such a pretty fellow. Pray that Captain Morrow takes a fancy to you. If he does, it will be much more bearable."

Smith jumped into his carriage, and the vehicle

whipped away, spitting up dust and rocks that pelted Archie in the face. A sailor traipsed over, and Archie was hoisted over the man's shoulder, but Archie was too shocked to resist or complain. Agog with dismay, he dangled upside down, as he was hauled up the gangplank and onto the ship.

He was thrown down a ladder into the hold, and he banged and hit as he tumbled to the bottom. Stunned, disoriented, aghast at the wretched turn of events, he huddled, quaking in the darkness. The orders were called to shove off, and the ship's timbers creaked as it was caught by the tide and swept away.

They reached the curve of the bay, and waves started slapping at the hull as it sliced through the water. He could visualize the shoreline fading, the coast of England being swallowed up by the evening's fog.

Quickly and quietly, Archie vanished without a trace.

❦

"Where have you been, Mr. Smith?"

"I can't say, Miss Reilly."

Patricia glared at Robert, vexed that he'd been absent for an entire week and that he refused to utter a word as to his destination.

"I assume you've relieved us of our unwanted cargo?"

"It's gone for good. We won't have to worry about it ever again."

"Fabulous."

They both knew she referred to Archie Mansfield. After the calamity, they'd spread the story that Bennett and Mansfield had plotted to kill Captain Westmoreland, then they'd fled to points unknown. They had so few friends and were so generally disliked that it was easy to persuade others that they'd have perpetrated such a terrible crime.

The country was buzzing with fury that their celebrated hero had been cut down by such a pair of scoundrels. Of course, each time the tale was told, Archie and Adrian grew more deranged, and no one at Mansfield Abbey did anything to quell the rumors.

People were searching for them everywhere, anxious to spot the appalling duo, to see them captured and executed. Patricia almost wished it could really happen. It would have been so enjoyable to observe at the gallows as the two men swung from their double ropes.

After Helen's failed wedding, as the servants had trickled back to their posts, Robert had kept Archie hidden until they could figure out how to be shed of him. Helen had had mixed feelings, wanting Archie punished, but she was extremely stricken and hating the notion of a public trial where details would have been bandied.

Robert had devised the perfect solution: In the dead of night, he'd spirited Archie away, not telling anyone— not even Patricia—where Archie was. In the years to come, as emotions and memories calmed, Helen would never have to fret over Archie's fate—because she would never know what it had been.

"Now then"—Robert removed his gloves and tossed them on a nearby table—"I have something to discuss with you."

"And *I* have something to discuss with you." In the frenzied days following the attack, they'd hardly had two seconds to talk. She gestured to his attire, to his untrimmed hair. He hadn't shaved, and his cheeks were shadowed with stubble. He looked tired, sexy, and dangerous. "What have you done to yourself?"

"I've found out how to be a man."

"I've seen you without your trousers. I never had any doubts."

"Well, I had them."

He was walking toward her, each step bringing him closer, and there was a feral air about him, as if he was ready to possess her in some way he never had previously. Butterflies swarmed in her stomach. When he gazed at her like that—as if she was beautiful and alluring—she couldn't resist him.

"I liked you just how you were," she insisted.

"You couldn't have."

"I did."

"Well, I like *you* better with all these curves and shapes. I didn't care for you as a man, at all."

"You didn't?"

"No."

"What are you trying to say, Robert?"

Her pulse was pounding, with dread, but also with expectation. Nothing had ever gone right in her life. No relationship had ever endured, no friend had ever stayed, and she couldn't trust the future. With his next comment, he could make her the happiest woman on earth or he could dash every dream. Which would it be?

"I learned to fight in London. The Captain taught me."

"What a marvelous legacy." She couldn't veil her sarcasm. She'd had enough fighting to last throughout eternity and didn't feel that an addition of brawling skills was any reason to brag.

"I'm not afraid anymore. Not of anything."

He was so proud of how he'd been transformed, so eager to have her welcome the alterations and be proud, too, so she would be. "I'm glad for you."

"I can protect you from any hazard. I can keep you safe."

He'd done all this for her? But she didn't want him to
be the person he'd become! She wanted her old Robert,
the funny, droll, humble man he'd been. Where was that
charming fellow?

"I never needed you to keep me *safe!* Did I ever demand it of you?"

"No, but *I* needed to know, for myself "—he clutched
a fist over his heart—"and now I do."

"Are you satisfied with how you've turned out?"

"Not yet." He fell to his knee and clasped her hand.
"Will you marry me?"

"What?"

"You asked if I was satisfied. I won't be until you say
yes."

"But . . . but . . . you claimed that we couldn't be together, that you hadn't any money, and that—"

"A few things have changed since then."

"What? What's changed?"

"My brothers sent me some cash—as reparation for
my losses. Actually, it was more than some; it was quite
a lot."

"How much is *quite a lot*?"

"Enough to have an excellent life with you."

She studied him, struggling over his declaration. He'd
received some funds, so he'd come back for her, as any
gentleman would, but he couldn't have thought through
his situation. For the moment, he was pretending to be a
brigand, but eventually, sanity would creep in, and he'd
pine for his tailored suits and ledger books.

She'd have no place with that man.

She began to tremble, and she pulled away and went
to peer out the window.

"Pat, what it is?"

He rose and walked over to stand behind her, and she could feel his consternation and concern.

"You don't want me."

"Why would you say so?"

"You want someone like . . . like . . . Helen." Gad, but it was so difficult to confess her greatest fear aloud. "You need someone like her. What would you do with me? You could never take me anywhere or introduce me to your snooty acquaintances. They'd laugh, and I couldn't bear to humiliate you."

After her outburst, there was such a protracted silence that she supposed he'd tiptoed out without her noticing. Finally, she peeked around only to see him evaluating her most peculiarly.

"You believe I could desire another more than you?" he inquired.

"I know you could."

"How could you have such a low opinion of me?"

"I don't. I think you're the finest man ever."

"Then give me some credit, would you? I know what I want."

"No, you don't," she countered. "You're wrapped up in this fantasy where you're strutting about like a bandit—it's as if you're acting out a part in a stage play—but you'll come to your senses and realize that you've made a terrible mistake, and then where will I be?"

"You'll be right beside me."

"With you hating me for being who I am! With you kicking yourself for doing something so stupid!"

"So . . . you're saving me from myself?"

"Absolutely."

"Pat?"

"What?"

"I don't wish to be *saved*. Haven't you figured that out?"

He drew her into his arms, and he kissed her forever, the embrace going on and on. He was staking his claim, proving his worth, and when he ended it, her knees were weak. She'd forgotten how good he was at kissing, and she could scarcely keep from sliding to the floor in a seduced heap.

"We're done talking," he advised, sounding so much like Captain Westmoreland that her heart ached.

"We are?"

"And I'm not letting you tell me *no*. You're being silly. There's a proposal on the table, and I'm accepting it for you."

Why wouldn't he listen? "You'll be miserable and unhappy and—"

"No, Pat," he interrupted. "You're wrong. I'm quite sure I'll be perfect."

He swept her off her feet, lifting her as if she weighed no more than a feather. When had he gotten so strong? He left the parlor and marched into the hall.

"Where are you taking me?"

"To bed."

"Why?"

"Do I need a reason?"

"Well . . . no, you don't."

"We seem to get on much better there, and besides, it's just occurred to me that I should spend some time changing your mind."

She assessed him. His expression was so steady and true. He really did want her—for now anyway. And who could predict what might happen? She would work so hard, would try so hard. She would be the best wife ever, would love and cherish and esteem, and if she was lucky, maybe he'd never have any regrets.

She smiled. "I don't imagine it will take very long to convince me."

"I disagree. I am positive it will take hours. Perhaps days."

He reached the stairs and started to climb.

25

Helen rushed down the garden path, and with the deteriorating weather she considered taking the shortcut through the trees, but she didn't. The grave was there, the place seeming to be haunted, and she couldn't bear to tiptoe past. Perhaps she'd never be able to, and she wondered why she hadn't had the spot moved farther into the woods.

Not that she'd been reasoning clearly at the time. Even now, her recollection of that terrible day was scattered and incomplete. She recalled some details but had blocked others entirely, with Patricia and Robert having to fill in huge pieces of the puzzle.

A brisk wind rippled her cloak, and she hurried on. The seasons had changed, winter nearly upon them. The sky was so stormy and forbidding that it looked as if it might snow.

Up ahead, she could see the house, and she stopped to study the empty flower boxes, the naked vines. It was amazing how much could happen over a single summer and autumn, how many dramas, heartaches, and joys could play out.

She vividly remembered the bright July afternoon when Luke had ridden into the yard. The servants had been lined up to greet him, trembling and fretting over the rumors they'd heard. He'd been so dashing and gallant, so scary and determined to make his mark.

At the memory she smiled and walked on, peeking in the downstairs windows as she passed. To ward off the gloom, a few lamps had been lit, but she didn't mind the waste of fuel. Previously, she'd have been frantic, but not anymore. With Adrian dead and Archie having disappeared, her ownership of the property was secure, and she'd never have financial difficulties again. If the maids wanted to burn some candles, or warm a room with a cheery fire, she was happy to allow it.

She hastened on, the letter that had arrived earlier clutched in her hand. She slipped in the rear door, then climbed the stairs to the master's suite. As she entered, she halted and frowned.

"Captain Westmoreland! What are you doing out of bed?"

"Hello, Helen."

Luke was sitting in a chair, fully dressed in clothes that Mr. Haversham had sewn for him. There was a sparkle in his eye and a rose in his cheek that had been absent for an eternity, and she was thrilled by the hints of a return to health, but at the same moment, she was unnerved.

There was a packed portmanteau at his feet, so apparently, he was intending to leave. The crazy oaf! What was he thinking?

"Well?" she challenged. "I asked you a question, and I expect an answer."

"I'm tired of lying around like an invalid."

"You *are* an invalid. You almost died on us."

On me, she could barely keep from wailing, but she pushed away the disturbing reflection. Throughout his recovery, he'd been extremely distant, and she wouldn't shame either of them by alluding to an affection she was positive he no longer felt.

"After such an injury," she scolded, "most sane individuals would understand that a lengthy recuperation would be required."

"I've had it with convalescing."

"Have you?"

"Yes."

"I know you assume you're invincible, but even Hercules rested occasionally. You're not supposed to be up."

"I'm not a baby," he snapped.

"I didn't say you were."

"I'm hungry, and I demand some food. Some *real* food—not that gruel you've been feeding me."

He was tremendously irritated, and she was glad to note that he was spry enough to complain. An increase of appetite and a display of temper were signs of an improving condition. She ought to have been rejoicing, but she wasn't. Obviously, the instant he was better, his initial act would be to abandon her again. What more proof did she need that his prior fondness had vanished?

She pulled up a chair and settled in, behaving as if naught were amiss, and she pointed to his satchel. "Are you going somewhere?"

He looked embarrassed, and he stared at a spot over her shoulder. "I have to be on my way."

"Really?"

"I must check on my ship and my crew."

"Robert already has. Everything is fine."

"I have other business in London. I have lawyers to meet and . . . and . . ."

"Then what?"

"Well . . ."

There was an awkward silence, as he struggled to conjure up excuses as to why he should go, but he couldn't conceive of any that would suffice.

"When all of your *business* is concluded," she pressed, "what will you do with yourself?"

He shifted about, wincing as his scar pained him, and she yearned to shake him. The foolish man could hardly get out of bed, yet he'd dare to jump on a horse and trot off to the city. Why . . . the jostling alone would probably kill him.

Did he detest her that much?

"I have to leave, Helen," he said quietly.

"Why?"

"It's time."

"According to whom?"

"To me."

"I disagree."

If he was determined to go, she wasn't about to make it easy on him. With scarcely a protest, she'd let him ride off once before, and she wasn't about to do so again. She would fight and plead, would dupe and coerce, would try every trick—whether fair or foul—to keep him, and if he still insisted on it being good-bye, at least she'd know she'd done her best to wrangle a different ending.

"Why must you go, Luke? Tell me."

"It's nothing, Helen. I just need to be away."

"Yes, yes, so you've said. To your ship and your crew and your lawyers, but what you actually want is to be away from *me*. That's why you're so bent on going. Have the courage to say so aloud. Put me out of this misery of waiting."

He nodded, breaking her heart. "Yes, I need to be away from *you*."

When the situation called for it, he could be so brutal. "Did I mean nothing to you then?"

He shrugged, a gesture that—given the tenor of the conversation—could have denoted a hundred responses, so she forged on.

"Why did you come back?"

"When?"

"On my wedding day. Why were you here? You never told me."

"Aah . . ." He couldn't answer, which she found encouraging.

"Do you want to know what I think?"

"Not particularly, but I suppose you're about to enlighten me."

The flip remark was so typical of the old Luke, the Luke she'd loved so desperately, and it should have been another moment for jubilation, but it ignited her temper.

"I think you came because you missed me, because you were sorry for how we separated. You came to see if you could have another chance."

"You're wrong."

"Am I?"

"Yes."

She held out the letter she'd brought, but he didn't reach for it. "Guess who wrote to me."

"Who?"

"Your father."

"The Duke?"

"Have you another father of whom I'm unaware?"

"No, but why would he contact you?"

"Would you like me to read it to you?"

"No."

"Aren't you curious as to what it says?"

"Not especially."

Despite his disinterest, she persisted. "He was worried."

"About what?"

"About you."

Luke scoffed. "Right."

"He heard the same horrendous stories as everyone else, and he's begged me to write and assure him that you'll recover."

"Will you?"

"Yes."

He frowned. "I wonder what he *really* wanted."

"He intimates that there was some trouble between the two of you, that you split on bad terms. I get the impression that he wasn't as kind as he could have been."

"Since kindness isn't a trait he possesses, that's laughable. He was just himself, as you'd warned me he'd be."

So . . . the Duke had lived down to her low expectations. With knowing how much the meeting had meant to Luke, she garnered no satisfaction in being correct.

"He claims that you declined an introduction to the Prince of Wales."

"I did."

"And that you spurned any potential offer of a knighthood."

He shrugged again, behaving as if the magnanimous, marvelous prospect had had no value to him, at all. "After I was in London for a bit, I decided I hated the folderol. I didn't belong there, with all of them."

"You've never belonged anywhere, have you?"

"No, I haven't."

The poignant, frank admission was unbearably sad. Perhaps that was the true reason he thought he had to leave, why he'd left before. He'd always been alone, had never had a place or a family to call his own, so he had no concept of how to stay.

His initial, incomprehensible drive to go to London now made sense and erased the anger she'd felt. It hadn't merely been a frivolous desire to socialize with his father but a deep and fervent hope that in the Duke he would find his way home.

How awful it must have been! The lofty aristocrat was too arrogant to accept Luke as a son, although with the letter she'd received, and with the Duke's demonstration of concern, there was certainly an opening for continued communication.

"Your father says the Prince is more eager than ever to speak with you."

"Bully for him."

"The Prince is a romantic at heart. Were you aware of that?"

"No, and why would I care?"

"He's heard the stories, too, about how you were almost killed while protecting me. He believes you're more of a hero than ever." She stood and stared him down, her scowl fixed, her tone firm. "He's still pondering that knighthood, so I'm writing to your father—on your behalf—to tell him we'll come to town as soon as you're able."

"You are not."

She patted his shoulder. "Don't fret over it, Luke. I'll go with you this time, and I won't let anything bad happen."

She snatched up his portmanteau, and she marched over and pitched it into the dressing room.

"What the hell are you doing?" he barked.

"I'm putting away your bag, so the footmen can unpack it."

"I need it. I'm leaving!"

"No, you're not."

"I am, too!"

"Oh, my darling, Luke"—she smiled—"quit being so tough. Let me tend you for a little while longer. I enjoy it."

"You don't."

"I absolutely do—although I can see that, as you heal, you'll be a difficult patient. But I can manage!"

She sat on his lap, and she'd imagined he'd hug her, or at least relax at having her so near, but he was rigid with restraint, grappling with every muscle to keep her at bay.

She kissed his forehead, and she wrapped her arms around him and fussed with his hair. Since the calamity, she hadn't touched him with any intent other than nursing, and it was fabulous to be caressing him again.

"While you were away," she said, "I learned a few lessons, and they were reinforced when you were so ill."

"What lessons?"

"Some things are worth having, and some things are worth fighting for." She kissed him on the mouth but couldn't generate a response. It was like kissing a block of wood. "*You* are worth fighting for, Luke."

"Me?" He snorted with derision. "You're mad."

"No, I'm more clear than I've ever been." She took his hand and rested it on her belly. "In your rush to flee, aren't you forgetting one small detail?"

"I haven't forgotten," he grumbled.

"That day you saved me, you didn't know about the babe, did you?"

"No."

"I waited for you, until I couldn't wait anymore. Didn't you get my letter?"

"You wrote to me?"

"Yes. I wonder what happened to it."

For a moment, he pondered the lost message; then he murmured, "I'm sorry."

"For what?"

"For failing you."

"*Failing* me? Is that what you think?"

"It's what I know. I was so excited to tot off to London, to put on airs and strut around with my nose stuck up my father's ass. I deserted you, and I never stopped to consider that you might be in dire straits. I was too busy pretending I was somebody important."

"You *are* somebody important, you silly man, and I need you more than ever. You have to stay."

He shuddered. "I couldn't bear to have the child born and to have your . . . your . . ."—since the murder, he hadn't uttered Adrian's name aloud—"late husband listed as the father."

"He won't be, and as far as anyone knows, I've never had a husband."

"What do you mean?"

"The vicar and my brother were the only witnesses to the ceremony. The servants were gone, so they all assume it never occurred. With my brother having permanently disappeared, Robert argued to the vicar that I shouldn't have to have any connection to Adrian as my legacy. He agreed, and the records were destroyed."

Actually, Robert had terrorized the young minister, then offered a hefty bribe. The pious, fiery fellow's vow of eternal silence had been bought for the price of a sporty new gig.

"So . . . ," Luke tentatively ventured, "there's no proof that you were ever married."

"No, and I find that I'm in desperate need of a husband.

Are you acquainted with anyone who might be interested in the position?"

She'd been certain he'd volunteer, but instead, he muttered, "I can't be a father."

"You already are!" she whispered, exasperated.

"I haven't a clue how to raise a child. Why would you want me here?"

"Don't you know?"

"No."

She was so glad to finally have the opportunity to confess. "I love you, Captain Westmoreland. I've always loved you."

"You couldn't possibly."

"I do!" He was so skeptical! She had to convince him that her feelings were genuine, and there were so many reasons as to why she cared for him that she couldn't fathom where to begin. Didn't he comprehend that he was her sun, her moon, her entire world?

When he'd left, she'd felt as if she couldn't breathe, couldn't see. When he'd nearly died, she'd suspected that she might die, too. A life without Lucas Westmoreland wasn't any sort of life, at all.

She slid off his lap and onto the floor, and she knelt before him, happy, humbled, and so grateful that he was with her. She took his hand in her own.

"Luke, will you marry me?"

"I told you I can't!"

"I'm having your baby. You can't refuse."

"I don't understand this, Helen."

"It's easy, Luke. I want to be your wife, to have your child and give it your name, so that the babe and I can love you forever." She leaned in, not letting him pull away, not letting him be separate. "You'll never be alone again, Luke. I swear it."

"I don't mind being alone," he stubbornly claimed. "Not really. You don't have to rescue me as if I'm a stray dog."

"Well, *I* hate your being alone, and it's recently dawned on me"—she snuggled closer—"that I can't live without you. Say yes. Say you'll marry me."

He studied her; then he ran a finger down her cheek. "You're serious."

"Of course I am. Do you presume that I've enjoyed humiliating myself by proposing when it's so evident that you don't want me?"

"I have to admit that I like having you down on your knees."

At the unexpected sexual innuendo, she chuckled. "You *are* feeling better, aren't you?"

"Yes, I am, and you're wrong about one thing."

"What's that?"

"You're wrong to assume that I don't want you." He tugged her back onto his lap. "I've always wanted you. I've always needed you."

"I know."

"Don't let me walk away."

"In case you haven't noticed, I'm trying my damnedest to stop you."

"Don't let me be stupid enough to go."

"I can't; I won't."

He kissed her, his lips falling lightly on hers, and it was the sweetest, most magnificent embrace they'd ever shared. It promised and pledged, accepted and enchanted, and after so much time apart, it was like coming together all over again.

When it ended, he was glimmering with desire and another deeper sentiment she couldn't define.

"I . . . I . . . love you," he said, the words seeming to

have been wrenched from the bottom of his soul. "I love you more than my life."

"I can't believe you finally realized it."

"I want it all. I want you, and this child we've made, and a dozen more." He swallowed, emotion threatening to swamp him. "I want a home of my own, that's my own place, where I can belong, where I'll always be welcome."

"Then it shall be yours, my dear, dear man."

"Will you have me, Helen?"

"Yes, I will."

"When?"

"We'll discuss the details later." She helped him up. "Now, let's get you into bed."

He raised a brow. "Only if you'll join me."

She saw a rekindled flicker of the randy, enticing knave who'd swept her off her feet, who'd stolen her heart and never given it back.

"For what?" she inquired.

"Why would you have to ask? After how well I taught you, I shouldn't have to explain it all over again."

"What would the doctor say?"

"The hell with him. What does he know?"

"Obviously more than you. I'm sure he wouldn't permit you to have company—at least not that type of company."

"Why?"

"You're rather fatigued, Captain."

"I am not. Suddenly, I'm feeling fit as a fiddle."

"You couldn't . . ."

"I could."

"You're exhausted."

"I might surprise you."

"You're an incredible optimist."

"I'm merely stating the facts, Miss Mansfield."

She rested a palm on the front of his trousers and was

amazed when his cock stirred. She shook her head.
"You're half-dead, yet you have the vigor to philander?"

"I was stabbed. Not castrated." He went to the bed and
stretched out, exhaling a satisfied breath as the mattress
cradled his body. "I'm going to lay here just like this."

"And what am I supposed to do?"

He grinned, his sexy, potent gaze wandering down her
torso. "I think you'll figure it out pretty fast."

She hesitated, then laughed. "I think I will, too."